The purchase of this item
was made possible by a
generous grant received
from

Don't Cry

Don't Cry

Stories by Mary Gaitskill

PANTHEON BOOKS, NEW YORK

The stories in this collection were originally published in slightly different form in the following: "The Agonized Face" in *Conjunctions;* "The Little Boy" in *Harper's;* "Mirror Ball" in *Index;* "Folk Song" on *Nerve.com;* "Don't Cry" and "An Old Virgin" in *The New Yorker;* "Description" in *Threepenny Review;* "College Town, 1980" in *Vice;* and "Today I'm Yours" and "The Arms and Legs of the Lake" in *Zoetrope: All-Story.*

Grateful acknowledgment is made to the following for permission to reprint previously published material: Alfred Publishing Co., Inc.: Excerpt from "La La (Means I Love You)," words and music by Thom Bell and William Hart, copyright © 1968 by Warner-Tamerlane Publishing Corp. and Nickel Shoe Music Corp., Inc. (BMI). All rights reserved. Reprinted by permission of Alfred Publishing Co., Inc · Hal Leonard Corporation: Excerpt from "Little Girl," words and music by Bob Gonzalez and Don Baskin, copyright © 1966 (renewed 1994) by Screen Gems-EMI Music Inc. and Duane Music Inc. All rights for the U.S. controlled and administered by Duane Music Inc. All rights for the world excluding the U.S. controlled and administered by Screen Gems-EMI Music Inc. All rights reserved. International copyright secured. Reprinted by permission of Hal Leonard Corporation.

Library of Congress Cataloging-in-Publication Data

Gaitskill, Mary, [date]
Don't cry : stories / Mary Gaitskill.
p.   cm.
ISBN 978-0-375-42419-9
I. Title.
PS3557.A36D66 2009   813'.54—dc22   2008025231

www.pantheonbooks.com

Printed in the United States of America
First Edition
2   4   6   8   9   7   5   3   1

FOR PETER

CONTENTS

Don't Cry

College Town, 1980

Dolores did not look good in a scarf. Her face was fleshy, her nose had a bulby tip, and her forehead was low. Her skin was coarse and heavy for a woman under thirty, and the tension in her face was such that a quick glance gave the impression that she was grinding her teeth, although she was not. She was attractive anyway because of her expressive, thick-lashed eyes and full mouth. When her hair was worn long, it was thick enough to draw attention from the fleshiness of her face, so that her eyes and mouth were more striking. Thus, it was not a good idea to pull her hair back with a scarf.

Dolores knew this. She hated wearing the scarf, but she'd recently pulled huge chunks of her hair out, and her head looked so weird that a scarf was necessary. It was the second episode of its kind in her life, and yet, now as then, she couldn't remember why it had ever been satisfying to pull her hair out, or even how it had felt, although you'd think it would have hurt. As if to remind herself, she'd actually kept the removed hair in a little box, until the sight of it sickened her one day. When she was in public, she was sometimes torn between the fear that the scarf had slipped and part of her head was showing and the urge to take it off and see what people did. Although, of course, she knew they'd only stare when they thought she wasn't looking.

She sat in the Oasis Café, before the picture window, next to a box of overwatered, crowded plants. She came to the Oasis every morning, sat down, and waited like a brute for coffee. She'd never had trouble getting it before. Now when Dolores raised her hand, the waitress looked at her and looked away.

Dolores knew the waitress. Her name was Teresa. She was a young, ungainly woman whose stomach seemed to be leading her around. She had a funny way of holding her forearms out in front of her at the waist, elbows bent, large hands dangling like flippers. Dolores knew that she had a snotty boyfriend, that she'd just graduated from the School of Public Health, and that she wanted to open an abortion clinic. She barely knew Dolores, and had no reason to dislike her.

Dolores glared at Teresa. It didn't work. She got two antidepressants from her bag and put them on the table so the waitress could see she needed something to swallow medicine with. Teresa sailed by imperiously, a full pot of coffee in her grip, nonacknowledging Dolores's "Excuse me" with an aggressive whap of her hip against the table, causing Dolores's antidepressants to roll off onto the floor. As Dolores bent to pick them up, Teresa ran back and yelled, "Are you ready?"

Dolores jerked up too quickly, dropped the pills, then had to reach for them again. She laughed nervously as she emerged from under the table a second time. "Are you ready to order?" asked Teresa.

"Hello," said Dolores.

Teresa stood there silently, one large hand dangling.

"I'd like a black coffee with—"

"What?" snapped Teresa.

"I said I'd like a black coffee with an apricot roll."

"We don't have any more rolls."

"All right. Just coffee."

When Teresa poured the coffee, she spilled some on Dolores's mulberry-colored gloves and didn't say she was sorry. A few minutes later, Dolores saw her traveling across the floor with a little plate of apricot rolls for another table, dangling hand wagging. Everyone else in the restaurant continued to smoke cigarettes, eat, and talk as if nothing had happened. Dolores began to feel depressed.

Teresa's friend Lindsay walked into the restaurant. Teresa cried "Linnnnn!" as if she hadn't seen Lindsay for months; they kissed and touched each other's arms. Teresa had incredibly thick, dark arm hair. Dolores remembered a girl from high school who, because of her thick body hair, shaved her arms. It had looked awful. Teresa and Lindsay walked to the counter with their arms around each other. They stood there giggling and whispering. Lindsay was a small, pretty girl who wanted to be a writer. She wore a black leather jacket and large black sunglasses. She came to the Oasis almost every day. She could sit there all day talking about how depressed she was to the various friends and acquaintances who would occupy the empty place beside her as the day went on. Dolores despised Lindsay for wearing ridiculous sunglasses and for letting her father support her. This, although Dolores's father had supported her until he went bankrupt.

Teresa and Lindsay turned to lean against the counter and stared at Dolores. They looked right at her, whispering and giggling. Dolores tried to think about how one of them was ugly and the other stupid. It didn't help. Under their eyes, she felt swollen and hideous at her little table in the sun. At least they were young and had boyfriends to get depressed about. She was an overweight twenty-nine-year-old in stretch pants and a scarf that hid her debased head, mentally ill, and unable to have orgasms, not even with herself, sitting in a college town with nothing to do but run around the phys ed building. She felt like the kind of retarded person who's smart enough to know she's retarded. Teresa and Lindsay looked and giggled; Dolores swelled, until she felt like a giantess barely able to hold the delicate little cup and utensils in her horrible fingers.

She no longer wanted to run around the track after her coffee. She drove back home, got in bed, and lay there while the sun gamboled over her body. She thought, This wouldn't be happening to me if Allan hadn't dumped me. She turned her head and her eyeballs took a rolling tour of the room. It had bright yellow wallpaper and plants in it. Baby pictures of her and her younger brother Patrick hung on the walls, Patrick looking dark and tiny and very solemn for a three-year-old. She had lots of pretty things—lacy lamp shades, linen dustcovers, vases and literature on the bookshelves. It would've been nice if someone else had lived in it.

When her father came to visit her in the mental hospital, right after Allan had dumped her, she'd said, "Daddy, I want you to beat me." He'd turned away and licked his lips. Dolores didn't see why he should balk at that; he'd been beating her mother for years, although it was true that it had never been a physical beating. Besides, the first time she'd been in a mental hospital, she'd asked him to kill her; this second request seemed reasonable in comparison.

She lived in a communal house with her younger brother, Patrick, his girlfriend, Lily, and Mark, a twenty-one-year-old philosophy student. Patrick was an acting student and a drummer in a local band that actually made a living; Lily was a journalism student. They were supposed to buy food together, but Dolores didn't like what Patrick and Lily bought, and nobody liked what Mark ate. They were supposed to split the bills four ways, but somehow bills got paid only after Patrick received a shutoff notice; then it took him months to collect from the others. The kitchen table was always covered with months' worth of bills, as well as papers scrawled with phone messages, cigarettes, ashtrays, pencils, and fruit, especially blackening bananas pulled apart from their bunch and ranging all through the mess in singular curves.

Dolores had never lived like this before. She'd never wanted to. But when Patrick came to visit her in the mental hospital, he'd said she could move in with him when he found a house, that he would take care of her. His large petal-shaped eyes were full of concern and puzzlement, and she was seized with a need to be near her brother, even though they did not get along, mostly because his gentle nature made her want to bully him.

Dolores liked Lily. Lily was a very pretty, very unpopular girl with a strange light-headed demeanor. She was very thin, and gave the impression that she walked on her toes. She had very black shoulder-length hair, narrow gray eyes, and a thin, severe mouth. She shied away from people, softly and indifferently as a cat. She had grown up in a foster home and had lived on her own since she was seventeen. Except for Dolores, she had no friends in Ann Arbor. She actually had enemies; Patrick's female friends were appalled when he first started to go out with her. Dolores was surprised to find herself associating with outcasts at such a late time in life.

On weekends, Patrick and Lily would sit around the kitchen for hours into the morning, cutting slices of rye bread for toast. After toast, they'd have tea and soft-boiled eggs, which Lily served in tiny porcelain eggcups with roses on them. Patrick would always finish his breakfast by peeling an orange or a grapefruit until every bit of white rind had been picked off it, then meticulously stripping the membrane off of each section with his teeth before eating it.

"You look like a kitten when you do that," said Lily. "A kitten playing with something."

"He is a kitten," said Dolores scornfully.

"Wash my dishes, slave," said Patrick. Since Dolores couldn't stand the idea of work yet, Patrick paid her rent. Because of this, he tried to push her around a little. "Slave? The dishes." He stretched his long neck out and grinned like a donkey.

"Give me some money, goon. I need cigarettes and medicine."

"I gave you twenty dollars yesterday."

"I need twenty more at least, fool."

But she was as touched by his beauty as anyone. He was tall, but girlishly slim and narrow-built, with the sensitive, angular face of a greyhound, a face heightened piercingly by large transparent eyes and a full emotional lower lip. When he played the drums, he sat straight and earnest behind the set, his eyebrows furrowed, listening terribly hard to something only he could hear, and hitting with a thrilling fierceness that seemed to come from the center of his small chest. Girls loved him, which was why they were outraged to see him with a creep like Lily.

He twisted his pliant neck to one side, shifted his slender hips, and dug into his pocket. He handed Dolores ten dollars. She snatched it and stuck it in her pocket.

Mark lumbered into the room and, without turning his head, flickered his flat gray eyes at the three of them. He was a tall boy with wide, heavy hips and coarse hair that stood up on his head, giving his pale face a shocked expression. He went to the counter and began preparing his breakfast of fried eggs, bacon, and toast with mint jelly.

"Bernie Gahan called me last night," said Dolores. "You know, from high school?"

"I remember," said Patrick. "He was sort of a geek, wasn't he?"

"Who's he?" asked Lily, smearing slabs of butter over her hot toast.

"That guy I saw just before I went into the hospital. That store clerk, the one who fucked me in the ass."

"I can't believe some of the things I hear in this house," said Mark. He violently mixed his eggs around in their frying pan.

"He's crazy," said Dolores. "The next morning, he had a fit when I put my coffee cup on his *Village Voice*. He said it proved how sick I was."

"Why did you go out with him?" asked Lily.

Dolores shrugged. "I don't know. He was cool in high school, but now he's getting fat."

"He was never cool," said Patrick.

Lily looked at Dolores over her toast, munching solemnly. Dolores could tell she wanted to hear more about Bernie Gahan.

"When he dropped me off at home, he put his finger on my nose and said, 'Catch ya later, kid!' God. I mean, I'm not a kid."

"It's too bad for you that you're not," said Mark. "The prognosis would be a lot better." He sat on the edge of a chair with his feet together and paused over his eggs. "I think it's the ultimate hypocrisy, Pat, for a vegetarian to smoke."

"Squeedle-de-bop," said Patrick. He tipped his head back and blew a mouthful of smoke at the ceiling.

"Don't give me that. You may be a great drummer, but you're a slob."

"And you're a grandmother," said Dolores. "A sexually frustrated grandmother."

"Just because sex isn't the be-all and end-all for me, Dolores."

"If you ever had it, it would be the end-all," said Lily.

"Why don't you try to seduce me, Dolores? Just try. I'll hurt your feelings."

"The only thing you'd hurt is your reputation—wait, do you have one?"

"I could really hurt you, Dolores."

Dolores doubted it. It would've made her feel better if she'd thought he could, but she knew he couldn't. She pushed through the papers and breakfast dishes and found her plastic bag of dried prunes. She picked through the prunes to find a soft one. "I saw your friend again," she said to Mark.

"Which one? *I* actually have more than one friend."

"The one who's going bald. The one who walks like a dinosaur." She found a prune and began eating it.

"Was she mean to you again?" asked Lily.

Dolores nodded. "Yes. She was mean to me."

"I'm sorry," said Mark. "I don't know why she does that."

"She's a bitch," said Dolores. "Maybe she knows Allan and he told her something about me."

"Do you sit in the Oasis and put on your false nails?" asked Patrick. He tipped his chair back until it stood on its hind legs. His T-shirt slid up and exposed his stomach, which he scratched.

"No. I don't put them on that early. Why?"

"A waitress might think they were disgusting. I wouldn't want to sit next to them. The glue stinks."

The next time she went into the Oasis, she brought a box of Dragon Lady fingernails, and two bottles of red polish. After she got her coffee and rolls, with the usual trouble, she took out the box and laid the flesh-colored spears on the table so Teresa would notice them and wonder what the hell was going on. She got the glue and began working, periodically stopping to hold the claws up to dry.

Teresa didn't notice, but the guy at the next table did. "I didn't know anybody wore those things anymore," he said.

"I do," trilled Dolores in a hideously affected voice. "I'm naked without them." Lily told her that she sometimes sounded like Blanche DuBois. She held up her taloned hands to her face and leered daintily.

"Oh, Dragon Lady," he said, "have mercy."

His friend laughed and scratched his beard.

I am a sexually potent woman, thought Dolores. Even if I am partially bald. During one of their last fights, Allan had said, "There's no love in you because there's no sex in you. Sex is light and fertility and life and communication! You only have this . . . pornography and submission and blackness and death! You're like a faggot!"

"You ass-wipe," she muttered. She couldn't help it if fertility didn't interest her in the abstract. It did interest her in the real. "Do you want to have children?" she asked the man next to her.

"Yeah, one day. Why?"

"Because I like to hear people say they want children. That's what would make me happy, I think, to have children. My room-mate is beautiful and she's not interested in having children."

"Your roommate is an idiot, that's why."

Sasha thumped against Dolores's table. She was a fat girl, and her fat was like the fur of a Persian cat. Her eyes were arrogantly flat and brown-gold, rimmed with black kohl. She wore a purple skirt with a gold hem and long green stockings with ducks on them. Of Patrick's friends, she was chief among the Lily haters. "How are you, darling?" she said.

"Bothering somebody. How are you?"

"I'm eating. I'm going from house to house eating my brains out. Now I'm here to get some home fries off the cook. It's the first day I've eaten in two weeks and I'm going to make the most of it."

"Where's George?"

"I don't know, getting chemotherapy." She sneered in an affected way that Dolores found absurd but exciting. "I don't know where the hell he is and I'm tired of people asking me. That's all I hear everywhere I go. 'Is she the one who's having an affair with George Hammond? Are they still together?' Are there any home fries, Eddie baby? With catsup and mayonnaise? Come sit by me and let me play with the hair on your chest. Only don't talk to me about George Hammond. I don't have anyplace to live. I lost my job at the art school and I couldn't pay my rent. I'd come stay with you except for your creepy roommate."

"Lily's not so creepy. You'd like her if you actually knew her."

"Is it true she bangs her head on the wall?"

"She might."

"Do you know what she said to me the last time I saw her? She was talking to John Francis about how, when she was fourteen, she used to want plastic surgery to change her lips and her eyebrows, and she turned to me and said, 'If you could get plastic surgery, what would you do?' Jesus Christ!"

"She didn't mean you *should* get plastic surgery."

"What are you doing to your nails?"

"Nothing."

"Oh, here's my home fries. Thanks, honey. Open your shirt. See you, Dolores. My life's in a shambles."

Dolores drank her coffee with even more sobriety. Everybody wanted to be depressed. But your depression was supposed to be funny, too, and that was what had proved too much for Dolores.

Sasha was sitting at the counter now, fondling the thin blond cook through his faded shirt, and skillfully nipping up mayonnaise-and-catsup-drenched fries, three fries at a time, with her pinkie extended. She was yelling about George Hammond. What would happen to Sasha? She almost had a degree in Russian, specializing in literature—but then she'd dropped out. Since then, she had been mulling around Ann Arbor in garish skirts and boots, sitting in bars and cafés gossiping all day.

Dolores was the same way, except that the degree she almost had was in history, and rather than gossiping in bars and cafés, she merely sat in them.

Teresa coursed by like a shark, her low forehead predomi-nant as a snout. Dolores felt impotent detestation. Teresa saw the false fingernails, now standing out from Dolores's hands like evil thoughts. Dolores stared at her nails, like a sea blob heaved up on a hot beach, dimly realizing that its soft, flat flippers won't help it get back into the water. Teresa sneered and began scribbling on her little gray pad. She ripped off Dolores's check and threw it at her, mumbling something about needing more table space.

Was strength the ability to make someone leave a restaurant, mostly because they couldn't bear to be in your presence any-more? Was it being big and loud and going to a bar with other big loud people and making more noise than anyone else there? Insulting someone? People insulted Lily often, and though she pretended not to be affected, Dolores knew she was hurt by it. But she couldn't stop them from doing it. Did that mean she was weak? On the other hand, Dolores sometimes pushed Patrick around and all he did was say "Dolores!" But he was a promising actor and a successful musician, and she was a flop.

She sweated wonderfully as she ran around the gym. Every day there were lots of other people sweating around the track with her, in headbands and sweatsuits. They were all trying to be strong. The day before, in the checkout line at Kresge's, Dolores had overheard a girl with pounds of wavy blond hair and bulging calf muscles say to her friend, "And I'm getting up every day and running!" like it was the best thing ever.

Anyone would do anything to be stronger. In the gym next to the track, college students took karate classes. Little teenage girls padded out of the dressing rooms in their white karate uniforms, some of them wearing small gold chains and nail polish. She could hear the instructor yelling at them. "Everyone wants to have control!" he shouted. "And to have control, you have to fight for it, work for it!"

Lily and Patrick were obsessed with working. Whenever you asked Lily how she was, she would either say that she was good, she'd been very productive, or that she was awful, she'd been so unproductive. All night, they would sit at the kitchen table eating toast and working on their projects. Lily had her work for school and her articles for local papers and magazines, and Patrick had his rehearsals and homework, plus his music to write. Lily worked with her long legs drawn up under her and her shoulders in a curl; Patrick sat on his tailbone, his legs spread and his cotton shirt open, his head hanging from his neck like a heavy flower.

After she ran, she stopped by Majik Market to shoplift several eyeliner pencils and a box of peanut brittle. Then she went home to share the candy with Lily. They sat at the kitchen table and ate big slabs of it out of the open box.

"People have told me that my sexuality is death-oriented," said Dolores, crunching her mouthful of candy.

"People have dumb ideas about sex," said Lily. "How long have you been having sex?"

"Twelve years."

"If your sexuality was death-oriented, you'd be dead by now." She was picking through the candy; it looked funny to see her serious face bent over it.

"Well, they didn't mean literal death. They meant death in the abstract."

"There's no such thing as death in the abstract. You're dead or you're not." Lily's hand dived into the box and emerged with a nut-encrusted chunk. "You can't have a facsimile of death." She leaned back in her chair like Patrick and popped the candy into her mouth. She sucked on it, her face slowly becoming tranquil.

"How do you know that if you don't know what death is like?" Dolores ran her tongue over her molars and found them coated with gnawed candy.

Dolores often wanted to die, even though she didn't know what it was like, either. Allan used to tell her about the recurring nightmares he had, in which his father humiliated him sexually. He said it was the same thing as dreaming about death. Dolores thought that if to be humiliated was to be dead, she would be decomposed beyond recognition. But she was crazily alive, stuffed with blood and muscles, going to the bathroom regularly, having conversations.

If she were dead, her blood wouldn't suffer the pain of struggling to sing while life's constant attack made it hurt to move in her veins at all. Why couldn't people be nice? Why did you go into a restaurant and get attacked by a bitch who hated you for no reason? Why did Allan's friends, when they saw her, look at her with that vague leer and the concern they thought they should have for a disturbed older woman, the expression that felt like a razor across her face? Allan's friends were young and loud, their bodies hideously forceful in the occupation of space. Even though he was in art school, most of them were law students, always apparently happy and grabbing. Just the sight of them, with their rough, healthy skin and big legs and heavy, porous head hair made her feel horrible, especially when one of them cornered her and tried to be nice. Sometimes she encouraged it, and she was always sorry later.

She remembered a time she'd met one of them at a student party. She and Allan had broken up a few days before. She was fairly drunk and slumped on a couch with a few kids whom she could no longer remember except as a mass of T-shirts and long hair. She was staring at a group of people stomping their way through a dance in the middle of the room. Harvey approached her and shouted through the music that he wanted to walk her home. She chattered to him all the way to her apartment, some grim inner monitor manipulating her shrill babble to impress him with her normality, her happiness. She told him about her projects, her courses at school. He made his voice go gentle; he touched her elbow, put a hand on her shoulder. They sat on her front porch steps, watching ants run in and out of their grainy little nest in the crack of the second step. He was very careful with the way he talked to her; he wanted to show that he respected her. He talked about books and art. He asked her, "But seriously, what is your favorite Faulkner novel?"

Allan had said, "I don't like people who feel sorry for themselves. In the past, I have had the patience of Job with weak and neurotic women. Not anymore."

But he was neurotic; he was weak. Once when they were arguing, she said, "And everyone in the art department hates you," even though she had no idea if that was true.

They were sitting on her front porch in the dark of night; she could not see his reaction, but she could feel it: He withdrew into himself and almost began to quiver with emotion. For a moment, she thought he would cry. "Not all of them," she said hastily. "Just a few." And he said, "Who? Who are they?"

And still he held her and said, "I want you to be a strong woman. I know you can be. I want you to be productive." He held her and she talked about her adulterous, alcoholic father as if he were a character on TV. "He ruined my mother financially and mentally. I don't even know where he is now. Somewhere in South America, trying to set up a tropical-fish business and fucking some fat eighteen-year-old who's in the Peace Corps. He's been through five failed businesses in the last eight years. He ruins everything he touches. Everybody said my mother was crazy when she went after him with the scissors. But I didn't think so."

Her mother was putting her life back together, even though she was murderously unhappy. Right after Dolores got out of the hospital, her mother invited her over for sandwiches cut up into four pieces. Her mother sat on the very edge of the couch and Dolores sat on the edge of a chair, with the sandwiches on a table between them. Her mother gripped her cream cheese and olive morsel like she had tweezers for hands. "The problem is that I just never asked 'What about *me?*' " she said furiously. "And now it's time for me. Me!"

Dolores had pitied her terribly.

But her mother was tough in her way. She ran her travel business and went to a yoga club and was even having an affair. She was strong, even if her face looked as if it were a mask held in place with staples.

Dolores lay in the dark of her room and said, "And now it's time for me! Me!" She said it as vehemently as she could, but she knew she had nothing but the dozens of eyebrow pencils and the nail polish and face cream she'd stolen and piled up on her dresser.

Lily and Patrick were having a fight. Dolores looked on with interest, although there wasn't much to watch. They were only eating breakfast, but they were doing it furiously. "You don't have to pretend that anything's normal," said Lily.

"I'm not." Patrick held up his slice of rye bread and spread it with apple butter evenly and meticulously. Lily was angry at Patrick for not telling off his friends who were mean to her. Maybe they would break up, and then Lily and Dolores could spend more time at the bar talking about how awful men were.

Lily got up in the middle of eating her soft-boiled egg and began sweeping the floor like a robot. "This place is fucking filthy," she said.

It was. Lily had already swept up a huge pile of dirt and dust and papers and food, and she hadn't even come close to finishing.

"You don't have to act like we're living in a nuthouse," said Patrick.

"We are." Lily threw the broom on the floor and went back to her egg, which sat in its rose cup. "It's not surprising that your friends treat me like shit, when it's obvious you don't have any respect for me. You let them do it. If I had friends who called me up and invited me to parties and wouldn't invite you, I wouldn't go. I wouldn't treat you like that."

"You could've gone."

"I wasn't invited. You and Dolores were. Sasha's always nasty to me anyway. You saw how she was last week."

Patrick put down his bread, picked up the knife, and began resmoothing the apple butter. "I saw how you were, too. You didn't extend yourself at all."

"Whenever I say anything, she ignores me or pretends to mis-understand. I'm tired of your dumb friends anyway, especially that dumb bitch Sasha. I'm tired of hearing these middle-class bitches who've never worked in their life, whose parents pay their rent and buy them college degrees, sit around and talk about how depressed they are. I don't have any parents and I don't have any friends and I've had to work for everything I ever got, which hasn't been much."

She was yelling now. Patrick's eyes had become very soft.

What a mess I live in, thought Dolores. Isn't it interesting, even though she could be talking about me.

Mark walked into the room with his hair on end and his shoulders knit together, his eyes flickering at Lily. "Oh God," spat Lily. She grabbed her eggcup, tossed the egg in the garbage, and left the room.

"It's so horrible living with two people who are involved in a relationship," hissed Mark at Dolores. "Especially when one of them is mentally ill." He raised his voice. "Who threw the broom on the floor?"

The bar was full of familiar, attractive people; plates of cheese sat on several tables, and plants hung above all heads. Dolores had been coming here almost every night. No waitresses were mean to her here. Lily was disappointingly calm, though, and only half-interested in talking about how awful men were.

"I know we have to break up eventually," she said. "I just don't want it to be about something as stupid as this. It's just gotten to the point that I can't tolerate it anymore. I mean the way his friends act toward me."

She wasn't showing anger at all. Her voice was flat, her expression blank. Dolores wondered if Lily looked that way because it was her nature or if the outside world had been so painful for her that she couldn't stand to be in it fully. She looked at Lily's long, slender fingers against the iced glass of her drink and felt touched by her vulnerability. Why should people dislike her? "It's really shitty," said Dolores.

"I don't know why it's happening."

Her passivity made Dolores feel a little contemptuous. She ordered another drink. "It's a small town. People like to gossip, and you're a natural subject because you're different."

"How am I different?"

Dolores sighed and looked at the ceiling, both hands on her drink. The question stirred memories of answering a professor's questions and loving the sound of her intelligent voice. "Because on one hand you seem completely unaware of people, completely self-contained and happy to be that way. And then you'll suddenly be so open and needy. I think the abrupt contrast disturbs people. And they can be aggressive with you because you're actually gentle. Even if you don't talk that way."

Lily didn't answer, but Dolores thought she looked pleased with the explanation.

"I'm sort of glad you're dumping Patrick. I know he's my brother and everything, but it's about time somebody dumped him. He's been picking up and putting down girls for years. It's sickening."

Lily shrugged. "He's told me all about what a heartbreaker he is. I guess it means I'm supposed to be the one to bring him down."

"You should. It would do him good."

"I don't see how it would do him good."

"Because it would teach him something about life. He's never been hurt before in that way. He thinks everything's so easy and that he's never been hurt because he's so smart."

"Being hurt doesn't teach anybody anything," said Lily. "It doesn't help. It just feels bad." She nipped up a piece of cheese and munched. "Although there is the Jesus stuff," she said through her cheese. "Suffering and redemption, suffering and purity."

"That's not what I'm talking about," said Dolores.

"What are you talking about?"

Dolores sighed abruptly; her eyes went ceilingward. "Morally, in the Christian sense, strength isn't necessarily a good thing. You're supposed to turn the other cheek, be sacrificed, you know? But I think that kind of meekness is weak, and when you think about it, weakness is really . . . evil in a way. It's like being connected with the ugly things in the world. You're the clubfooted straggler endangering the herd. You make people depressed and sentimental."

"Did you vote for Reagan? That's his whole thing; he's for strength. People despised Carter for being weak."

"No. No, no. I didn't vote for anybody. I'm not talking about anything political. I don't mean you should despise people for being weak, if it's a kind of weakness they can't help. But when they're weak on purpose, it's another thing. When they don't even try. When they let people hurt them and don't fight back. It's gross. It's letting down the whole human race."

"Oh. I think I see what you mean." Lily looked out the window for a minute. "It's funny. When Reagan won, I was secretly relieved. Even though I hate him. Secretly, some part of me must feel like he's right. Even though I think Carter is the better one." She turned to face Dolores. "Tell me again why you think I should dump Patrick."

"Well, to . . . to make him see that he could be weak and damaged like anybody else."

Lily smiled. "That would just make Patrick stronger."

"Think so?"

"Some people are like that. Patrick is like that. The more he was hurt, the stronger he'd get. It's like Ann Landers says: 'The same heat that melts butter tempers steel.' "

"If it's that way, maybe you really should dump him."

Lily made a face. "The thing is, I don't want to hurt his feelings." She played with the wheat crackers on their plate. "I wonder how many other people feel that way about Reagan? Even if they hate him?"

Dolores had begun to work on her history papers so she could graduate. There were only three weeks left to get them done, and she hadn't even started her research, so she had to get up very early in the morning. She went to the Oasis before many people had a chance to get there and start gossiping. She smoked and drank coffee and read about socialism in England. It was wonderful to be constructive. No wonder Lily clung to it so. Dolores wondered if it would change her appearance the way masturbating had. After Lily and Patrick broke up, she masturbated for the first time in six months. People kept telling her how relaxed she looked all of a sudden. Lily said her "energy" had changed. Maybe doing her history papers would have an even greater effect.

At night, she went to the bar and saw Sasha and her friends. Sasha looked fat and tragic, her eyes bitterly flat and smeared with kohl. Dolores told her about the papers. "Good girl!" said Sasha. "I never did my papers. Is it true that Lily and Patrick broke up?"

"For a few days now. I think they might get back together, though. They're being very seductive at breakfast."

Dolores was surprised when Sasha didn't say anything nasty. She just started telling about how she'd gotten kicked out of her best friend's apartment after a fight, and how she had to stay with George Hammond as a result. "Of course, he'll probably kick me out as soon as he gets tired of me. He loves me most when I start talking about moving to Chicago."

Lindsay walked in wearing her little black leather jacket. Her large, heavy brown eyes looked smug and almost crossed under her tortoiseshell glasses, and her little nose was in the air. "Sasha!" she cried, advancing toward them. "Hi, you look great."

"Being an outcast is very becoming," replied Sasha. "I hear you're going to New York."

"Yeah, I'm going to become a disc jockey. I know people there who can get me connected. At least I hope they can. Hi, Dolores."

"Oh, you'll do great. You're the kind of person who's successful."

"I can just hear her on the radio in New York," said Sasha after Lindsay had left. "Have you heard her show? It's called 'No Feelings' and she reads her poetry on it. All this stuff about splinters of night reaming her eyes. She's retarded. She'll probably get a great job in New York. Every pretentious asshole I know went to New York and got a job in film or publishing."

"I'm an asshole and I don't have a job in film or publishing."

"That's because you're not pretentious. You wouldn't even be an asshole except you can't get out of Ann Arbor. And who am I to talk? I've been trying to get out for years."

"I'm going to get out soon," said Dolores.

Dolores rolled her car windows down as she drove home, so she could feel the spring air and look at the little residential houses. She drove her car up onto the lawn and almost over the tulips. She heard herself thunder across the porch like an ogre.

As soon as she walked in the door, she knew that Lily and Patrick had gotten back together. She heard their voices coming out of the kitchen in low, intimate sounds, and when she put her head around the corner, she saw them sitting amid their papers. On the table were little dishes with pieces of toast on them and an open package of butter with a knife still in it.

She turned and padded away. She went upstairs and threw her books and papers on the floor. She got into the bed and lay there, swollen and drunk. She reviewed the situation: Her hair was growing out so well, it was almost okay to take the scarf off. She was working on her papers. She was masturbating and having orgasms. Lily was right. Ann Landers was right. She was one of those people who just got stronger and stronger, no matter what you did. Her strength was like the steel structure of a bombed-out building, stripped but imperious and stern. She couldn't feel anything inside herself now but flat metallic strength.

Folk Song

On the same page of the city paper one day:

A confessed murderer awaiting trial for the torture and murder of a woman and her young daughter was a guest on a talk show via satellite. His appearance was facilitated by the mother's parents, who wanted him to tell them exactly what the murder of their daughter and grandchild had been like. "It was horrible," said the talk-show hostess. "He will go down in history as the lowest of the low." There was a photograph of the killer, smiling as if he'd won a prize.

A woman in San Francisco announced her intention to have intercourse with one thousand men in a row, breaking the record of a woman in New Mexico who had performed the same feat with a mere 750. "I want to show what women can do," she said. "I am not doing this as a feminist, but as a human being."

Two giant turtles belonging to an endangered species were stolen from the Bronx Zoo. "This may've been an inside job," said the zoo president. "This person knew what he was doing, and he was very smart. We just hope he keeps them together—they're very attached." The turtles were valued at three hundred dollars each.

It was in the middle of the paper, a page that you were meant to scan before turning, loading your brain with subliminal messages as you did. How loathsome to turn a sadistic murder into entertainment—and yet how hard not to read about it. What dark comedy to realize that you are scanning for descriptions of torture even as you disapprove. Which of course only makes it more entertaining. "But naturally I was hoping they'd report something grisly," you say to your friends, who chuckle at your lighthearted acknowledgment of hypocrisy.

And they did report something grisly: the grandparents of the murdered girl who wanted to know what only the murderer could tell them. You picture the grandmother's gentle wrinkled chest, a thick strip of flesh pulled away to reveal an unexpected passage to hell in her heart.

Then you have the marathon woman right underneath, smiling like an evangelist, her organs open for a thousand. An especially grotty sort of pie-eating contest, placed right beneath the killer, the pure vulnerability of an open body juxtaposed against the pure force of destruction. Why would a woman do that? What do her inane words really mean? Will she select the thousand? Is there at least a screening process? Or is it just anyone who shows up? If he had not been arrested, could the killer himself have mounted her along with everybody else? If she had discovered who he was, would that have been okay with her? Would she have just swallowed him without a burp?

You picture her at the start of her ordeal, parting a curtain to appear before the crowd, muscular, oiled, coifed, dressed in a lamé bathing suit with holes cut in the titties and crotch. She would turn and bend to show the suit had been cut there, too. She would "ring-walk" before the bed, not like a stripper, more like a pro wrestler, striking stylized sex poses, flexing the muscles of her belly and thighs, gesticulating with mock anger, making terrible penis-busting faces.

Might the killer enjoy this spectacle if he could watch it on TV? He may be a destroyer of women, but his victims were regular, human-style women: a concerned mother trying to connect with her daughter on a road trip in nature—the trip that delivered them into the hands of the killer. You picture the mother reading *Reviving Ophelia* the night before they left, frowning slightly as she thinks of the teenage boy years ago who fucked her mouth and then took her to dinner at Pizza Hut, thinks also of her daughter's coed sleepover last week. Getting out of bed to use the bathroom with only the hall light on, peeing in gentle darkness, remembering: Grown-up pee used to smell so bad to her, and now the smell is just another welcome personal issue of her hardworking body, tough and fleshy in middle age, safe under her old flowered gown. The daughter is awake, too, and reading *Wuthering Heights.* She is thirteen, and she is irritated that the author has such sympathy for Heathcliff, who abuses his wife and child. What does it mean that he is capable of such passionate love? Is this realistic, or were people just dumber and more romantic back then? She doesn't think that the mean people she knows are the most passionate; they just want to laugh at everything. But then she remembers that she laughed when a boy in class played a joke on an ugly girl and made her cry. Sighing, she puts the book down and lies on her back, her arm thrown luxuriantly over her head. On the ceiling, there are the beautiful shadows of slim branches and leaves. She does not really want to take this trip with her mother. Her mother tries so hard to help her and to protect her, and she finds this embarrassing. It makes her want to protect her mother, and that feeling is uncomfortable, too. She rolls on her side and picks up the book again.

————

Thought and feeling, flesh and electricity, ordinary yet complex personalities, the like of which the killer had found impossible to maintain inside himself from the moment of his birth—and yet which he could erase with the strange, compulsive pleasure of an autistic child banging his head on the wall. You picture him as a little boy alone in an empty room, head subtly inclined, as if he is listening intently for a special sound. In the top drawer of his dresser, there are rows of embalmed mice stacked neatly atop one another. At age twelve, he has killed many animals besides mice, but he embalms only the mice because uniformity satisfies him. He likes embalming because it is clean, methodical, and permanent. He likes his mind to be uniform and inflexible as a grid. Below the grid is like the life of animals—sensate and unbearably deep.

There are people who believe that serial killers are a "fundamental force of nature," a belief that would be very appealing to the killer. Yes, he would say to himself, that is me. I am fundamental! But the marathon woman on TV would be fundamental, too. She would not show her personality, and even if she did, nobody would see it; they would be too distracted by the thought of a mechanical cunt, endlessly absorbing discharge. However, with her lamé bathing suit and her camp ring walk, appealing to everyone's sense of fun, she would be the fundamental female as comedy: The killer could sit comfortably in the audience and laugh, enjoying this appearance of his feminine colleague. Maybe he would feel such comfort that he would stand and come forward, unbuckling his pants with the flushed air of a modest person finally coming up to give testimony. Safe in her sweating, loose, and very wet embrace, surrounded by the dense energy of many men, his penis could tell her the secret story of murder right in front of everyone. Her worn vagina would hold the killer like it had held the husband and the lover and the sharpie and the father and the nitwit and every other man, his terrible story a tiny, burning star in the rightful firmament of her female vastness.

Hell, yes, she would "show what women can do"!

In the context of this dreadful humanity, you think, The poor turtles! They do not deserve to be on the same page with these people! You think of them making their stoic way across a pebbled beach, their craning necks wrinkled and diligent, their bodies a secret even they cannot lick or scratch. The murdered woman, in moments of great tenderness for her husband, would put her hands on his thighs and kiss him on his balls and say to him, "Secret Paul." She didn't mean that his balls were a secret. She meant that she was kissing the part of him that no one knew except her, and that the vulnerability of his balls made her feel this part acutely. That is the kind of secret the turtles are, even to themselves.

But now all natural secrets have been exposed, and it is likely the turtles have been sold to laboratory scientists who want to remove their shells so that they can wire electrodes to the turtles' skin in order to monitor their increasing terror at the loss of their shells. You think, This idea is absurd and grotesque. It isn't even possible to remove a turtle's shell without killing it! Yet with science, anything is possible. With science, rats have been tortured by electroshock each time they press a lever to get a food pellet. Rabbits have been injected with cancerous cells and then divided into control groups, one of which was petted and the other not, in order to investigate the role of affection in healing. Scientists do these experiments because they want to help. They want to alleviate physical suffering; they want to eradicate depression. To achieve their goal, they will take everything apart and put it back together a different way. They want heaven and they will go to hell to get there.

But still, there is grace. Before the mother met the murderer, her vagina had been gently parted and kissed many times. Her daughter had exposed her own vagina before her flowered cardboard mirror (bought at Target and pushpinned to the wall), regarding her organs with pleased wonder, thinking, This is what I have.

And maybe the turtles were not kidnapped, but rescued: There are actually preserves for turtles, special parks where people can take turtles they have found or grown tired of, or rescued from the polluted, fetid fish tanks of uncaring neighbors. Or maybe they were simply set free near the water, wading forward together as the zoo spokesman had hoped, eyes bright in scaly heads, each with the unerring sense of the other's heartbeat, a signal they never knew to question.

And maybe she didn't start the marathon in a gold lamé suit. Maybe she appeared in a simple white gown with a slip and a bra and stockings and beautiful panties that the first man (hand-selected for his sensitivity) had to help her take off to the sound of "The First Time Ever I Saw Your Face." Maybe they even took time to make out, acknowledging romantic love and the ancient truth of marriage. It would be the stiff and brassy acknowledgment of showbiz, but deep in the brass case would be a sad and tender feeling—sad because they could stay only a moment in this adolescent sweetness, could not develop it into the full flower of adult intimacy and parenthood. But this flower comes in the form of a human; it must soon succumb to disease, atrophy, ruined skin, broken teeth, the unbearable frailty of mortality.

The marathon woman is not interested in mortality or human love. Right now, the marathon woman has infinity on her mind. Roberta Flack's crooning fades. The first man mournfully withdraws. Then: the majestic pounding of kettle drums and brisk, surging brass! It's *2001: A Space Odyssey*! The lights go up! The silhouettes of naked men are revealed on the screen behind her bed, above which spins a giant disco ball! Men step from behind the screen and array themselves about the bed, splendid in their nakedness, even the ugly ones, like gladiators poised to wade in! This one now, number two, is very short and muscular, covered with hair. His face is handsome; his body exudes physical swagger shadowed by physical grief. The woman cannot know that, at eighteen, he was a gunnery mate on a PT boat in Vietnam, or that *Time* once ran a photograph of him posed with his machine gun, the brim of his helmet low across his eyes, a cigarette sticking up at a jaunty angle from between his clenched, smiling lips. She can't know it, but she can feel it: the stunned cockiness of an ignorant boy cradling Death in one arm, cockiness now held fast in the deep heart of a middle-aged man. Just before he enters her, she pictures his heart bristling with tough little hairs. Then she feels his dick and forgets his heart. He pulls her on top of him and she feels another man ready to climb up her butt while number four bossily plants himself in her mouth, one hand holding his penis, the other on his fleshy hip. The referee, a balding fellow in a smart striped shirt, weaves deftly in and out of the melee, ensuring that real penetration is taking place each time. The music segues into hammering dance music, the kind favored by porn movies, only better. The music is like a mob breaking down a flimsy door and spilling endlessly over the threshold. It celebrates dissolution, but it has a rigid form and it hits the same button again and again. It makes you think of Haitian religious dances where the dancers empty their personalities to receive the raw flux of spirit—except this music does not allow for spirit. This is the music of personality and obsession, and it is like a high-speed purgatory where the body is disintegrated and reanimated over and over until the soul is a whipsawed blur. It is fun! People dance to this music every night in great glittering venues all over the world, and now the woman and the men fuck to it. They are really doing it and it is chaos! The referee furrows his brow as he darts about, occasionally giving the "Roll over" signal with his forearms, or a TKO hand sign barring a man who's trying to sneak in a second time.

And because it is chaos, there are moments when the woman's mind slips through the bullying order of the music and the assault of the men. There are many trapdoors in personality and obsession, and she blunders down some of them—even though she doesn't realize that she has done so. Like the killer, she is now able only to occupy her surface because extraordinary physical demands are being made on her surface. By turning herself into a fucking machine, she has created a kind of temporary grid. But underneath, in the place of dream and feeling, she is going places that she, on the surface, would not understand.

What no one would guess about this woman who is having intercourse with a thousand men: She is afraid of men. Her father was a weak, ineffectual man; his own weakness enraged him, and so his daughter grew up surrounded by his silent, humiliated rage. Her mother smothered her own strength in order to make her father look strong; that didn't work, so the girl grew up with her mother's rage, too. She had no way to put male and female together inside herself without rage. This is the core of her fear. Her fear is so great that she cannot afford to recognize it. It is so great that it has taken on a thrilling sexual charge. Because the woman is courageous by nature, she has always gone directly toward what she most fears. When she began to have sex with boys, it was as if she were picking up a doll marked "Girl" and a doll marked "Boy" and banging them together, hoping to unite herself. As she grew older, the woman inside her became more insatiable and the man became more angry. He became angry enough to kill.

Because this woman is decent, she will not kill. But in deep sleep, she dreams of terrible men. In the worst of these dreams, the men rape and murder women over and over again and they cannot be stopped. The dreams are so terrible that the woman forgets them before she wakes. But they are still part of her: the male who would kill and the female he wants to kill. Deep inside, she is still trying to bring them together. And for one moment, down a special trapdoor, she has found a way. If the corporeal murderer who appeared on the talk show had been fucking the marathon woman at this moment, he might've had a feeling of *anxiety:* For she has entered the deep place of sex and it is not a place the killer wants to be. This is a place without form or time. There can be no grid here. Even the shape of his closed heart will no longer hold; it will be forced to open. Sorrow, terror, hate, love, pity, joy: All human feeling will come in and he will be unable to bear it. He will dissolve. His killing nature will be stripped to abstract movement, a bursting surge overtaking the weaker prey, the principle of pouncing and eating. In this place, all pouncing and eating are contained, because this place contains everything. This place is her ovaries and her eggs, bejeweled with moisture, the coarse, tough flowers sprouting in her abdomen, the royal, fleshy padding of her cunt. Some people say that nature is like a machine. But this is not a machine. This is something else.

When male turtles fuck, they thrust deep inside their mates, they stretch out their necks, they throw back their heads, and they scream. They don't have to drop through trapdoors or travel down layers. They are already there. Animals want to live because they are supposed to. But they know death better than a human killer. Life and death are in them all the time.

The marathon woman is more than halfway through, and she is tired. You are tired, too, just from thinking about it. The theme from *Chariots of Fire* is on the sound system, but you are hearing a very old song from the Industrial Age called "John Henry." It is about a steel driver of great strength who outperformed the machine invented to replace him. He won, but in doing so, he died. The song ends, "He laid down his hammer and he died." This song is not about sex or about women. The marathon woman is not going to die, nor is she going to win. She has no hammer to lay down. But she is like John Henry anyway because she is trying to make herself into a machine. A machine can never be hurt or raped or killed. But no matter how she tries, she will not succeed in becoming a machine. Because she is something else.

An Old Virgin

Laura was walking around her apartment in a flannel nightgown with green-and-yellow flowers on it, muttering, "Ugly cunt, ugly cunt." It was a bad habit that had gotten worse in recent months. She caught herself muttering while she was preparing her morning coffee and made herself stop. But it's true, she thought to herself. Women are ugly. She immediately thought of her sister, Anna Lee, making herself a chicken-salad sandwich to have with a glass of milk. Anna Lee was not beautiful, but she wasn't ugly, either. She thought of her mother, frowning slightly as she sat at her kitchen table, drawing a picture of fruit in a dish. If anyone had said "ugly cunt" to her sister or her mother, Laura would have hit him. She would hit anyone who said it to almost any of her friends. Well, she didn't really mean it when she said it. At least not in the normal way.

She put her foot up on the table and drank her coffee out of a striped mug the size of a little bowl. She had to be at her job at the medical clinic in half an hour; she wasn't even late, and still, her body was racing inside. Even though she'd been at the clinic for five years, every morning her body worked like the crew of a sinking ship, when all she had to do was get out the door in the morning. This was even truer since her father had died. The death had turned her inside herself. Even when she was in public, talking to people, or driving through traffic, or carrying forms and charts and samples in the halls of the clinic, she dimly sensed the greater part of herself turned inside, like a bug tunneling in the earth with its tiny sensate legs. All through the earth was the dull roar of unknown life-forms. She could not see it or hear it as she might see and hear with her human eyes and ears, but she could feel it with her fragile insect legs.

She finished her coffee and got out the door. Houston in the summer was terribly hot and humid, and the heat made her feel grossly physical. She gave a tiny grunt to express the feeling; it was the kind of grunt her cat made when she lay down and settled in deep. She opened her car; there were cassettes and mixed trash on the floor and the passenger seat, and she thought there was a sour smell coming from somewhere. She let the air conditioner run with the door open, sitting straight up in the seat with her legs parted wide under her tented uniform skirt.

Across the street, there was a twenty-four-hour flower market in an open shack; she could dimly see the proprietor inside, wiping his brow with a rag. He looked like he was settled deep into something, too.

Last night, she had dreamed of two men in a vicious fight. At first, they had been playing basketball. One of them seemed the apparent winner; he was tall, handsome, and well developed, while his opponent was short and flabby. Watching the game, Laura felt sorry for the little one. Then the game became a fight. The men rolled on the ground, beating each other. The little flabby one proved unexpectedly powerful, and soon he had the tall, handsome man pinned on the ground. As Laura watched, he pulled out a serrated knife and began to cut the top of the handsome man's skull off. The handsome man screamed and struggled. Laura ran to them and took the knife away from the small man. He pulled out another knife and tried to stab her. She cut him open from his neck to his crotch. He remained standing, but blobs of brown stuff fell from his opened body.

Laura lit a cigarette and closed the door. Her father had been a small man. When he was younger, he would strike boxing poses in front of the mirror, jabbing at his reflection. "I could've been a bantamweight," he'd said. "I still have some speed."

Laura lived in a slow, run-down neighborhood, but today there was heavy traffic. She talked to herself as she negotiated the lanes, speeding and slowing in a lulling rhythm. When she talked to herself, she often argued with an imaginary person. This time, she argued about the news story concerning the president's supposed affair with a twenty-one-year-old intern. "Personally, I don't care," she said. "If it were rape, or if the girl were twelve, I would want him in jail. But if it's consenting adults . . ." Stopped at the red light, she glanced at the people waiting for a bus. They looked tenacious and stoic as a band of ragged cats, staring alertly down the street or pulled tidily into themselves, cross-legged and holding their handbags as if they were about to lick their paws. "When things are private like that, it's hard to tell what really went on between the two people anyway," she continued. "Sometimes things that look really ugly on the outside look different when you get up close." Or feel different.

She had gone to see her father in the hospital in Tucson. Of the daughters, she was the last to arrive, and by the time she'd gotten there, her sisters were fighting with the doctors about their father's treatment. He was too weak to eat, so they'd stuffed tubes down his nose to feed him something called Vita Plus. "His body doesn't want it." Her sister Donna was talking to the nurse. "It's making him worse." It was true. As soon as Laura looked at her father, she knew he was going to die. His body was shrunken and dried, already half-abandoned; his spirit stared from his eyes as if stunned, and straining to see more of what had stunned it. "I know," said the nurse. "I agree with you. But we have to give it to him. It's policy."

"Hi, Daddy," said Laura.

When he answered her, his voice was like a thin sack holding something live. He was about to lose the live thing, but right now he held it, amazed by it, as if he had never known it before. He said, "Good to see you. Didn't know if you'd come."

His words struck her heart. She knelt by the bed. "Of course I came," she said; "I love you."

She paused at a crosswalk; there was a squirrel crossing the street in short, halting runs. She stopped traffic for a minute, waiting for it. A woman sitting on a public bench smiled at her approvingly. In her pointy shoes, her feet were like little hooves. It made sense she was on the squirrel's side.

They brought their father home to be cared for by hospice workers. By that time, he was emaciated and filled with mucus that he could not discharge through his throat or nose. It ran out of his nostrils sometimes, but mostly they heard it, rattling in his lungs. He couldn't eat anything and he didn't talk much. Because he was too fragile to share a bed with their mother, they put him in the guest bedroom, in a big soft bed with a dust ruffle. The sun shining in the window made his skin so transparent that the veins on his face seemed part of his skin. He blinked at the sun like a turtle. They took turns sitting with him. Laura stroked his arm with her fingertips, barely grazing his fragile skin. When she did that, he said, "Thank you, honey." He had not called her that since she was a little girl.

When the hospice workers had to turn him, he got angry; his skin had become so thin that his bones felt sharp, and it hurt him to be moved. "No, leave me alone. I don't care, I don't care." He would frown and even slap at the workers, and, in the fierce knit of his brow and his blank, furious eyes, Laura remembered him as he had been, twenty-five years ago. He'd been standing in the dining room and she was walking by him and he'd said, "What're you doing walking around showing your ass? People'll think you're selling it." She had been wearing flowered pants that were tight in the seat and crotch.

She arrived at the clinic early and got a good place in the parking garage. On the way up to the seventeenth floor, she shared the elevator with Dr. Edwina Ramirez, whom she liked. They had once had a conversation in the break lounge, during which they both revealed that they didn't want to have children. "People act like there's something wrong with you," said Dr. Ramirez. "Don't they know about overpopulation? I mean yeah, there's biology. But there're other ways to be a loving person." She had quickly bent to take her candy bar out of the machine. "You know what I mean?"

Ever since then, Laura had felt good around Dr. Ramirez. Every time she saw her, she thought "ways to be a loving person." She thought it as they rode up in the elevator together, even though the doctor stood silently frowning and smoothing her skirt. When they got to their floor, Dr. Ramirez said, "See you," and gave Laura a half smile as they strode in opposite directions.

Laura went to the lounge to get a coffee. Some other technicians and a few nurses were sitting at the table eating doughnuts from a box. Newspapers with broad grainy pictures of the White House intern lay spread out on the table. In one of the pictures, the girl posed with members of her high school class at the prom. She stood very erect in a low-cut dress, staring with focused dreaminess at a spot just past the camera.

"She's a porker," said a tech named Tara. "Just look at her."

Laura lingered at the little refrigerator, trying to find the carton of whole milk. Everybody else used 2 percent.

"It makes me sympathize with him," said a nurse. "He could have anybody he wanted, and he picks these kinds of girls. Definitely not models or stars."

"That makes you sympathize? I think that makes it more disgusting."

"But it might not be. It might mean he wants somebody to be normal with. Like somebody who's totally on his side who he can, like, talk about baseball with."

"What? Are you nuts? She was a homely girl sucking his dick!"

Laura had to settle for edible oil creamers. She took a handful, along with a pocketful of sugars and a striped stir stick. She walked down the empty hall whispering, "Ugly cunt, ugly cunt."

The day they brought their father home, the plumbing in the bathroom backed up. Sewage came out of the bathtub drain; water seeped into the chenille tapestry their mother had put up around the window. It was like snot was everywhere.

Laura lay with Anna Lee on the foldout couch in the living room. She and Anna Lee had slept close together in the same bed until Laura was fifteen and Anna Lee thirteen. Even when they got separate beds, they sometimes crept in together and cuddled. Now they lay separate even in grief.

Anna Lee was talking about her six-year-old, Fred, an anxious, overweight child with a genius IQ. The kid couldn't make friends; he fought all the time and usually lost. He'd set his room on fire twice. She was talking about a psychiatrist she had taken him to see. In the light from the window, Laura could see her sister's eyelashes raising and lowering with each hard, busy blink. She could smell the lotion Anna Lee used on her face and neck. The psychiatrist had put Fred on a waiting list to go to a special school in Montana, a farm school with llamas the children could care for and ride on.

"I hope it helps," said Laura.

There was a long silence. Laura could feel Anna Lee's body become fractionally softer and more open, relaxing and concentrating at the same time. Maybe she was thinking of Fred, how he might get better, how he might grow happy and strong. Laura had met the child only once. He'd frowned at her and looked down at the broken toy in his hand, but there was curiosity in his mien, and he was quick to look up again. He was already fat and already bright; he seemed too sorrowful and too angry for such a young child.

"I had a strange thought about Daddy," she said.

Anna Lee didn't answer, but Laura could feel her become alert. Even in the dark, her eyes looked alert. Laura knew she should stop, but she didn't. "It was more a picture in my head," she continued. "It was a picture of a woman's naked body that somebody was slashing with a knife. Daddy wasn't in the picture, but—"

"Oh for crying out loud!" Anna Lee put her hands over her face and turned away. "Just stop. Why don't you just stop."

"But I didn't mean it to be—"

"He's not your enemy now," said Anna Lee. "He's dying."

Her voice was raw and hard; she thrust it at Laura like a stick. Laura pictured her sister at twelve, yelling at some mean boys who'd cornered a cat. She felt loyalty and love. "I'm sorry," she said.

Anna Lee reached back and patted Laura's stomach with her fingers and half her palm. Then she withdrew into her private curl.

Laura lay awake through the night. Anna Lee moved and

scratched herself and spoke in urgent, slurred monosyllables. Laura thought of their mother, alone upstairs in the heavy sleep brought on by barbiturates. Tomorrow, she would be at the stove, boiling Jell-O in case her husband would eat it. She didn't really believe he was dying. She knew it, but she didn't believe it anyway.

Carefully, Laura got out of bed. She walked through the dark house until she came to her father's room. She heard him breathing before her eyes adjusted to the light. His breath was like a worn-out moth feebly beating against a surface. She sat in the armchair beside his bed. The electric clock said it was 4:30. A passing car on the street filled the room with a yawning sweep of light. The wallpaper was covered with yellow flowers. Great-Aunt's old dead clock sat on the dresser. Great-Aunt was her father's aunt, who had raised him with yet another aunt. Two widowed aunts and a little boy with no father. Laura could see the boy standing in the parlor, all his brand-new life coursing through his small, stout legs and trunk. The dutiful aunts, busy with housekeeping and food, didn't notice it. In his head was a new solar system, crackling with light as he created the planets, the novas, the sun and the moon and the stars. "Look!" he cried. "Look!" The aunts didn't see. He was all alone.

Another car went by. Her father muttered and made noises with his mouth.

No wonder he hated them, thought Laura. No wonder.

Behind the reception desk, there were two radios playing different stations for each secretary. One played frenetic electronic songs, the other formula love songs, and both ran together in a gross hash of sorrow and desire. This happened every day by around 1:00 p.m. Faith, who worked behind the desk, said it was easy to separate them, to just concentrate on the one you wanted. Laura, though, always heard both of them jabbering every time she walked by the desk.

"Alice Dillon?" She spoke the words to the waiting room. A shabby middle-aged man eyed her querulously. A red-haired middle-aged woman put down her magazine and approached Laura with a mild, obedient air. Alice was in for a physical, so Laura had to give her a preliminary before the doctor examined her. First, they stopped at the scale outside the office door; Alice took off her loafers, her socks, and her sweater to shave off some extra ounces. A lot of women did that, and it always seemed stupid to Laura. "Five four, one hundred and twenty-six pounds," she said loudly.

"Shit," muttered Alice.

"Look at the bright side," said Laura. "You didn't gain since last time."

Alice didn't reply, but Laura sensed an annoyed little buzz from her. She was still buzzing slightly as she sat in the office; even though she was small and placid, it struck Laura that she gave off a little buzz all the time. She was forty-three years old, but her face was unlined and her eyes were wide and receptive, like a much younger person's. Her hair was obviously dyed, like a teenager would do it. You could still tell she was middle-aged, though.

She didn't smoke, she exercised three times a week, and she drank twice weekly, wine with dinner. She was single. Her aunt had diabetes and her mother had ovarian cancer. She had never had an operation, or been hospitalized. Her periods were regular. She had never had any sexual partners. Laura blinked.

"Never?"

"No," said Alice. "Never." She looked at Laura as if she was watching for a reaction, and maybe holding back a smile.

Her blood pressure was excellent. Her pulse rate was average.

Laura handled her wrist and arm with unusual care. A forty-three-year-old virgin. It was like looking at an ancient sacred artifact, a primitive icon with its face rubbed off. It had no function or beauty, but it still felt powerful when you touched it. Laura pictured Alice walking around with a tiny red flame in the pit of her body, protecting it with her fat and muscle, carefully dyeing her hair, exercising three times a week, and not smoking.

When the doctor examined Alice, Laura felt tense as she watched, especially when he did the gynecological exam. She noticed that Alice gripped her paper gown in the fingers of one hand when the doctor sat between her legs. He had to tell her to open her legs wider three times. She said, "Wait, I need to breathe," and he waited a second or two. Alice breathed with her head sharply turned, so that she stared at a corner of the ceiling. There was a light sweat on her forehead.

When she changed back into her clothes, though, she moved like she was in a women's locker room. She got up from the table and took off the paper gown before the doctor was even out of the room.

"She's probably really religious, or maybe she's crazy." That's what Sharon, the secretary, thought. "In this day and age? She was probably molested when she was little."

"I don't know," said Laura. "I respected it."

Sharon shrugged. "It takes all kinds."

She imagined her father looking at the middle-aged virgin and then looking away with an embarrassed smile on his face. He might think about protecting her, about waving at her from across the street, saying, "Hi, how are you?" sending protection with his words. He could protect her and still keep walking, smiling to himself with embarrassed tenderness. He would have a feeling of honor and frailty, but there would be something sad in it, too, because she wasn't young. Laura remembered a minor incident in a novel she had read by a French writer, in which a teenage boy knocked an old nun off a bridge. Her habit was heavy and so she drowned, and the writer wondered, with a stupid sort of meanness, Laura thought, if the nun had felt shocked to have her genitals touched by the cold water. She remembered a recent news story about a nut job who had kidnapped a little girl so that he could tie her to a tree and set a fire around the tree. Then he went to his house to watch through binoculars as she burned. Fortunately, a neighbor called the police and they got there in time.

Instead of going back to the waiting room, she went to the public bathroom and leaned against the small windowsill with her head in her hands. She was forty; she tried to imagine what it would be like to be a virgin. She imagined walking through the supermarket, encased in an invisible membrane that was fluid but also impenetrable, her eyes wide and staring like a doll's. Then she imagined her virginity like a strong muscle between her legs, making all her other muscles strong, making everything in her extra alive, all the way up through her brain and into her bones.

She lifted her head and looked out the small window. She saw green grass and the tops of trees, cylindrical apartment buildings and traffic. She had not wanted her virginity. She'd had to lose it with three separate people; her hymen had been stubborn and hard to break.

She brushed the dust and particles from the windowsill off her elbows. "I was a rebellious girl," she said, "and I went in a stupid direction."

She thought of the Narcotics Anonymous meetings she had attended some years ago. People talked about the things that had happened to them, the things they had done on drugs. Nothing was too degrading or too pathetic or too dull. Laura had talked about trying to lose her virginity. Her friend Danielle had told a story about how she'd let a disgusting fat guy whom she hated try to shove a can of root beer up her vagina because, he'd suggested, they might be able to fill cans with heroin and smuggle them.

Laura smiled a little. After the meeting, she'd asked Danielle, "Who tried to stick it in, you or him?"

"Oh," said Danielle, "we both tried." They laughed.

Such grotesque humility; such strange comfort. She remembered the paper plates of cookies, the pot of coffee at the low table in the back of the room at NA. She loved standing back there with Danielle, eating windmill cookies and smoking. Laura looked at herself in the bathroom mirror. "A stupid girl," she said to her reflection.

Well, but who could blame her? When she was still a teenager, out of nowhere her mother asked Laura what it had been like to lose her virginity. She wanted to know if the experience had been "special." It was late and the living room was dark. They had been watching TV together. Laura was startled by the question. "Was it someone you loved?" asked her mother.

"Yes," replied Laura, lying. "Yes, it was."

"I'm glad," said her mother. She still looked straight ahead. "I wanted you to have that."

What a revolting conversation, thought Laura. She couldn't quite put her finger on why; her mother had only been expressing concern. But her concern seemed somehow connected with the nun in the water, and the dirtbag trying to set the little girl on fire.

She went back to the waiting room and got the grouchy middle-aged man. He didn't bother to take off his shoes when he weighed himself. He was there, he said, only because his wife had made him come. He had taken off from work and shot the whole day. "My wife loves going to the doctor," he said. "She had all those mammo-grams and she lost her breast anyway. Most of it."

"Well, but it's good to come in," said Laura. "Even if it doesn't always work. You know that. Your wife's just caring about you."

He gave a conciliatory snort. With his shirt off, he was big and flabby, but he carried it as if he liked it. His blood pressure was much too high. Laura let her touch linger on him as she worked because she wanted to soothe him.

When the man was gone, she asked Dr. Phillips if she could go outside on her break. He usually didn't like her to do that because she was always a little late getting back when she went out, but he was trying to be extra nice since her father died. "Okay," he said, "but watch the time." He turned and strode down the hall, habitu-ally bristling, like a small dog with a dominant nature.

Outside, the heat was horrible. She started sweating right away, probably ruining her uniform for the next day. Still, she was glad to be out of the building. The clinic was located between a busy main street and a run-down little street occupied by an old wig shop, a children's karate gym, and a large ill-kept park where aging home-less men sat around. She decided to walk a few blocks down the park street. She liked the trees and she was friendly with a few of the men, who sometimes wished her good afternoon.

She walked and an old song played in her head. It was the kind of old song that sounded innocent and dirty at the same time. The music was simple and shallow except for one deep spot where it was like somebody's pants were being pulled down. "You got nothin' to hide and everybody knows it's true. Too bad, little girl, it's all over for you." The singer laughed and the music laughed, too, and the laughter was spangled all over with sexiness.

Laura had loved the song; she had loved the thought of it being all over and everybody knowing. A lot of other people must've loved it, too; it had been a very popular song. She remembered walking down the hall in high school wearing tight clothes; boys laughed and grabbed their crotches. They all said she'd sucked their dicks, but really she'd only screwed one of them. It didn't matter. When her father found out, he yelled and hit her.

"Was it someone special?" her mother had asked. "Was it someone you loved?"

She stopped at a curb for traffic. Her body was alive with feelings that were strong but that seemed broken or incomplete, and she felt too weak to hold them.

A car pulled up beside her, throwing off motor heat. The car was full of loud teenage boys. The driver, a Hispanic boy of about eighteen, wanted to make a right turn, but he was blocked by a stalled car in front of him and cars on his side. He was banging his horn and yelling out the window; his urgency was hot and all over the place. Laura stared at him. His delicate beauty was almost too bright; he had so much light that it burned him up inside and made him dark. He yelled and pounded the horn, trying to spew it out, but still it surged through him. It was like he was ready to kill someone, anyone, without any understanding in his mind or heart. That thought folded over unexpectedly; Laura pictured him as a baby with his mouth on his mother's breast. She pictured his fierce nature deep inside him, like dark, beautiful seeds feeding off his mother's milk, off the feel of her hand on his skull. She thought of him as a teenager with a girl; he would kiss her too hard and be • rough, wanting her to feel what he had inside him, wanting her to see it. And, in spite of his roughness, she would.

He turned in his seat to shout something to the other boys in the car, then turned forward again to put his head out the window to curse the other cars. He turned again and saw Laura staring at him. Their eyes met. She thought of her father showing his aunts the stars and all the planets. You are good, she thought. What you have is good. The boy dropped his eyes in confusion. There was a yell from the backseat. The stalled car leaped forward. The boy snapped around, hit the gas, and was off.

Laura crossed the street. How to explain that? she thought. How to know what it even was? She thought, I told him he was good. I told him with my eyes and he heard me.

Well, tonight she'd call Danielle and tell her about it; Danielle had a lot of strange emotional moments with, say, a lady standing in the prescription line next to her at the drugstore, or a guy in the car behind her who'd yelled at her because she couldn't figure out the parking gate right away. Except it probably wouldn't seem like a story by the time the day was over.

She walked up the block sweating, feeling so replete and grateful that she wondered if she was crazy. She pictured the middle-aged virgin, this time at home at night, doing her meticulous toilet, rubbing her feet with softening cream. She pictured herself at home, curled on the couch, watching TV and eating ice cream out of the carton. She pictured the men in her dream, fighting. She pictured herself kneeling to hold the handsome man's cut-open head. She would pass her hand over his broken skull and make an impenetrable membrane grow over his exposed brain. The membrane would be transparent, and you would be able to see his brain glowing inside it like magic stones. But you could never cut it or harm it.

She pictured her father, young and strong, smiling at her, the planets all around him. She thought, I love you, Daddy.

She saw the homeless men moving about deep in the park, their figures nearly obscured by overgrown grasses and trees. For a moment, she strained to see them more clearly, then gave up. It was time to go back. She was late, but it would be okay, probably.

The Agonized Face

A feminist author came to talk at the annual literary festival in Toronto, one of the good-looking types with expensive clothes who look younger than they are (which is irritating, even though it shouldn't be), the kind of person who plays with her hair when she talks, who always seems to be asking you to like her. She was like that, but she had something else, too, and it was that "something else" quality that made what she did so peculiarly aggravating.

Before I go any further, it must be said that I arrived at the festival tense and already prone to aggravation. I have been divorced for five years. I am the mother of a ten-year-old girl. My ex-husband is stalwart in his child-support payments, but he is a housepainter who is trying to be an artist, and out of respect for his dreams, his payments are not large. We met in graduate school, where I was studying creative writing, a dream-cum-memory rolling monotonously near the bottom of the subthought ocean. After years of writing in-brief book reviews, plus fact-checking and proofreading for an online magazine, I have recently begun writing full-length reviews (which means a little more money and a lot less time for playing "The Mighty Michelle" with Kira); for the first time, I have been assigned to "do" something light and funny on the social scene at the literary festival. The idea of proximity to so many actual authors may've caused some more intense than usual subthought rolling, which is perhaps why a fight with my daughter got nastier than it had to this morning. It did not help that it was a fight about whether or not she can, at ten, bleach her hair "like Gwen Stefani," and that the fight then had to turn into a discussion with Tom about how he had to be sure that while staying with him this afternoon, she did not somehow get hold of boxed bleach and take charge of the bathroom. Or, furthermore, that she not be allowed to persuade him that red might be okay if blond was not.

Still, for the most part, I was able to clear my mind of all this once I arrived at the festival. Writers from all over the world were there, people from Somalia, Greece, Israel, the United States, Italy, and Britain. There were writers who'd been forced to flee their countries, writers from police states, writers from places where everybody was starving; writers who wrote about the daily problems of ordinary people, the obscenity of politics and the pain of the lower classes, glamorous writers who wrote about the exciting torment of the fashionable classes. Writers with airs of gravity or triviality, well-heeled or wearing suits they had probably rented for this event, standing at the bar with an air of hard-won triumph, or simply looking with childish delight at all the glowing bottles of delicious drinks and trays of foodstuffs. I glimpsed a smart blond woman on the arm of a popular author and fleetingly thought of my daughter: If she could see me here, she would feel curiosity and admiration.

But getting back to the "feminist author"; it is not really right to call her that, as she was not the only feminist there, as, in fact, her presence may have annoyed other, more serious feminists. She was a feminist who had apparently been a prostitute at some point in her colorful youth, and who had gone on record describing prostitutes as fighters against the patriarchy. She would say stupid things like that, but then she would write some good sentences that would make people say, "Wow, she's kind of intelligent!" Some people may've said she should not have been at the festival at all, but why not? An event such as this is dazzling partly in its variety; it is a social blaze of little heads rolling by in a ball of light, and all the heads have something to say: "No one should ever write about the Holocaust again!" "Irony is ruining our culture!" Or in the case of the feminist ex-prostitute, "Women can enjoy sexual violence, too!" *Well.* I had been asked to write something funny, and the feminist author sounded pretty funny. I pictured her in a short skirt and big high heels, standing up on the balls of her feet with her legs bowed like a samurai, her fists and her arms flexed combatively, head cocked like she was on the lookout for some patriarchy to mount. An image you could look at and go, Okay, now for the author who says, "We live in an entertainment society and it's terrible!"

She was reading with two other people, a beautiful seventeen-year-old Vietnamese girl who wrote about rapes and massacres, and a middle-aged Canadian who wrote touching stories about his daughters. First the Vietnamese girl read about a massacre, then came the feminist writer. She immediately began complaining, but she did it in a way that made her complaint sound like a special treat we might like to have. Her voice was sweet, with a sparkling rhythm that made you imagine some shy and secret thing was being gradually revealed. I felt caught off guard; she wore a full-length skirt and little glasses and round-toed clog-style boots.

She wasn't going to read, she said; instead, she was going to give a talk about the way she had been treated by the local media, as well as by the festival organizers, who had described her in an insulting, unfair way in their brochure. I had not even read the brochure—I perhaps should've read it, but the information in such pamphlets is usually worthless—and from the look on other people's faces, they

hadn't read it, either. The author, however, didn't seem to realize
this. The brochure was not only insulting to her, she continued; it
was an insult to all women, to *everyone,* really. They had ignored the
content of her work completely, focusing instead on the most sen-
sational aspects of her life—the prostitution, the drug use, the stay
in a mental hospital, the attempt on her father's life—in a way that
was both salacious and puritanical. "It isn't that these things aren't
true," she said in her lilting voice. "They are. I was a prostitute for
six months when I was sixteen and I spent two months in a mental
hospital when I was eighteen. But I have also done a lot of other
things. I have been a waitress, a factory worker, a proofreader, a
journalist, a street vendor! I am forty-five years old and now I
teach at Impala University West!"

There were cheers, applause; a woman in the back fiercely
hollered, "You go, girl!" The author blinked rapidly and adjusted
her glasses. "I can even understand it," she continued. "It's exciting
to imagine such a kooky person off somewhere doing unimagin-
able stuff! I like the idea myself! But I am not that person!" It
seemed to me that she kind of was that person, but right then
it didn't matter. "And when we do that," she continued, "when we
isolate qualities that seem exciting, but maybe a little scary, and
we project them onto another person in an exaggerated form, we
not only deny that person her humanity but we impoverish and
cheat ourselves of life's complexity and tenderness!"

This wasn't funny. This was something wholly unexpected. We
were all feeling stirred, like we were really dealing with something
here, something that had just been illustrated for us by a magical,
elfish hand. We felt like we were being touched in a personal place,
a little like our mothers would touch us—a touch that was emo-
tionally erotic. Like a mother, she seemed potent, yet there was
something of the daughter there, too, the innocent girl who has

been badly teased by an importune boy, and who comes to you, her upturned face looking at you with puzzlement. Yes, she seemed innocent, even with her sullied, catastrophic life placed before us for the purpose of selling her.

She must've sensed our feelings, because she cut short her speech. We had been so kind, she said, that she wanted to give us something. She was going to read to us after all—in fact, she had her book right there with her, and she even had a story picked out. It was a story about a middle-aged woman dressing in sexy clothes to attend a party for a woman who writes pornography, which is held in a bar decorated with various sex toys. A good-looking boy flirts with the middle-aged woman, who allows that she is "flattered."

What had happened to the mother? Where was the injured girl? The voice of the author was still lilting and girlish, but her words were hard and sharp, the kind of words that think everything is funny. The middle-aged woman invites the young man to her home, gives him a drink, and then pulls his pants off while he lies there gaping. For the next several pages, she alternates between fellating him and chattering cleverly while he tries to leave.

This was the feminist author we had heard about, all right. Her readers smiled knowingly, while the readers of the Canadian and Vietnamese authors looked baffled—baffled, then angry. And I was feeling angry, too.

I am not really a feminist, probably because, at forty, I am too young to have fully experienced the kinetic surge of feminism that occurred in the seventies, that half-synthetic, half-organic creature with its smart, dry little mouth issuing books, speeches, TV shows, and pop songs. None of it is stylish anymore, and, in fact, feminists have come in for a lot of criticism from female pundits. Some of these pundits say that feminists have made girls think they have to have sex all the time, which, by going against their girlish nature, has destroyed their self-esteem, and made them anorexic and depressed. Feminists have made girls into sluts! Others, equally angry, say that feminists have imposed restrictive rules on nubile teens, making them into morbid neurasthenics who think they're being raped, when they're actually just having sex. Feminists have neutered girls by overprotecting them! I don't know what I think of any of it; it's mostly something I hear coming out of my radio on my way to work. But I do know this: When I hear that feminism is overprotecting girls, I am very sympathetic to it. When I see my fashion-conscious ten-year-old in her nylon nightie, peering spellbound before the beguiling screen at the fleeting queendom of some twelve-year-old manufactured pop star with the wardrobe of a hooker, a jerry-rigged personality, and bulimia, it seems to me that she has a protection deficit that I may not be able to compensate for. When she comes home wild with tears because she lost the spelling contest, or her ex–best friend called her fat, or a boy said she's not the prettiest girl in class, and I press her to me, comforting her, even as that day's AMBER Alert flashes in my brain, it is hard for me to imagine this girl as "overprotected."

Which is, in some indirect way, why the feminist author was so affecting and so disappointing. She was a girl who needed to be protected, and a woman standing to protect the girl. But then she became the other thing—the feminist who made girls into sluts. She sprouted three heads and asked that we accept them all! She said she had been a prostitute, a mental patient, that she had tried to stab her father. She said it in a soft, reasonable voice—but these are not soft or reasonable things. These are terrible things. Anyone who has seen a street prostitute and looked into her face knows that. For her to admit these things, without describing the pain she had suffered, gave her dignity—because really, she didn't have to

talk about it. We could imagine it. But the story she read made
what had seemed like dignity look silly and obscene. Because the
voice of the story was not soft. It was dry and smart as a dance
step—but what it told of was neither dry nor smart. While the
voice danced, making scenes that described the woman and the
youth, an image slowly formed, taking subtle shape under the picture created by the scenes. It was like an advertisement for cigarettes where beautiful people are smoking in lounge chairs, and
suddenly you see in the cobalt blue backdrop the subliminal image
of a skull. Except the image behind the feminist author's words was
stranger than the image of a skull, and less clear. It made you strain
to see what it was, and in the straining you found yourself picturing
things you did not want to picture. Of course, it can be fun to picture things you don't want to picture—but somehow the feminist
author had ruined the fun.

After the reading, we all went for refreshments in the hospitality
lounge. The Vietnamese girl and the Canadian father, as well as
the feminist author, were there, signing books and talking with
their readers. There were other authors present, too, including an
especially celebrated Somali author known for an award-winning
novel of war and social disintegration, and an American woman
who had written a witty, elegant, clearly autobiographical novella
about a mother whose child is hit by a drunk driver and nearly
killed. The feminist author appeared more relaxed in this setting
than she had been onstage; she smiled easily and chatted with the
mostly young women who approached her. And yet again I sensed
a disturbing subliminal message bleeding through the presenta-
tion: a face of sex and woman's pain. The face had to do with dis-
grace and violence, dark orgasm, rape, with feeling so strong that it

obviates the one who feels it. You could call it an exalted face, or an agonized face; in the context of the feminist author, I think I'm going to call it "the agonized face." Although I don't know why—she doesn't look like she's ever made such a face in her life.

There was only one more person waiting to talk to her, an animated girl with ardently sprouting red hair. I got in line behind her. When I got up close, I saw that the author's eyes were not sweet, innocent, or sparkling. They were wary and a little hard. As she signed the animate red girl's book, I heard her say, "Sex has been let out of the box, like everything is okay, but no one knows what 'everything' is."

"Exactly!" sprouted the ardent girl.

Exactly. "I liked the talk you gave," I said, "*before* the reading."

"Thank you," she said, coldly answering my italics.

"But I'm wondering why you chose to read what you read afterward. If you didn't like what they said about you in that brochure you mentioned. I didn't read it, but—"

"What I read didn't have anything to do with what they said."

No? "I'd love to talk more with you about that. I'm here as a journalist for *Quick!* Would you be able to talk about it for our readers?"

"No," she said. "I'm not doing interviews." And she turned her back on me to sign another book.

I stood for a moment looking at her back, vaguely aware of the Somali author talking into someone's tape recorder. With a vertiginous feeling, I remembered the days right after graduation, when Tom was an artist and I was a freelance journalist hustling work at various small magazines. We slept on a Salvation Army mattress; we ate and wrote on a coffee table. "The grotesque has a history, a social parameter," said the Somali author. "Indeed, one might say that the grotesque *is* a social parameter."

Indeed. I took a glass of wine from a traveling tray of glasses and drank it in a gulp. On one of those long-ago assignments, I had interviewed a topless dancer, a desiccated blonde with desperate intelligence burning in her otherwise-lusterless eyes. She was big on Hegel and Nietzsche, and she talked about the power of beautiful girls versus the power of men with money. In the middle of this power talk, she told me a story about a customer who had said he would give her fifty dollars if she would get on her hands and knees with her butt facing him, pull down her G-string, and then turn around and smile at him. They had negotiated at length: "I made him promise that he wouldn't stick his finger in," she said. "We went over it and over it and he promised me, like, three times. So I pulled down my G-string, and as soon as I turned around, his finger went right in. I was *so* mad!" Then bang, she was right back at the Hegel and Nietzsche. The combination was pathetic, and yet it had the dignity of awful truth. Not only because it was titillating—though, yes, it was—but because in the telling of it, a certain foundation of humanity was revealed; the crude cinder blocks of male and female down in the basement, holding up the house. Those of us who have spouses and/or children forget about this part—not because we have an aversion to those cinder blocks necessarily, but because we are busy on the upper levels, building a home with furniture, decorations, and personalities in it. We are glad to have the topless dancer to remind us of that dark area in the basement where personality is irrelevant and crude truth prevails. Her philosophical patter even added to the power of her story because it created a stark polarity: intelligent words on one side, and mute genitals on the other. Between the poles, there was darkness and mystery, and the dancer respected the mystery with her ignorant and touching pretense.

Which is exactly what the feminist author did not do. I drained my second glass of wine. The feminist author—she told and then read her disturbing stories as if she were a lady at a tea party, as if there were no mystery, no darkness, just her, the feminist author skipping along, swinging some charming little bag, and singing about penises, la la la la la!

Another server wafted past, a young woman with her mind clearly on something else. I reached for another glass of wine, then changed my mind. Of course, someone might say—I can picture a well-dressed, intellectual lady saying it—well, why not? And rationally, there is no reason why not. These things are accepted now; these things are talked about in popular comedies on television. So why not? Because everyone knows such television shows are nonsense. Because glib acceptance does not respect the profound nature of the agonized face.

I reconsidered having another wine; looking for a server, I noticed that the Somali author, momentarily unpestered, was looking at me with a kindly expression. He was handsome, well dressed, and elegant. Impulsively, I crossed the room and introduced myself. His hand was long, dry, and warm. He had come from New York, not Somalia. He came every year. When I told him it was my first time, he smiled.

"Are you enjoying yourself?" he asked.

"Yes," I said, "though it's been a long time since I've had two quick drinks this early in the day."

He laughed, raised his wineglass, and sipped from it.

"And you?" I asked. "Do you enjoy this?"

"Oh yes," he said. "One meets such curious people. And, of course, interesting people, too."

"What about her?" I indicated the feminist author, now chatting with her back to us. "What did you think?"

"Oh!" The Somali author laughed. "I've heard what she has to say many times—it's nothing new. But I did admire the panache with which she said it. Did you see Binyavanga speak on cultural rationalism?"

But we were interrupted by more people wanting his signature, and then it was time for his reading. "I hope you will come," he said.

The Somali author read from his award winner, the novel about civil war and familial bonds. He skipped through the book, reading excerpts from several chapters, starting with a tender love scene between a husband and his wife, who magically has two sets of breasts, the normal set augmented by a miniset located just under her rib cage. Their young son runs in and cries, "Are you going to give me a sibling?" Then the author jumped ahead, and suddenly there it was again: the agonized face. The son, now grown, is being pursued by a fat, whorish girl who claims he owes her a baby, even though she has AIDS and he is engaged to someone else. We learn that this very girl, an orphan who was briefly taken in by the family when she was fourteen, once sexually attacked the grandfather, who responded by righteously kicking her in the face. When the mother learns that this slut is back again, she decides to get a gun, humiliate the girl, and then kill her. The grandfather, though, does not want the mother on the street during the escalating civil unrest. "Leave her to me," he counsels; "there is, after all, something unfinished between us." He goes to the son's house to lie in wait, and sure enough, the slut comes calling. She's looking for the son, but when she finds grandpa, it doesn't matter; she wants his baby, too. He pretends to be asleep while she masturbates him. She thinks, How beautiful his penis is! She longs for his children! She mounts him, and the grandfather reports, with a certain gentlemanly discretion, that he and the slut "went somewhere together." But nonetheless, almost as soon as they are done, the girl is mystically stricken with discharge and gross vaginal itching; she runs down the road, scratching her crotch as she screams, "I itch! I smell!" The son is happily reunited with his fiancée, and the wife, his mother, finds new tenderness with her husband. The grandfather meditates on history.

If he had been an American or a Canadian man saying these things, he might've been booed as a misogynist. But an African man—no. It was wonderful, especially the way he read it—with the *earned* hauteur of a man who has seen war, persecution, and the two sides of the agonized face: the mother who is poignant in her open-legged vulnerability, and the visage of the female predator. Because for all its elegance, his voice—unlike the voice of the feminist author—did not try to hide reality: the pain and anger of the unsatisfied womb grown ill from lack of wholesome use, a fungal vector of want, thick with tumors, baby's teeth, and bits of hair inside each fibrous mass. Pitiful, yes, but also nasty, though we in the antiseptic West don't say so.

"Motherhood is the off-and-on light in the darkness of night," concluded the author, "a firefly of joy and rejoicing, now here, now there, and everywhere. In fact, the crisis that is coming to a head in the shape of civil strife would not be breaking in on us if we'd offered women as mothers their due worth, respect, and affection; a brightness celebrating motherhood, a monument erected in worship of women."

The audience went wild.

In the big reception hall, we celebrated the Somali author with more drinks, and I caught up with the American novelist whose son actually *had* been nearly killed by a drunk driver. She was a good egg, hawk-nosed and plainly dressed, and she was having a stiff one. When I asked her, she said she'd disliked writing about the accident, but that if she hadn't written about it, she never would've been able to pay the medical expenses. We gossiped; we admired the Somali author. "I can't imagine an American writer saying something like that," she said. " 'A monument erected in worship of women.' "

"I know," I said, "it was lovely." *As long as you're the right kind of woman,* I didn't say. I glimpsed the feminist author across the room from us, standing by herself, eating a fistful of grapes. The American writer was saying something about how irony is the most human of artistic methods, but I was thinking of something else. I was thinking of a girl I had known in high school named Linda Phoenix. She was a thin girl with a stark, downy back, who fucked every boy, plus some girls. Jeff Lyer, an angry fat kid, brought pictures to school of her drunk and sucking someone's penis, and people passed them around the cafeteria, laughing or feeling sorry or just looking.

Across the room, two reporters approached the feminist author with their tape recorders. I thought of the blurred pictures of Linda Phoenix. I thought of my daughter, standing before the mirror, pushing her lower lip out, making seductive eyes. I thought of her sitting at the kitchen table, drawing scenes from her favorite book, *Magic by the Lake.* I thought of her frightened awake from a nightmare, crying, "Mommy, Mommy!" I remembered washing her as a baby, using the spray hose from the kitchen sink to rinse shit from the swollen petals of her infant slit—a hole she may fall down if she opens it too early, a dark Wonderland of teeth and bones and crushing force. The hole in life, a hole we cannot see into, no matter how closely we look.

I had had too much to drink and too little to eat, and for a drunken instant the hall became a courtroom, the authors and journalists members of a jury overspilling the box to cry out: Now hold on a minute! Are you completely out of your mind? It is one thing to express disdain for this so-called feminist, who may deserve it. Even the muddled atavism about rotten wombs full of baby teeth—well, it is loony and gross, but in the locked closet of our inmost heart, we can see how you might feel that way. But your daughter? What kind of mother are you? Leave her out of this grotesquerie, please!

And of course the imaginary jury was right. I would love Kira no matter how many boys she did what with, or girls, for that matter. Things are not like they once were. *Sex and the City* is on TV. Still, when I think of her as she will be—dripping with hormones and feelings, nursing the secret hurt of a seed about to burst into flower—it makes me uneasy. To think of her opening her warm spring darkness to any lout who wants it makes me feel sadness, followed by a surprising surge of anger (anger that includes an even more surprising burst of sympathy for my mother's anger, sympathy even for the time she slapped my face after she caught me and Donald Parker doing it in the rec room). But even as I feel the anger, even with my mother's anger crowding behind it—my mother, also single, now a mild alcoholic in old age, calling me to give me a piece of her mind about the latest nonsense on the news—even as I feel the anger, love rises up to enclose it. Inside love, anger still secretly burns—but it is a tiny flame. I can hold it like I once held my daughter in my body, a world within a world.

But just now I allowed myself to enter the little flame and feel it all the way. I did it in the spirit of the feminist author—and to show her up, too. So, she can be the innocent girl and the prostitute and the author, eh? Well, imagine a full deck of cards, each card painted with symbols of woman—the waif, the harlot, the mother, the warrior, the queen—until the last card, on which we see Medea, a knife in her raised, implacable hand. Yes, there I am and there any woman can be, even though we don't stand up on stages and make a fuss about it. And we can skip lightly back through the deck, carelessly touching each card as we do, before returning to the card of the good mother, or the lover, or, in my case at this moment, the stolid female worker in my brown skirt and flat shoes. Every woman knows all about everything on those cards, even if her knowledge is wordless and half-conscious. It is wordless knowledge because it is too big for words. Sometimes, it is too big for us. Stand up onstage and put words on it and you make it small—and then you say it's sexist when people don't like it.

Except that, if I am going to be honest, I have to admit something that weighs in on the side of the feminist author *just slightly.* The anger and upset that I let myself feel, that mere hot pinprick in the ardent wetness of love—when you let yourself feel it, when *I* let myself feel it, it is, was, very strong. Strong and primitive. Enter in through that tiny spot of fire and come out in a hell of shape-shifting and destruction. In that hell lives a beast that will devour anything in front of it, and that beast is especially partial to woman. Why not split her open all the way, just for the pure animal joy of rending and tearing? For a woman even to skirt this place is dangerous because she has the open part. She needs rules, structures, intact shapes to make sure the openness doesn't get *too* open. For a man, it is different—he can align his strength with the monster and tear the prey with its teeth. For a second, he can walk triumphant in a place of no place. Then he can say the woman lured him there.

That is why the grandfather in the Somali author's book wants to fuck the slut. He tells his son that because she has no children, he feels sorry for her, that he is fucking her out of sympathy. But he does not seem to feel sorry for her. He wants her; you could even say he needs her, for through her he can descend into a terrible, thrilling world and then come back in his suit and tie and be good. The Somali author almost acknowledges this in his frank fascination with the slut. For if she were not there, how could he go to that place of no place? He would have to discharge his anger and contempt on Mom with Double Boobs, and this would be more than anybody could bear—for, like me, he has more love than anger. How unfair that men get to go to this mysterious place and come back whole. How noble that the feminist author stands up onstage and tries to speak for the sluts they go there with, even if she fails. Even if her story makes something terrible into something light and silly, even if she herself is light and silly.

This is what I was thinking as I sat in the hospitality lounge, nursing a seltzer water with lemon, after attending a reading by a man from the prairies who had written a prizewinning novel about a heroic woman who rescues an orphan from an abusive foster parent. I was sitting by the window, and, in the sunlight, the room seemed composed of impossible purple and mahogany hues. Caterers discreetly moved in and out, replacing platters of food and trays of drinks.

Soon I would leave, pick up my daughter, and take her for pizza. We would go home and watch *Buffy the Vampire Slayer*. And then maybe that strange anime show, the one we stumbled on last week—a show where the heroine, the good girl, has no arms and the sexy villainess is powerful and crude. It looked like the cartoon slut was trying to kill the heroine and steal her boyfriend. But instead, in the middle of a gun battle between hero and villain, the slut (admiring the armless girl's purity) took a bullet to save her and died with the heroine in her arms. When the embrace broke, the good girl magically stood up with arms of her own and proceeded to beat the crap out of the bad guy. "Yeah, there's gonna be some changes around here!" she announced. Rock music played.

"Weird," said Kira, and, yes, it was.

I drank my seltzer water and reviewed my notes.

Early in my career, I did a piece on the then-burgeoning phenomenon of TV talk shows, focusing on a particular show, a show that at the time had made its reputation by sympathetically telling the stories of victims, stories that had once been too shameful to tell. Rape was a mainstay of the show, and I was present on the set for an episode that featured two women who had been raped by coworkers in the workplace, one of whom had succeeded in pressing charges, while the other had lost her case. The successful woman was a flamboyant redheaded beauty who came on yelling, "I just want to say I've got a shotgun ready for any sumbitch who tries it again!"

But first came the defeated one, a chubby middle-aged woman who tried to hide her identity by sitting with her back to the camera and wearing an ill-fitting wig. The man she'd accused of raping her was there, too, and he had a lot to say. "She go like this," he said, "on the desk!" He stood up and bent over, putting his hands out as if bracing himself. "And I say, 'No! I don't want that!' "

The awful thing was, you could totally picture her bent over the desk. Even viewing her from the back, we could see her bending nature—the mild, gentle slope of her shoulders, the sweetness of her excess flesh, the way she turned in her chair to yell, "No! That's not the truth!" Her anger was like a clumsy animal, and you could hear in it the soft puzzlement of a person who does not understand cruelty.

"You are an alcoholic!" yelled the accused rapist. "Everybody knows!"

"I offered you one drink!" she cried. "I thought you were lonely!"

"You are a whore! You give VD!"

"No!" cried the woman. "No!" And then she just wept.

A stout little woman came on to talk about rape. She planted her feet, set her small barrel body in a "no bull" stance, and gave it to us straight: Rape was bad, and she was prepared to duke it out with anyone who said it wasn't.

"I agree!" screamed the accused rapist. "I agree!"

The wigged woman continued to weep. Nobody looked at her. In swept the triumphant redhead, who bellowed about her rights. "And I just hope the rapists who are watching the show right now understand that we aren't going to take it anymore!" she cried. The audience cheered. The wig woman wept. The talk-show hostess strode about the set, blond and bristling with savoir faire. She had featured progress, but she had not forgotten the agonized face. Unlike the feminist author, she had put it right up there on the screen.

But wait! The feminist author was not talking about rape, was she? Being a prostitute is not the same thing as being raped, is it? And of course they are not the same. But for the purposes of my discussion here—for the deepest layer of my discussion—they are close enough! The rape victim on TV was treated like a prostitute on an official pro-victim show, and the feminist author—well, it probably wasn't fair to talk about her that way in the pamphlet, even if nobody read it, even if it was true. Can you blame her for not wanting to be like the poor, hurt woman on the talk show, preferring to prance around, swinging her little handbag, instead? Can you blame her for trying to put a good face on it? For talking so loudly about things that have been used to shame women for centuries?

Wordless knowledge can be heavy and dark as the bottom of the ocean. Sometimes you want the relief of dryness, of light, bright words. Sometimes you might be on the side of a smart-aleck middle-aged woman who thumbs her nose at the agonized face and fellates a snotty, sexy man, just for a dumb little thrill. Sometimes you wish it could be that easy.

I looked at my watch. I drank my seltzer and felt myself return to sobriety. I listened to the prairie author entertain a group with a story about how he had been so drunk the previous night that, in a muddled attempt to find the bathroom, he had left his hotel room naked and had roamed the halls until a "beautiful woman" from room service had escorted him back. Everyone laughed. A harried caterer wiped her hand on her rumpled white shirt and made a disgusted face. I looked out the window; people strolled the sidewalks like sensitive grazing animals, full of trust that what they needed was to be found there on the grounds of the hotel. I heard the prairie writer cry, "And she had the most incredible ass!" There was delighted laughter.

Suddenly, I was flooded with goodwill toward the feminist author. I didn't even care that she had refused to speak with me. She wrote well enough and she was an articulate, perhaps even socially significant, figure. Why should she be dismissed, while a man who ran around naked in public and yelled about people's asses was coddled? And yet . . . some part of me was still troubled by the issue of the agonized face. Because the face is not only about rape and pain.

I remember how it was with my husband sometimes, or, rather, how it was on occasion, or, really, maybe just once. It was before I became pregnant with Kira. We had not been getting along, and we were trying to have a special time together. We lit a candle and we undressed and lay on the bed, outside the covers. We rubbed each other with oil. It was relaxing, and awkward, too—it would feel really good and then he would have a sneezing fit. Or I would turn his foot at a strange angle during the foot massage and he would open his eyes and tactfully try to pull it a more comfortable way. When he touched between my legs, I wasn't even thinking about sex anymore. His presence was physical and insistent, like the smell of a wild animal, like a bear, grunting and searching for food, picking berries with the elegant black finger of its tongue—but my mind had wandered away. It wandered like someone browsing a junk store, its attention taken this way and that by each gewgaw, the faded, painted face of each figurine: an argument with my sister, a birthday gift for a friend, the novel I was supposed to review, and, like a tiny reflection on the curve of a glass, a scene from the novel (hero and heroine in tense conversation on a fire escape at dusk, red flowers climbing the wall, traffic darting below). Every few moments, my attention would return to my husband, and I would feel what he was doing, and caress his rough fur and then dart away again. Except with each return, I darted away more slowly, and then I didn't dart at all. His touch had entered my nervous system without my knowing it. The images in my head softened and ran together, colorful, semi-coherent, and still subtly flavored with the novel. The blunt feelings of my lower body came rolling up in dark, choppy waves. He put his hand on my abdomen and said, "Breathe into here." I did. He didn't have to touch me anymore; the flesh between my legs was hot and fat. He touched me with his genitals. I took his large bony head in my hands. We kissed, and we entered a small place sealed away from every other place. In that place, my genitals were pierced by a ring attached to a light chain. He held the chain in his hand and we both looked at it, smiling and abashed—*Whoa! How did that get there?* Then I became an animal and he led me by the chain. We entered into stunning emptiness; we emerged. He moaned and bit my shoulder with his hot, wet mouth.

Afterward, we smiled, rolling in each other's arms, laughing at ourselves, laughing at the agonized face. But we couldn't laugh at the emptiness. It was like entering an electrical current, passing first into a landscape of animate light, and then into pitch-darkness, warm with invisible life, the whispering voices, the dissolving, re-forming faces of ghosts and the excited unborn. Everything horrible to us, everything nice to us. We did not conceive Kira at that time; I think that happened one sleepy morning when, without even realizing it, we entered emptiness again and brought a tiny female out of it.

My husband and I are not friends, but we are amicable. Once, after we split up, I called him late at night, after I'd had a terrible dream, and I was glad for his kind response. But I have never called him like that since, and I'm sure he is glad of it. He is now another wholly separate creature with whom I can negotiate, chat, joke, fight, cooperate with or not. But I remember that moment between us, and it is represented to me by the agonized face. It is

easy to be ashamed of the face—and sometimes the face is shameful. But it is also inextricably bound up with the royalty of female
nature. It symbolizes our entry into emptiness because it is a
humiliation of our personal particularity, the cherished definition
of our personal features. Men don't go there because they can't or
because they are too scared. (Okay, maybe gay men go there. I'm
sure they'd say they go there. But somehow I doubt it.) So they
pretend to look down on us for it—but really, they know better.

It is this weird combination of pride and shame that makes you
want to snap at the feminist author, like a dog in a pack. Perhaps
it is also what gives her an audience; I don't know. But for her to
raise the issues that she sweetly raised in her earnest elf voice—the
middle-aged woman pretending that humiliation is an especially
smart kind of game, together with the casual mention of her experience with prostitution—and yet to leave out the agonized face?
No way. If she had told the same story, even with the prostitution
attached, and let us see the face—that would've been one thing.
We could've sat back and nodded to ourselves, a little contemptuous maybe, yet respecting the truth of it. But to tell those stories
and pretend there's no agony—it makes you want to pinch her, like
a boy in a gang, following her down the street while she tries to act
like nothing's wrong, hurrying her step while someone else reaches
out for another pinch. It makes you want to chase her down an
alley, to stone her, to force her to show the face she denies.

Which in a metaphorical sense is what I did with my article.
When I turned it in, the managing editor said, "Whew! She sure
pissed you off, didn't she?" And I said, "Do you think it's too
much?" And the editor said, "No, if that's what you feel . . ."
Although, of course, I didn't say what I "feel." I couldn't, because it
could not be printed in a newspaper. I had to speak in the fast

brute code of public discourse and count on people to see the sub-
tler shapes moving in the depths below the conventional grid of
my words.

The day after my piece appeared, there was some discussion
among the younger girls at *Quick!* who did not like it that I had
failed to "support" a woman artist, who felt that I used unfair, sexist language. And, privately, when I think of the feminist author,
standing there at the podium in her long skirt and her glasses,
blinking nervously, I almost agree that it was not fair. But fair or
not, I was right. The agonized face and all it means is one of the
few mysteries left to us on this ragged, gutted planet. It must be
protected, even if someone must on occasion be "stoned." Even if
that person is someone for whom we feel secret sympathy and
regard.

And besides, she wasn't really stoned. She will go on writing her
books, making her money, standing up on stages. She will probably
do better than I. I think of the night Kira and I watched the
strange anime story about the armless heroine, and the villainess
who dies. As Kira was getting ready for bed, I asked her if she
found the story scary.

"No," she said, yawning. "But it was sad the other girl had to
die." She paused, climbing into bed. I bent to pull the covers up
to her chin. "But even if she died, she won anyway," she continued.
"Because it was her arms that beat the bad guy."

"That's right," I said, and kissed her. *That's right.* As I turned out
the light, I thought fleetingly about an article I might write on
what you can learn from your children. Then I went to make
myself a drink before preparing to get started on the next day's
work.

Mirror Ball

He took her soul—though, being a secular-minded person, he didn't think of it that way. He didn't take the whole thing; that would not have been possible. But he got such a significant piece that it felt as if her entire soul were gone. As soon as he had it, he not only forgot that he'd taken it; he forgot he'd ever known about it. This was not the first time, either.

He was a musician, well regarded in his hometown and little known anywhere else. This fact sometimes gnawed at him and yet was sometimes a secret relief; he had seen musicians get sucked up by fame and it was like watching a frog get stuffed into a bottle, staring out with its face, its splayed legs, its private beating throat distorted and revealed against the glass. Fame, of course, was bigger and more fun than a bottle, but still, once you were behind the glass and blown up huge for all to see, there you were. It would suddenly be harder to sit and drink in the anonymous little haunts where songs were still alive and moving in the murky darkness, where a girl might still look at him and wonder who he was. And he might wonder about her.

It was at one of these places that he met her. She was drinking with a friend of a friend. She was slim and elfin, with dark hair, long fingers, and tapered fingernails. She held her drink as if she held a bit of liquid flame. She smiled at him; he smiled back. The friend of a friend started talking about a movie she had seen, a complicated fantasy in which a hero and heroine fall into a hidden world running parallel to ours, and discover that the two worlds are on a collision course. The elfin girl punched him lightly on the hip. "We should go," she said. There was a loud crash behind the bar. They both started and turned to look. They turned back to face each other at the same time.

They went to the movie that weekend and then to a bar afterward.

It must be said: She should not have shown him her soul. She flashed it again and again, as if it were a bauble meant to entice him, or a hand mirror flashing signals from a dark and lonely place. Everybody knows about dark and lonely places, he thought. But why was she sending these signals without knowing who he was and if he cared to read them? Still, her constant flashing was dramatic and attractive. Images from the movie they had just seen hovered about her. A woman in black strode through the city with a gun; a woman in white fell on her knees before a killer. The camera lingered on her terrified face; the hero pounded on the door. The girl's eyes flashed like her bright, nervous soul.

"Do you know that vintage-record store on Sanchez and Eighteenth?" he asked.

She shook her head and smiled.

"It's got a mirror ball in the window. It flashes over the whole street at night. Your eyes remind me of it."

She looked down, her small lips in a sweet pinch. Her soul was very visible, and right then, he didn't care why; it seemed natural and lovely. He embraced her, and for a moment he felt that holding her was like holding a bit of liquid flame.

"I'll show it to you," he said. "It's right around the corner from me."

She looked up. "Yeah, right," she said, and the sweet pinch
became a pungent smirk. She took her glass and swallowed the rest
of her drink with a tart little face. He felt annoyed, but he walked
her home anyway.

It was a cold fall night with a feeling of secret pockets and moving shadows. They walked past a park full of human shadows,
drunks, crackheads, and vagrant kids, half-visible and half-audible
in the dark. Cars rolled through pools of street light; blurred faces
and pale hands appeared and vanished, on their way somewhere
else. She put her cold little hand in his pocket, taking the tips of his
fingers in her grip, and he felt as if he were in a fairy tale where the
hero is led into the forest by an enchanted ball of light. She looked
up at him and said something, and once again her soul flashed in
her eyes.

When they reached her door, she invited him in, and her invitation had the same tart face he'd seen at the bar. He followed her
slim figure down a long dark hall that smelled of onions. Squalid
electronic music came from behind a door. The door opened
and a roommate emerged, wearing a short robe with a cat face
on it. She was introduced in motion, and her gleaming eyes went
from the girl to him and back as she continued down the hall.
Another girl sat before the TV in the living room and yet another
was in the kitchen making instant macaroni and cheese. There
were dirty dishes, a shiny garbage pail, fruit on the counter, notes
tacked up on the fridge with colored magnets (magenta and
orange).

The enchanted ball of light paled in the bright room; he glanced
at his watch. The macaroni roommate was telling him how much
she'd loved his last record. She had forthright blue eyes and a muscular red arm that stirred the milk into the glass bowl while he
talked. His elfin date smiled and petted the sharp-cut hair at her

temples with both cold hands. She glanced at him, and there it was again—the forest and the ball of light.

Who was she that she should have this? He sincerely wanted to know.

When she led him to her room behind the kitchen, he followed. She lay on her bed, eyes full of invitation. He sat beside her. He said, "I usually like to get to know a girl better," even though it wasn't true. "Why?" she said. "Can't this just be for now?" He felt insulted, although he didn't realize that was what he felt. She lay like she was posing in a mirror, except that she was trembling slightly under the pose. He felt like he wanted to take her and throw her away; he didn't realize that, either. He kissed her. She rose through her body to meet him. He touched between her legs; she opened her pelvis and recklessly unfurled her soul. He felt like a man in a small boat under which a huge sea creature has passed, causing the boat to pitch gently. Like a man in a boat, he could chase it or run from it, and he picked chase. If he felt it on her lips, he put his mouth on her lips. If he found it on the palm of her hand, he opened her hand and licked it up. Her soul darted here and there, sensitive as any creature, tipping her center of balance back and forth as it oscillated.

She liked this, and if she had any fear, she did not take it seriously. He liked it, too, so much that he could barely concentrate on the chase. Sensation nearly overwhelmed him; his will strained almost to the breaking point when he felt her soul gather its vastness in one small spot, pulling so hard that it yanked him off the boat. He felt her all about him in a tingling feminine myriad; out of this myriad appeared formless spirit that lived in the form of their bodies, touching their eyes, their mouths, their limbs, their genitals. The unknown rose up through their souls and became joined with the known in the form of feelings. Something hot and glow-

ing flew from her. It was joined with Ardor, and it compelled him;
it compelled the part of his soul that was joined with Hunger. He
reached for it, and she did not hold it back. She cried out, delirious
and ignorant of her danger. Hunger snapped shut its jaws, and her
soul, which should have filled the room with her, contracted and
went silent. Her cry was clipped off with a sharp, bewildered gasp.
Her liquid flame was out, and she was just another girl who shared
a flat with too many other girls.

Still—he was not indecent—he felt tenderly toward her body,
and toward his own body, too, and he held her close while she
buried her face against him. He could sense her diminishment, and
that made him feel protective toward her. He meant it when he
kissed her good night and told her he'd call her. But out in the hall
(which still smelled of onions), he changed his mind. He weighed
her good qualities as he walked home in the interesting light of
4:00 a.m., but he did it like a man counting pocket change, yawning and half-interested. When he got home, Hunger yawned, too.
He dropped her soul on the floor, where it quickly became invisible
to him. He forgot her.

Because the dark-haired elfin girl was also a secular-minded person, she didn't know he'd taken a part of her soul any more than
he did. But she knew she would not hear from him again. And
she knew something was gone. She woke the next day feeling
bereft and heartsick. She sulked and drooped around her flat while
her roommates exchanged knowing glances. She vacillated between anger and contempt and terrible longing, and a sense that
she must see the young man again no matter what. Because she
was a rational person, she was sure that her feelings were illusory.
Because she was a proud person, she was determined that she should

not act on her feelings and call him. Rational and proud, she
controlled her feelings by categorizing them in terms of obsession
and projection. "I don't even know him," she said. "I'll get over it."
And she waited for it to pass, much as she might wait for the end of
a flu.

What made it worse: Her soul was connected to her through her
brain. This was not a fault or a virtue; she was just born that way.
Heart, viscera, genitals, brain—none is better than the other; it's a
matter of where the soul has found a place to cling. The brain is not
higher in moral or celestial terms, nor is a person with a soul connected to the brain always unusually bright. But such connection
can give the soul a kind of shocking electricity that will make it stay
up talking its head off for nights on end. Now he had it and it was
talking to him.

　He did not understand where the talking was coming from and
he did not like it. The soul spoke in images of sight and sound that
were quick and multiple, and which changed form by blending into
one another. Because the young man had seized a piece of the soul
linked to Ardor, many of these images were about love. But the
glowing unknown attached to Ardor was, in the soul of this girl,
Effacement. And so the pure, exquisite voice of her soul's love
could flowingly transform, for instance, into the shape of a naked
woman on her hands and knees, holding a knife in her hand, poised
as if to cut her own face. In the physical world, a picture like this
would describe insanity and suicide. In the world of this particular
soul, it described a mystery of Ardor and Effacement, a mystery
the girl was expressing in human form on the night she invited the
boy to have her. The soul addressed itself to the girl, innocently
and literally mirroring her actions—and she could still hear it,

albeit dimly. She did not hear it with her conscious mind; she heard it like she heard her own breath, without being aware of it. And because the young man had possession of it, he heard it, too— and it was not like his breath.

He did not see the naked woman in his mind's eye; he would never have allowed himself to become conscious of something so violently ugly. But he sensed it in his body, and sensed why it was there. Thoughts of the girl came to him, and with those thoughts, fear that he didn't understand. Because he didn't want to be afraid, he had contempt for her. He thought that would work.

The girl tried to feel contempt for the boy, too, but it is hard to have contempt for a person who's made off with part of your soul. She went about her life—her job at a used-clothing store, her once-a-week volunteer stint at the Outreach Center for home-less youth, her evenings out with friends. Outwardly, she did not appear much changed by the misalignment; the first layer of her thoughts was more or less the same, logical and competent enough to get her through the day. But the next layer down, her mind was slowly becoming disintegrated and febrile, unstable on its primary support. Her perception was both heightened and dulled; she would suddenly weep at the sight of an old woman on the bus, or bewilder a friend with her excited analysis of a television character. But the intensity of feeling was misplaced and did not satisfy her. Her mind seized on triviality and substance without being able to tell the difference between the two; she went through it all like a computer on a search, looking tirelessly for what she lacked with-out knowing what it was.

And constant through it all was the memory of the boy she had so casually taken into her body. He was now always present for her,

more overtly than she was present for him. She thought of him
against a vast, open sky, with a halo of piercing white. She thought
of him astride a leopard, light and graceful in mid-leap. She
thought of him moving in an aura of electrical fire, his heart huge
and glowing with blue fire. She did not realize that these pictures
came from her own soul, which was steadfastly signaling her from
the boy's room. She thought she was seeing the boy's fantasti-
cal nature. And so she overruled her pride and called him. In two
weeks, she left two messages on his answering machine. They went
unreturned. She thought, I was very stupid just to have sex with
him. I loved him, and I degraded us both. I am a terrible woman.
I love him and now I will never see him again. Tears ran down
her face.

Meanwhile, the young man was having his own difficulties. Although he was quick to be insulted by a girl who didn't seem
to take him seriously, he generally didn't take girls seriously. But
serious or not, he'd regularly made off with prize bits of their
souls: One (Gentleness) sat quietly, chewing its cud, one (Forbearance) grew up his wall like ivy, and one (Instinct) blundered
dazedly around in the closet, looking for release. They were pacific
and untroublesome, subtle feminine presences that soothed and
grounded him—until now. The newly stolen soul was so talkative,
so increasingly restless, that it had gotten all the others going; if he
could've seen the female souls clustered in his room, they might've
looked like sexy juvenile delinquents hanging around a street corner, smoking and muttering. It wasn't just the girls, either. His soul
was starting to get in on it, too. The new captive was talking to it
and it was beginning to talk back—or at least half of it was. For this

was a young man with a soul in two parts; he'd split it up so it would be harder to get.

He'd done this when he was about two. He'd done it at his mother's advice; she had done it early in life herself. She advised her son to follow her example after his father had walked away and left them in their small brick house. His mother was glad she had kept part of her soul back from her former husband, and she thought her son should learn to do the same. When she sat on his bed at night, singing lullabies and pop songs, he heard her advice, not in the songs, but in her supple voice. Her words would say, "You've got to hide your love away," but he understood that meant "hide your soul." Not all of it, just the vulnerable part. And, as he lay on the verge of dreams and sleep, she would show him how. One half of her smiled and bent to kiss him, and the other vanished in the dark like a cat. And, in the moment between waking and sleep, he followed her lead. The bright, strong half of his soul smiled back at his mother and received her kiss, and the weak part of him withdrew, even deeper than she. For although he took after his mother enough to follow her advice, he could not split so easily. His fragile soul hid too deep inside itself. It made the darkness into which it fled a thing of shape and substance: a tiny model of his childhood home, except the model had no windows and only one door, which was always locked. The strong soul, out in the world of light and movement, forgot his fragile brother. The dark house became a prison and the soul inside a shapeless, nearly voiceless mass of pain that did not stir except in the young man's deepest dreams.

Until now, that is. The chattering soul of the infernal brain girl was everywhere, including outside the prison, tapping on the walls and whispering through the bricks. Her terrible pictures penetrated the thick walls of the prison and the soul inside saw and understood—for he had been effaced for a very long time. The pictures did not seem terrible to him; on the contrary, their violence gave him hope because they confirmed what had happened to him. In the language of the soul, his eyes spoke to the girl through the prison wall in feelings, words, sights, and sounds.

Naturally, this response only increased the girl's pain. On top of her own soul calling out to her, she was hearing from him, too, in the most confusing way possible. She heard him like the American sailors searching the Baltic for a wrecked Russian submarine at the bottom of the ocean heard, with their elaborate sonar, cryptic tapping, which they could not be sure of as signals, and which did not help them rescue the doomed crew. The signals of his soul were like this tapping, which could be anything or nothing, and they haunted her day and night. Day and night she heard him, and nothing she knew about obsession and projection could help her.

She wanted desperately to buy his records and bathe herself in his voice; she didn't because she knew that would only enflame her. But now all music was about him, and she heard his voice in every singer. And she craved music almost as much as she craved the boy. Where her soul had once held space, there was now a ragged hole, dark and deep as the pit of the earth. At the bottom of it ran boiling rivers of Male and Female bearing every ingredient for every man and woman, every animal and plant. Without the membrane of her soul to buffer and interpret the raw matter of the pit, her personality was now on the receiving end of too much primary force. Music temporarily filled the empty space, soothing her and giving shape to the feelings she could not understand.

She went with her friend Angelique to see a live band with a

powerful woman singer. The woman sang like her songs were giant
weird-shaped things pulling her this way and that as they came
through her body and out her mouth. Her songs rose through the
room in huge moving tableaux that dissolved in the darkness, then
rose again—fantastic pictures heard as sound by the clumsy ear, but
seen vividly by the souls present. The songs reflected these souls
and spoke their language: Emotion, thought, sound, image, word-
lessness, and words mixed together in the place between the life of
this world and the pit.

But because the girl's soul was missing, the music didn't reflect
her; rather, it filled her, and she reflected those around her. She
experienced these reflections as a feast, as if she were a clear pool
with senses and a mind, glutted on the sights that passed through
it. She wandered away from her friend into the live darkness,
blooming with the painted eyes and lips of a hundred stories. The
rest room was a burst of light and filth, rushing water and voices. A
young pregnant woman in high-heeled boots and a fur collar
laughed and shook water off her fingers, as if she were scattering
tiny jewels into the air. A sparkling bracelet flashed on her wrist.
She smiled into the mirror and rubbed her belly, and this double
reflection was delicious to the girl.

Still, she was full of humiliation and pain. She was full of anger
at the boy and fear of him because she believed he'd caused her suffering. But because she still heard, without knowing what she was
hearing, the plaintive message of his trapped soul, her abjection
and anger were strangely mixed with tenderness and pity. She
came out of the bathroom staggering a little; she already felt drunk.

Meanwhile, onstage, the singer was singing about love. She
stood still with her naked legs apart, as if the song were splitting
her open and offering her, whether she was wanted or not. Offering layer by layer, until she was splayed so wide that her spine was

made to offer its long, sensitive nerves. It was not an abject song; it was proud. It said, See how I can open. And at the end, when she put her legs together with a quiet "Thank you," it said, See how I can close again. The crowd was still and rapt, receiving her, honoring her, acknowledging all things that open, including themselves. Bouncers and bartenders presided with nimble grace and witness. They had been there a thousand nights and they knew it already.

But the girl, who had opened with the song, could not close again. She found Angelique standing alone with her arms wrapped around herself, her teeth clamped against the rim of her paper cup. When she saw the girl, she took her teeth off the cup, leaving a dark, blurred imprint of her lips. "What's wrong?" she said.

"Oh!" Heavily, the girl put her arms around her friend and laid her head on her shoulder. She rubbed her cheek against her denim jacket and, shuddering, felt the movement of every stranger's reflection flitting through her. Especially, and gratefully, she felt Angelique.

Angelique was a chunky redhead with a beautiful face: big lips, scarred skin, and green eyes that were watchful and passive at the same time, like an animal's. Except her eyes were sad, too. Once they'd gone to L.A. and stayed on Venice Beach for a few days with some Mexican boys they'd just met. The boys had renamed them. They looked at the girl and said, "You'll be . . . Prestige." To Angelique, they said, "And you're Infinity." They were joking, but they were also right: Angelique had a window in her soul and Infinity poured through it, slow and sorrowful as dust. But while Infinity can be sorrowful, it can be calming, too. Right now, for the girl, that desolate calm was like a draught of opium. She shuddered again; in this borrowed Infinity, the boy was just one tiny star among thousands, speeding past.

Abruptly, Angelique shrugged her shoulder and stepped away.

"What's wrong?" she asked again. The girl looked up, to see Infinity staring at her with the face of a worried office mate.

"Nothing," she said, straightening. "I'm just drunk." She looked at the stage, but instead of seeing the singer, she saw the boy, sitting next to her at the bar. He was talking about the movie they had seen. In amazement, she gazed at this ordinary boy who had apparently destroyed her. Help me, she said to him. Please help me. I don't understand what is happening.

And he heard her. Her soul, still in his possession, made sure of that. He was sitting in a bar, half-listening to his drinking partner talk about the ghosts in his apartment while he brooded about his music. His songwriting had not been going well. He was used to writing music that was light and lovely; it had no weight because all the young man's darkness and heaviness was concentrated in the prison house. It could've been a good thing artistically that he was finally hearing from the forgotten soul inside it; he could've used the weight of sorrow in his songs. But since it had been awakened by the foreign agency of the hijacked female, its effects came through an alien sensibility and were distorted. He felt chaotic inside, his thoughts like tiny boats scattered on a strange sea with a cold, unknowable heart.

The ghosts, his friend said, had come out of their usual corner and had taken to floating up around the bed as he lay in it, even floating between him and the books he read before going to sleep. The young man smiled.

"Why don't you try slamming a book on them?" he asked.

The friend said something, but he didn't hear it. He thought the ghost thing was ridiculous, and anyway, he had noticed a girl sitting across from him. She was beautiful, with dark, heavy-lidded eyes exaggerated by makeup, and an almost overly full mouth. She looked at him, frank and confident in her beauty. There was a black bat tattooed on her clavicle.

Well, chaos was not unfamiliar to him. In daily life, his emotions were chaos. He let himself become a vessel for them, letting feeling roar through him, pulling him around like a kite, boiling him like water in a kettle, dissolving him in a whirl of elements. Except that normally he could go into his studio and make order. He could make songs that were satisfying containers, for the kite, the kettle, the whirl of elements—he could put each in its place. The things he was feeling now did not fit into the songs he was used to making.

Thinking he had smiled at her, the bat girl smiled back. Her smile slit open her personality, and out of it tumbled sultry little demons with black curly hair, bright eyes, and naked bottoms. He let himself be distracted. He dropped down into another layer of drunkenness. One of the little demons hiccoughed and sat down heavily.

That's when he heard her say *Help me.* He receded more deeply into drunkenness, and, with a little shock, felt her acutely. She was reaching out to him, but he didn't know for what. He stepped deeper into himself, into the little swift-moving stream of music that always played inside him, a stream of songs running together with memory. His mother's smile was there, the one she had smiled when she was young and beautiful and ready to disappear into the dark. Her smile ran together with the smiles of girls he had loved, or tried to. Mother became an old radio song that cascaded into dozens of songs, sweet and cheap, with something real hidden inside each of them. Still he heard the call—slow and repeated— for help.

He had no ill will toward the girl. On the level that he heard her, he would've been willing to help her. But he had no idea how. He propelled himself back up into his personality and stopped hearing her.

At three in the morning, Angelique had gone home, leaving the girl alone and very drunk. She was sitting on the pavement in the door-way of the vintage-record store at Sanchez and Eighteenth, the one with the silver mirror ball spinning in its window. The mirror ball was full of light from the dimly illuminated store, and out of it flew a horde of ghost lights, skimming dark walls and sleeping windows in a slow, shimmering curve. Secret and tucked away, the girl knelt beneath the curve of light, her hand on the pavement for balance. Her tapered nails and sparkling rings were fascinating against the concrete, which appeared wonderfully porous and soft, as if it had magically absorbed all the softness of the night. She was waiting for the boy to walk by. Even if she couldn't talk to him, she wanted to see him.

It was a sad situation and might've been a disastrous one, except for one thing: It had caused the girl's heart to come open. This had never happened before. Because of the way her soul was hooked into her brain, whenever it had been touched by love, her brain had taken control and overruled her heart. But because of the missing place in her soul, her brain was in too much chaos to control her heart. And so it had come open for the first time. It was as if she had just discovered a hidden door leading to a place inside her-self she'd never known to exist. This was a marvelous thing. Of course, she did not experience it that way; because her openness had come for someone who did not want her, she felt it as painful. And yet she made no attempt to close it. Her mind was still strong enough that she could've tried, but she didn't. The stolen piece of her soul silently compelled her to let it stay open. Her soul did this so that if it got loose, it would have a way back in. And so, without knowing what she was doing or why, the girl obeyed. She was steadfast and loyal, and she did not know it. She thought she was just a lovesick bitch. Because of what she thought, it shamed her to keep her heart open. But she did.

The ragged man approaching her on the street could see all of this from almost a block away. Significant pieces of his soul had been missing for years, and his endless search for them had caused his normal sense of sight to grow an invisible, voracious eye, which tirelessly scanned places most people would not wish to see. He saw her emptiness sucking at everything around it. He saw her open heart, full of feeling and pouring it all out. Emptiness and fullness, pulling in and pouring out with equal and opposite force, gave her an extraordinary psychic discharge more visible to him than the ghost lights. It made him curious. When he got close enough to see her, he was even more curious; she did not look like that kind of person.

Meanwhile, the boy was heading home in a taxi, bat girl in tow. He was in a philosophical mood. She was talking nonsense about art. That was okay with him. Her talk was like a glimmering curtain pulled back to reveal a stage with costumed people on it—and he was one of them. The curtain was moth-eaten and torn at the bottom, but that only made it better. The taxi turned down the mirror-ball street. He interrupted the girl. "Do you know why this is my favorite block in the city?"

She looked out the window, then looked back at him. He could tell she was thinking hard about it. He looked past her out the window; the dancing lights flirted with him and ran away. There were homeless people huddled in the dark storefront. He felt pity, plus curiosity. What was it like for them?

"Oh!" said the girl. "The record store?"

In fact, the ragged man was not homeless. He had a room in a tiny, rotting hotel with a hot plate, a buzzing box refrigerator, and stacks of magazines piled up against a wall. People assumed he was homeless because he stank and was ragged, because he asked for change, and because he was empty like the girl. His soul hadn't been stolen; he had lost it, gradually, over a period of years. He had lost much more than she had. Unlike hers, his soul had been connected to his heart. Because his heart had been deranged by the loss, he'd tried to call back his soul by opening his mind. It didn't work, and he had been without so much of his soul for so long that his open mind was like a gaping wound. His openness had made him wise, but it was not a wisdom he could do anything useful with. His mind hurt him all the time, and the constant hurt made him full of pity for everything that hurt. But because his pity came through his mind, it translated as a thought disturbance rather than feeling, and so was hard to express. He stood before the kneeling girl full of sympathy he couldn't feel and didn't know how to express.

"Do you want money?" she asked.

"Could you help me out?" He hadn't known what else to say. Reflexively, he extended his hand.

"Um, hold on." She opened her purse and pawed through it. Absently, she wondered if the man might rob her. She found her wallet, pulled a dollar from it, and handed it up to him. He took it and paused, as if trying to decide what to do. The circle of whirling lights enclosed them like a spell cast long ago and forgotten, all the force gone out of it but still haunting its spot. He was trying to remember how to talk to girls.

"That's all I can give," she said. "I'm not rich."

He saw she had no idea what was happening to her. Even if he could talk to her, she would not be able to answer. Sorrow and loneliness roared through him—so much force that came to nothing. He decided to try anyway. "You aren't what you think," he said.

"I don't know what I am," she answered.

You are a sack of things without a sack, he thought, but the thought sped by too fast. "Six farts going off in a bag," he said. "Broke the bag and fell out."

She gave a short, nervous laugh. Making a girl laugh—that was good. Grateful for her laughter and wanting very much to help, he decided to show her what was inside him. If you had been looking at him, you would've seen him open his coat and stand as if he were sexually exposing himself. But that gesture was symbolic. Hoping that the girl would have eyes to see, he made his coat the cover for his daily self and, in opening it, revealed the disfigurement of his soul. He did it like a leper might stand in mute greeting before another leper. He did it to show understanding and also to warn.

Her personality didn't see, let alone recognize, what she had been shown; her personality just saw a homeless guy holding his coat open. But beneath her personality, her soul saw what he was showing and shrieked in fear. A block away, the missing piece came awake so suddenly that the other souls trapped in the room with it started and stirred, like restive animals. Do not let that happen, it signaled her. Do something—now! NOW!

At that moment, the boy and his guest walked into his room. Even though the boy was drunk, he was sensitive enough to feel the agitation present there. Not guessing what it was, he mistook it for his own excitement, and he thought he was more attracted to this girl than he was. The girl felt it, too, but, likewise, mistook it for the intensity of the boy himself. Within moments, they were stretched out on his bed, kissing. This girl had no intention of revealing her soul. But in the charged atmosphere of the room, she couldn't hold it back altogether, and it floated to her surface, where he could feel it, just under her skin, delicious and tantalizing. She closed her eyes and arched her neck, and he saw the subtle beauty of her eyebrows, the elegant bone of her nose, the down that covered her face. He felt like he loved her, even though he knew he didn't.

The ragged man sighed and closed his coat. He thought he saw a flicker of recognition, but she just sat there, staring at him. He tried another approach.

"Why don't you go home?" he asked. "You shouldn't be out here."

"I'm waiting for someone."

"Oh," he said. "A . . . boyfriend?"

"Yeah."

His memory became a tunnel of girls, and he fell down it. Some of them were shouting angrily, others were indifferent, and some were laughing with happiness and kissing him with warm, live mouths. One was crying because she was pregnant and too young to have a baby. He sighed again. Now here was this one before him, pert and pretty and torn down the middle. Of course this boyfriend had something to do with her predicament, but what could he do about it? He gave up. "Well," he said, "don't wait too long, sweetheart."

"I won't," she said. She watched him walk down the street, hunched as if subtly crippled. There was a drunk scream from the next block over, and she heard it as a refrain: *Do something—now! Now!* She took her cell phone out of her pocket and dialed the boy's number.

When he picked up the phone, a dark little silence followed his hello and he knew who it was. "Hello?" he said again. The girl on the bed propped her head up with her hand and looked at him. Wonderful: her deep eyes and her blunt-tipped nose and the sharp angle of her elbow.

"We have to talk," said the voice from the phone.

At the sound of it, her captive soul unfurled itself again, and a wave of urgency passed through the room.

"It's four in the morning," he said.

"I know. We need to straighten some things out."

"Well, we can't do it now. I have company." Her soul rolled through the room, crashing like Rip van Winkle's ninepins. He couldn't hear it, but his soul, which was getting nervous, roughly and quickly translated it to his mind as *Give me back my Golden Arm!*

"You treated me like shit!" cried the girl.

"I don't know what you're talking about," he said. "I treated you like you treated me."

She didn't say anything. She gazed at the new place inside her, longing to enter it with him. She thought, I love you, I love you, I love you.

He sensed the new place, but he didn't see what it had to do with him. He sighed. "Call me tomorrow and we can talk," he said. "But right now, I'm busy." He hung up and the ninepins crashed again as her soul flung its full weight against the prison door inside him. The girl on the bed sat like an alert cat, sensing an invisible war.

"An old girlfriend?" she asked.

"No, just somebody I went out with once."

Give me back my Golden Arm!

"I hope she's not a stalker," he added. He sat on the bed; his guest sat up and watched him intently. Deep inside him, deeper than dreams, a drum was beating. It had taken several hours for the girl's call for help to filter down to the bottom of the boy's soul; it had just now gone through the prison wall and reached the prisoner inside. He recognized her voice instantly. He rose and gripped the handle of the prison door. With all his strength, he pulled from the inside while the female pushed from the outside. The boy's inmost foundation began slowly to rock. Debris was loosed. The pit was disturbed.

"Do you want me to go?" asked the tattooed girl.

"No," he said. He meant it; he didn't want to be alone.

The girl lay against the storefront door, her open lips pressed against the tiny, hateful phone, her eyes closed, her face knit tight with pain. Day was coming. In the shallow dark, the mirror-ball lights swarmed biliously. Her heart felt swollen and grotesque, as if it were taking over her whole body, including her head. Her mind felt nearly gone. But the ragged man had helped her after all. Because a tiny bit of her had seen what he showed and had the sense to fear it, she made herself stand up. "Don't wait too long, sweetheart," she muttered through her teeth. "Don't wait too long, sweetheart." She imitated the ragged man's voice as she walked home, hunched in the cold and nearly growling.

The girl from the bar was naked before the boy, as he was before her. She had the turgor of a healthy plant, dense with moisture, so aroused that she was already lost in it. Her soul moved beneath him, luxuriantly turning in her fecundity. The crashing inside him was matched by the hard, socketed joining of their bodies; he pushed from the outside, she from the inside. Deep things were roused and driven toward the surface: Bits of primary matter joined with feeling, memories, and dreams swarmed upward like bats from a dark shaft. The girl beneath him released her own darkness like a wave of perfume. Overwhelmed without knowing why, the boy pressed into her body as if for refuge. She gave it to him, hot and jumping. Her little demon consorts punched their fists in the air and cheered. He let go of everything but the feeling of her body and the sight of her face, her lips parted just enough to show a sliver of teeth. The prison broke. The boy had a sensation of flying as his freed soul shot up and up and up. The boy rolled off the girl, so moved that he nearly passed out. He touched her face with astonished fingers. "Who are you?" he whispered. She smiled. His awe was misplaced, but that scarcely mattered.

Between sleep and wakefulness, he remembered the soul of the girl he'd taken and thrown away; it was like you might suddenly remember something strange that you'd done during a blackout drunk. He got up to look for it, and, to his amazement, bumped into several others before he found it. It was clear what was called for—and yet, as he looked at them, he realized he had grown attached. He had to sit for some moments, just looking at them— Gentleness, Forbearance, Instinct, and Ardor—before he could herd them into the hall and out the door. Perhaps some of them were attached to him, too, for, once outside, instead of dispersing right away, Forbearance and Gentleness clustered at the door, giving off an air of doelike confusion.

But the intrepid soul attached to the brain of the girl who had knelt under the mirror ball that night did not hang around. As soon as he released it, it made a beeline toward its proper owner, who was mercifully still asleep, and so was spared the strange sensation of reentry. The window of her heart was just open enough for it to slip in.

Almost a year later, they passed each other on the street. They might have tried to avoid meeting, except that neither recognized the other until it was too late. This was because the appearance of both had been subtly altered. Each of them was vaguely aware that the other had changed, but neither suspected that the other had a thing to do with it. Each merely recognized the other as an enemy with whom they were no longer at war, and they both had tentative, tolerant eyes that said, I like you fine as long as you don't start anything. They said, Hi, how are you?" on the approach and "Good!" on the way past. Both of them turned to look at each other, got caught, and quickly turned back. Neither of them saw their souls, unfurled in the sun and glimmering at each other with recognition and regard.

Today I'm Yours

I dreamed of Dani only once that I can remember, but it was a deep, delicious dream, like a maze made of diaphanous silk, or a room of hidden chambers, each chamber nested inside the previous one—except that according to the inverse law of the dream, each inner chamber was bigger, not smaller, than the last.

In the dream, I was alone on the streets of Las Vegas, surrounded by speeding traffic and huge streaming lights advertising monstrous casinos. There were thousands of people pouring in and out of the monstrous advertised mouths, but I didn't know any of them. I went to my hotel. The walls of its lobby were made of artificial forest, with animals and birds moving inside them. I went to my room; its walls seemed to shift and flux. Dani came out of the bathroom wearing a leopard-print minidress and black high-heeled shoes. The room stirred as if surprised; though she sometimes wore lipstick, Dani never wore a dress or high heels. She wore pants and clunky boys' shoes; she liked her lovers to wear dresses. But in the fluxing chamber of my dream, she walked toward me with a leopard-print dress purring on her haunches. Her slender little body was like a cold-blooded eel with electricity inside it; her movements, too, had the blithe, whipping ease of an eel traveling in deep water. But her flashing eyes were human. She came toward me as though she were going to kiss me, but instead she walked past me, opened a door in the wall, and disappeared. I looked out the window and saw cities and countries; I even saw private rooms in other countries; I saw things that had happened hundreds of years ago. But I couldn't see Dani, even though she was inside my room.

A week later, I was walking down the street in Manhattan, and there she was. It was during the first autumn of the Iraq war. It was a time of decay and disillusion. On the newsstand, a magazine cover read WHY WE HAVEN'T BEEN HIT AGAIN: TEN REASONS TO FEEL SAFE—AND SCARED. In the middle of town, a building fell down and crushed people to death, and before sadness, there was relief that it was merely more decay, and not terrorism. A bus stop advertisement for bras read WHO NEEDS INNER BEAUTY? and someone had written across it in black marker YOU DO ASSHOLE.

I was carrying wine and fuchsia flowers, and the flowers nervously waved their wobbling fingers over the top of my bag. It was a humid afternoon and the air was heavy with the burnt tang of fresh-laid asphalt and hot salted nuts. I walked past a wall layered with many seasons of damp movie posters; the suggestion of a circus seeped up under the face of an actress, until a torn half tiger leapt, roaring, through the hoop of her eye. Loud, clashing music poured out car windows and ran together in a muddy pool of sound, with a single bell-like instrument sparkling in and around the murk. I looked up, my mind suddenly tingling with a half-remembered song, and there she was, looking at me. An eerily smiling beggar wandered between us, jiggling the coins in his cup, and I remembered that when we first met, she had put her finger on my sternum, lightly run it down to my navel, and turned away. "Hello, Ella," she said.

She was on her way home from her job as an editor of a small press distinguished mainly by its embroilment in several lawsuits. I was preparing for a dinner party my husband was giving for some pleasant people who had once been well regarded in bohemian literary circles. She knew I was married, but still, when I said the word *husband,* she let contempt touch her eyes and lips. We clasped hands and I kissed her cool, porous cheek. Dani used contempt like a clever accessory, worn lightly enough to beguile and unsettle the eye before blending into otherwise-ordinary clothing. I've never seen her without it, though sometimes it fails to catch the light and flash.

During the last ten years, we've met several times like this. When we first met, nothing was like this. That was fifteen years ago. I had just published a book that was like a little box with monsters inside it. I had spent five dreary years writing it in a tiny apartment with a sink and a stove against one wall and a mattress against the other, building the box and its inhabitants out of words that ran, stumbled, posed, and pirouetted across cheap notepaper like a swarm of hornets were after them. I neglected my family. I forgot how to talk to people. I paced the room while feverish tinny songs poured from a transistor radio with a broken antenna and fantasized about the social identity that might be mine if the book were to succeed.

I did not realize I had made monsters, nor how strong they were, until the book was published and they lifted the roof off my apartment, scaled the wall, and roamed the streets in clothes I never would've worn myself. Everywhere I went, it seemed, my monsters had preceded me, and by the time I appeared, people saw me through their aura. This could've worked for me socially; monsters were and always will be fashionable. But in my mind, my monsters and I were separate. Painful and complicated situations arose, and I lacked the skill to handle them with finesse. I left the monsters behind and moved to California, where I rented a cottage in a canyon heavily grown with trees. I purchased a rug with large, bright polka dots on it and a red couch, on which I sat for hours, hypnotized by the prize of my new social identity. It was an appealing thing and I longed to put it on—but when I did, I couldn't quite make it fit. Hesitant to go out in something so ill-fitting, and uncertain how to alter it, I stayed home with the cat, who accepted my private identity as she always had.

Back in New York, several new acquaintances became concerned. They gave me the names of people I might introduce myself to in San Francisco, and one day I took the bus across the Golden Gate Bridge to meet one of them. The warm, dim, creaking old coach traveled low on its haunches, half-full of adults heavily wrapped in their bodies and minds, plus light-limbed, yawping teens, bounding and darting even as they sat in their seats. On the highway, the bus accelerated, and with a high whinging sound, we sprouted crude wings and flew across luminous bay on humming bridge, between radiant, declaiming sky and enrapt, answering sea, flecked with flying brightness and lightly spangled with little tossing boats. We barreled along a winding avenue thickly built with motels (the stick-legged ball of a smiling sheep leaping over the words COMFORT INN still leaps somewhere in my brain) and squat chunks of fast-food stores. The distant ocean flashed and brimmed at intersections. We turned right, climbed a hill; at the top, fog boiled through the air on wings of mystery and delight. Down the hill, lit slabs of business rose up into the coming night. Floods of quick, smart people surged along with the hobbled and

toiling; the felled sat beached and stunned against buildings in
heaps of rags. Turn and turn again. Glancing out the window, I saw
a strip club with a poster on its wall featuring one half-naked girl
walking another on a leash. The leashed girl looked up and raised a
paw in a patently ironic expression of submission and desire. I was
meeting Dani in a neighborhood of bars and old burlesque clubs, a
place of cockeyed streets like crooked mouths lined with doors
like jack-o'-lantern teeth. The fog lolled in the sky, sluggish as a fat
white woman on rumpled sheets. I was in a place where people
dressed up as monsters, and after going to so much trouble to
make them, I'd left mine behind. Feeling small and naked, I walked
under big neon signs: a naked woman, an apple, a snake. It was not
frightening. It was a relief to feel small and naked again.

I entered the appointed spot, a dive with a slanted, vertiginous
floor. It took a moment to figure out who she was, but I believe
she saw my nakedness at once. So did the man sitting with her, a
middle-aged academic with a red shelflike brow. "Your stories are
interesting for their subject matter," he peevishly remarked to me.
"But they aren't formally aggressive enough for me." He went on to
describe his formal needs while Dani listened with droll courtesy,
then turned to me with an amused grin. She put her cold finger on
my sternum and ran it lightly down to my navel, then turned back
with mock solemnity as her companion put down his drained glass
and held forth again. He left minutes later, banging a table cockeyed as his curled arm and flipper hand worried the torn sleeve of
his jacket.

"I'm sorry about that," she said. "I just ran into him. He's lonely
and he talks too much when he's drunk."

She was twenty-five. I was thirty-three. She was already editor
in chief of a venerable avant-garde press, a veritable circus of caged
monsters and their stylish keepers. She spoke with a combination

of real confidence and its flimsy counterfeit. Monsterless, I barely knew how to speak at all, and what I could say was timid and unctuous. It didn't matter. She wore a heavy silver necklace over her white T-shirt, under which her small breasts gave off dark, glandular warmth. Behind the bar, a mountain of green, blue, and gold bottles glimmered before a murky mirror lake. On the television above the bar, a rock star in an elaborate video drew a door in the air with a piece of chalk, smiled, and stepped through it. Jukebox music rose up, making a forest of sound, through which young girls traveled on their way to the bathroom. Above us, the fog traveled, too, laughing and quick. The bathroom door creaked loud and long; slim thighs went past, along with a swinging little wrist loaded with shining jewelry. We were hungry for this, all of this, and for each of us, "this" took form in the other. We ate each other with our eyes and, completely apart from our inconsequential words, our voices said, How delicious. We impulsively kissed, and separated quickly, laughing like people who had accidentally brushed against each other on the sidewalk. Then with a nervous toss of her head, she glided in close again. Soft heat came off her face, and then there was the dark, sucking heat of her mouth. She said, "I'd take you to dinner, but my girlfriend is expecting me."

She drove me to the bus stop in front of a doughnut place and stood waiting with me. She lived with her girlfriend, she said, but they had an understanding. Gum wrappers and plastic bags stirred in the cold, light-echoing wake of night traffic. Behind the glass of the doughnut place, a dark woman with rhythmic arms labored over golden dough. On the street, a hunched man with a sour face strutted back and forth, displaying the masking-tape words on the back of his jacket—COPS ARE TOPS—I'M A BOTTOM—plus an arrow pointing at his butt. Really, I said, an understanding? Yes, said Dani, though it had been difficult to maintain. How had they arrived at it? I asked. How had they talked about it? They had not talked about it, she said. She thought it was more powerful for not being talked about. Bottom scowled as we kissed again. Golden doughnuts continued to fry. The bus arrived; I crossed its black rubber threshold, sat in the back, and almost immediately went to sleep.

Asleep on the bus, I dreamed that while watching a magic show I was plucked, blank and tingling, from the audience and led by a white-gloved assistant up onto the stage, where I was suddenly drenched with color and identity: I was the girl to be sawed in half. My heart pounded. I woke on the winding avenue thickly built with hotels, their signs now rapt and glowing in the velvet dark.

Naturally, it was nonsense about the understanding. That was just a door Dani had drawn in the air with her finger. But when we tried it, it opened, and so in we went.

We met almost every week for five months. Our time alone was as light and pleasantly shocking as her casual touch to my sternum, but with its meaning now thoroughly unfolded. We attended film screenings, dinner parties, the dull receptions that follow literary panels—and somehow we would always find an unused room, an inviting stair, a hallway that would magically rearrange its molecules to become a sweet little seraglio and modestly revert as soon as we left it, smoothing our clothes and hair. We would have dinner somewhere, and then she would drive me back home to Marin. We drove without talking, the tape deck playing and the landscape making dark curved shapes all about us, shapes that would part to reveal the stars, then the ocean, then clusters of fleeing light. I remember a tape she played a lot, a song that went "Let your love come through / Love come through to you." It was a lush and longing song, and after it, the silence between songs seemed dense and deep. It was during this silence that Dani asked, "What are you thinking?" And so we began to talk.

We talked much like we made love—false and sincere, bold and fearful, vulnerable and shielded. I knew that her mother had had several face-lifts, a tummy tuck, and liposuction. I knew that after an especially grueling set of operations, she had declared triumphantly to her daughter, "You have inherited an excellent set of healing genes!" She knew that my father had screamed to my mother, "I'm done with you, you phony! I'm going to find me a black lady with big flat feet and a hole up her butt!" I knew that one Thanksgiving her mother had burst into tears, run into the kitchen, and stuffed the turkey into the garbage, shouting, "And I wish I could do this to every one of you!" When Dani tried to comfort her, she turned away, shouting, "No! No!" Dani told this story not with self-pity but with laughter and love in her voice. When I showed her a picture of my parents taken at an ancient local studio known for its funereal tinting and suffocating airbrush technique, she said, entirely without irony, "They look great! They look so real!"

"She means we look like hell," said my father when I told him what my "friend" had said.

"She meant you don't look like you've had a face-lift," I replied.

"I would if I could afford it."

I repeated that to Dani, with laughter and love in my voice. We love our parents, our stories said to each other. We are people who can love. At thirty-three, I used my parents to explain me—to make me something more real than the outline of a woman drawn in the polluted air of a bar by the most casual of fingers. The thought makes me sad and a little ashamed, and yet our confidences were not entirely false. Standing on the street fifteen years later, we still felt the silken warmth of our stories breathing between us, a live tissue of affectionate trust that appears to give us shelter each time we meet.

The light changed, but instead of crossing the street toward my destination, I went the other way with Dani, as if she had led me, even though she hadn't. I asked about her latest girlfriend, a poet as fashionable as Dani's orange hip-hugging jeans. "Yasmin is in L.A. for the month," she said, and paused while we recognized an actress striding toward us on starved stick legs, a little black poodle with a beautiful red tongue peering haplessly from the tensile cave of her bosom. "She's teaching a poetry workshop," added Dani. "And how is David?"

A grainy smell of gas rose off a torpid snake of traffic and snakily wound through the scent of damp bark and leaves. A taxi driver with his arm out the window beat out a song on his section of snake. Already it had formed, our invisible shelter, its walls hung with living pictures.

"So," said Dani lightly, "are we going somewhere?"

And of course we are: down the hall and to the right, past the picture of Dani in her office, talking on the telephone to her father; he is in San Francisco and wants to see *Tosca* with her. Dani is wearing black-and-white-checked stretch pants and bright red lipstick, and her glossy hair is flush against her wide cheekbones. "Okay, Daddy," she says, and her voice is softer and more seductive than it ever was with me.

We walk down the street in San Francisco, holding hands; a creamy-skinned young girl with a rosy smile rides up on a lavender bike and says, "Dani!" She and Dani talk, the girl's long bare leg bracing tense and beautiful against the curb. Dani promises to call soon; the girl rides away in a wake of lavender and rosy eagerness. I ask, "Who's that?" and Dani smiles. "Oh," she replies, drawing it out, "just some girl."

In my bedroom, we lounge on a summer afternoon. The air is thick with heat and earthen smells: cat piss, armpit, rug mold, fruit, cunt; in the world around us, fibrous green and fungal life unfurls to offer its inmost odor to the sun. We are naked, and my blue comforter is rolled back like a parted wave; the cat walks in and out with her tail up. I am showing Dani a picture of my father holding me in one arm and bending his head to kiss my infant foot. My mother is a blur of breast in the background, and my breast, just scored by Dani's teeth and tongue, echoes hers. Dani had called and asked me to meet her and I'd said no because I had a cold. An hour later, she showed up with a plastic bag of oranges and echinacea tea, and I was surprised and touched to realize she thought I might be lying.

I should not have been surprised: Dani's confidence lay almost entirely in her social identity, a smart, well-secured area, beyond which lay hidden a verdant private world longing for and afraid of form—hidden even from her. When she broke up with her girl-friend (a pretty blonde with pink, allergic eyes whom I was fated to run into at parties for the next dozen years), Dani said this woman, with whom she'd lived for two years, had never known her. "I feel like people accept the first thing I show them," she said, "and that's all I ever am to them." A month later, she broke up with me.

I said, "Do you have time to get a drink?"

"With your bag?"

"Why not?" I said. "It's easily checked."

"Umm."

A freckled girl walked by in a red raincoat, smiling to herself, and there was that same papered-over circus poster on another wall, this time showing a ghostly tiger leaping from a shouting model's open mouth.

"I dreamed about you last week," I said.

"Yes?" Her sidelong glance was piercing in the eye, but watchful in the heart; her dark hair was rough-textured, and layered in a ragged way, which gave a casual carnality to her lips and jaw.

"I dreamed we were in Las Vegas again, and you were wearing high heels and a dress."

"Really!" She laughed, a hot, dry little sound, and—how ridiculous—on yet another wall a circus elephant dourly paraded across an advertisement for a rock concert against cancer, apparently holding another elephant by the tail. "So," she said, "where do you want to go?"

Back to that first dive with its passing girls, its flavor of fog and forest of music; or the sweet sad cave next to a vacant lot strung with darkish-colored bulbs; or that odorous cavern glittering with earrings and rhinestone studs and sweat on the tossing hair of some dancer under a dirt-swarming light; that velvety cubbyhole like an emerald jewelry box with a false back, a secret compartment that, when we found it, revealed a place where we belonged together.

"Café Loup?" I said. "It's quiet."

Six months or so after the first time we broke up, we met again at the book fair in Las Vegas. I was there because my new book was coming soon; Dani was there as an editor. During the day, the book fair was a bland caravan parked inside a pallid amphitheater tented with beige, a series of stalls and tables draped with colorless cloth and laden methodically with books. At night, it was a giant Ferris wheel whirring ecstatically and predictably, each club, restaurant, and gaming room its own tossing car, blurred with lights and screaming faces while the sober carnie worked the machine. In this tossing blur, I kept glimpsing Dani; walking down a hallway to an obligatory event, I glanced into a passing room and saw her crossing it with the feral stride particular to her—her hips never swaying, but projecting intently, rather coldly forward. I thought I saw her slender back and butt impatiently squeeze between a pair of outsized hams and heads in order to get to the bar, but more hams and heads crowded in and buried her before I could be sure. I was at a party for an author, who has since become an actress, when I saw Dani politely listening to someone I couldn't see, eyes flashing through the politeness as if in response to the flattered speaker—a fool who would not recognize the instinctive flashing of an eel in deep water. It was a few minutes later that she came up behind me while I was scooping a fingerful of icing off the author's cake. Later that night, in front of a display of white tigers trapped behind the glass wall of a hotel lobby, I leaned against her and whispered, "Let's pretend we don't know each other." She embraced me from behind and roughly rubbed her head on mine. A brilliantly colored bird flew behind the glass; one tiger snarled at another, which had come too close to it.

In my room, we ordered a bottle of scotch. An hour or so later, in a torrent of furious drunkenness, we used each other on the floor. I remember pungently but only dimly the terse movement of her lean arm and its maniacal shadow, my splayed leg, the gentle

edifice of her chin, her underlip, the soft visual snarl as she turned
her face sharply to the side. Amazement briefly lit my drunkenness
as she gathered me in her arms and carried me to the bed. "I love
you," I said, and sleep came batlike down upon us.

The next day, we ordered breakfast from a huge menu in a fake
leather book and I apologized for that intimacy—we were not,
after all, supposed to know each other. "Oh, that's all right," she
said. "People who don't know you are always saying that." For the
rest of the book fair, we were together every night, holding hands
and kissing at strip shows, casinos, and a women's boxing match.
Then we went back to San Francisco, and broke up again.

During that breakup conversation, I reminded her of what she'd
said about no one really knowing her. "Don't you see why that is?" I
said. "You've gone out of your way to create a perfect, seductive
surface, and people want to believe in perfection. If they think they
see it, they don't want to look further."

"Do *you* want to?"

If I said yes, I meant it, in a way. But in another way, I didn't. If
social identity was her great strength, it was my great weakness.
And so of course I loved to see myself reflected in her shiny surface. I loved to appear in public as that reflection—even if the
reflection was that of a stupidly smiling woman in a sequined
costume, waiting to be sawed in half.

Café Loup is an elegant establishment with a low ceiling, dim
lighting, and a melancholy feeling of aquarium depth that subtly
blurs the diners seated at the white-draped tables in the back—the
elderly gentleman with his gallant fallen face and his pressed shirt,
his companion's lowered white head and dark linen dress, her pale

arm quivering slightly as she saws the leg off a small bird. I checked my bag at the door and we chose a table, even though the polished bar was almost empty. Dani ordered a martini with no olive; I had red wine. The waiter, a middle-aged man with a heavy face, silently approved of the elegant manner with which Dani placed her order. Silently, with upturned eyes, she accepted his approval. Then she turned to me and said, "So, how long has it been?"

Months passed; I moved from Marin County to San Francisco. I saw Dani for dinner every now and then, or went with her to the movies. We were only friends, but still her face froze when, over pomegranate cocktails with lime, I told her I couldn't meet her later because I had to meet my boyfriend. Seeing her expression, I became so flustered that I nearly began to stammer. She turned her head and became absorbed in the view—chartreuse shrubbery below, blue and hazy sky above, a watercolor with a purple blur spreading luridly across its middle.

After that, our invisible shelter became less substantial, more like a pavilion or a series of tents gently billowing and hollowing in the night air. When I saw her at a poetry reading/performance that I attended with my boyfriend, it was almost not there at all. While he wandered through the room with an affable air, I sought out Dani, half-afraid to find her. When I did, she saw my fear, and rushing to press her advantage, she tried and failed to curl her lip contemptuously. Perhaps to steady her quavering mouth, she took my extended hand. "Hello," she said softly. Hello, said the heat of her hand. It was around then that she took up with another writer, a preposterous person who once took offense at something I said or didn't say, and, to my relief, refused to speak to me ever after.

And suddenly there were long distances between one tent and the next, and I found myself walking under the stars, alone on dark wet grass.

Dani sipped her martini and nibbled at a dish of nuts. She talked about Yasmin, with whom she had lived for the last three years—longer than anyone else. Her posture was erect and alert, her small shoulders perfectly squared. But her hair was rough by then, not glossy. She was swollen under the eyes, and there were deep creases on either side of her mouth and between her brows; her lips were bare and dry. Her once-insouciant slenderness had become gaunt and somehow stripped, like a car or motorcycle might be stripped to reveal the crude elegance of its engine.

"I don't want to be unfaithful anymore," she said. "I want to stay with Yasmin. I want to take care of her."

I smiled and said, "You're like a man. You've always been that way." Her smile in return was like a blush of pleasure. "Yeah, I guess it's true," she said.

In San Francisco, I wandered into a maze that was sometimes peopled and sometimes empty, sometimes brightly lit and sometimes so dark that I had to grope my way along it with my hands, heart pounding with fear that I would never find my way out. I quickly became lost, and it seemed like almost everyone I met was lost, too. Sometimes it seemed to me an empty life, but that wasn't really true. It wasn't empty; it was more that the people and events in it were difficult to put together in any way that felt whole.

———

Before she met Yasmin, Dani said, she did not court or date or screw any girls for over a year. She was thirty-six and she felt very old. She did not want to be the "older lesbian" going after young girls. She did not have the heart for it. But she was very lonely, more lonely than she had ever been. She felt she didn't belong anywhere. She thought she would die. I didn't ask her why she hadn't called me, because I already knew. Instead, I glanced down at my watch, saw that I needed to go, and ordered another drink.

At the end of the show, the magician goes home. And so does the girl who was sawed in half. She changes out of her costume into her jeans and sneakers and leaves by the back door, crushing a cigarette under her foot as she goes.

It is a low form of performance, and a tawdry metaphor for any kind of affair. And yet shows are wonderful. Even for jaded performers, they have a sheen of glamour, no matter if the sheen is threadbare and collecting dust. And in that sheen, there may be hidden, in the sparkle of some stray rhinestone or store-bought glitter, the true magic that will, as the synthetic curtain opens, reveal a glimpse of something more real than one's strange and unreal life.

The curtain opened again at a boring book event in L.A.; I walked in, and there was Dani, lying eel-like on a leather love seat, nodding at someone I couldn't see. She must've felt my gaze, because she turned, saw me, and said, "Of all people—," her voice loud enough for me to hear her across the room. I knocked down a lamp as we stumbled into her room, a funky little box that my fun-house memory has given three walls instead of four. To steady me, she took my hair in her fist. "We really *don't* know each other now," she said. The next day, I woke alone in my room, where a lustily roaring hotel shower brightly stippled my bruised flesh. The curtain opened again that evening; silently she offered me her smartly clad arm, and silently I accepted.

Halfway through her second martini, Dani asked, "Does David take care of you?"

"Yes," I said. "We take care of each other."

"Good," she said. "I'm glad."

In the back of the restaurant, the elderly couple slowly rose from their seats, the man taking the woman's arm at the elbow. We paused to watch them. Ceiling fans with large wooden blades solemnly turned over our heads.

Each scene covers and is covered and shows through the others, fractured, shifting, and shaded, like bits of color in a kaleidoscope. I moved to Houston to teach; she moved to New York to work for a former jazz singer who wanted to write a memoir. She traveled often to L.A. to visit a woman she was courting there; I traveled often to New York to visit no one in particular. We were nothing to each other, really. I rarely thought of her, and although she said otherwise, I doubt she thought of me except when she saw me. And yet from time to time, in a little pit with a shimmering curtain, we would discover a room with a false back, and through the trapdoor we would willingly tumble, into a place where we were not a mere addendum to another, more genuine life—a place where we were the life, in this fervid red rectangle or this blue one.

———

Slowly, the elderly couple moved past our table, the man still holding the woman's arm, the woman's small silver handbag dangling a
little rakishly from her gentle, wrinkled hand. Dani watched them,
her eyes softening even in profile.

Her strength, her social identity, had been stripped from her as
time had stripped her youth. But her private world had moved forward to fill the empty space. I thought, This is why I always trusted
her. Because my private identity was my strength, I could sense
hers even when I couldn't see it, and I knew it could be trusted.

Time and again, the curtain parted: Served by stylish hostesses, we
sat in ornate chairs, drinking martinis and eating caviar on toast. A
lurid dream of music surged around us, mixed with the globule
voices of strangers bent double, triple with personality. We held
hands and kissed across the table; Dani said, "If we have sex again,
I don't want us to be drunk." Drunk already, I took a ring out of my
pocket, a flat amethyst I had bought that day. I had not bought
it for her, but I gave it to her. "I love you," I said. "We can't be
together, and maybe we'll never even have sex again. But I love
you." Rosy young heterosexuals burst into laughter, gobbling olives
and peanuts and beautiful colored drinks in shimmering glasses.
Another time, we sat side by side in a modest music hall, my arm
around her low back, feeling the knobs of her fiery spine. We were
there because Dani knew the singer in the band, a sexy blonde no
longer in her first youth. She sang "Today I'm Yours" and the music
made shapes for her words: a flower, a rainy street in spring, an
open hand, a wet, thumping heart. Each shape was crude and colored maybe a little too vividly with feeling. But we wanted those
shapes and that feeling. My father was dead, and the writer Dani

had once left me for was dead, too. We were not young anymore. "Today I'm Yours." It was a crude and romantic song. But human feeling is crude and romantic. Sometimes, it is more vivid than anyone could color it. In some faraway badly smudged mirror, Dani's striking arm flashes again and again; her face is in an almost featureless trance, and my twisted mouth is the only thing I can see of myself.

"Here," she said, handing the taxi driver a bill. "Wait until she gets in the door, okay?" The cab bucked forward, and her hard, dear face disappeared in a rush of starless darkness and cold city lights. I woke sprawled half-naked in a room with all the lights on, the phone in one hand, my address book in the other, open to the page with Dani's number on it.

"I'm sorry about something," she said. "I've always wanted to tell you." We were waiting for the check. Playfully laughing waitpeople lingered at the warmly lit kitchen door; for them, the evening was about to begin. "I wish I'd been a better friend to you," she said. "In San Francisco, I mean. I knew you were lonely. But I couldn't. I was too young and I just couldn't."

"It's all right," I said. "It would've been difficult." I looked down at the table; it was gleaming and hard, and there was a shining drop of water or alcohol graying the tip of Dani's spotless napkin. Soon my husband and I would be making chicken for five people. There would be little bowls of snacks and flowers and drinks. But how private the knobs of Dani's spine had been when she was next to me and my arm was around her low back. How good it was to sit across from her and see the changes in her face. How heartless and foolish we had been together, how obscene. How strange if ten years from this moment, David and Yasmin were gone and instead

Dani and I were living together. The image of this, our life together, winked like a piece of glitter with a whole atomic globe whirring inside it, then vanished like the speck it was. The check came. We counted out the money. I paid the tab; Dani left a generous tip.

We came out onto the street and saw it had rained. The pavement was steamy and darkly patched, and traffic moved with a shadowy hiss. The sky was pale, but gold light rimmed the rumpled horizon of old brick apartments, restaurants, and shops that had changed their names a dozen times in ten years. Dani said she'd walk me home. We walked past the wall layered with movie posters, and I saw that the circus tiger leaping through the rubbed-away eye of an actress had itself been rubbed away by the rain, leaving the image of a pale blue eye staring through rippling black stripes. I remembered the song "Today I'm Yours," and I asked Dani if she knew what the blond singer was doing now. "I don't," she said. "We lost touch somehow." We walked in silence for a while. Another piece of glitter winked; in it I saw my parents, smiling at each other, kissing and embracing. Like an afterimage, I saw Dani's parents embracing, too. Tonight, David and I would make food for people; we would talk and there would be music. We would smile, kiss, embrace. Before we lost touch, or turned into something else, another person or a spirit or ashes or bones in the dirt with a stone on it.

Forgetting to look at the light, I stepped off the curb into traffic. A car swerved and braked as Dani yanked me back against her. The driver, remarkably dressed as a clown but without the red nose, shook his clown-gloved fist out the window as he sped past. We laughed. We let go. She said, "It's great to see you"; she said it like she always had. Then she walked away to be with Yasmin, and I walked away to be with David, hurrying now because I was late.

The Little Boy

Mrs. Bea Davis walked through an enormous light-fluxing corridor of the Detroit airport, whispering to no one visible: "I love you. I love you so much." The walls of the corridor were made of glowing translucent oblongs electronically lit with color that, oblong by oblong, ignited in a forward-rolling pattern: red, purple, blue, green, and pale green. "I love you, dear," whispered Mrs. Davis. "I love you so." *You didn't love him,* said the voice of her daughter Megan. *You had nothing but contempt. Even when he was dying you—* Canned ocean waves rolled through the corridor, swelling the colors with sound. "You don't understand," whispered Bea. The ocean retreated, taking the colors solemnly and slowly back the other way: pale green, green, blue, purple, red. Red, thought Bea. The color of anger and accident. Green: serenity and life. She stepped onto a moving rubber walkway behind a man slumping in his rumpled suit. "I love you like I loved him," she whispered. Very slightly, the rumpled man turned his head. "Unconditionally." The man sighed and turned back. A woman with a small boy passing on the left peered at Bea curiously. Does she know me? thought Bea. "What a wonderful idea," she said out loud. "These lights, the ocean—like walking through eternity."

The woman smiled uncertainly and continued past; her little boy turned his entire torso to stare at Bea as his mother pulled him on. Maybe she did know me, thought Bea. We lived here long enough. She smiled at the little boy until he turned away, a calf tethered at his mother's hips.

They had not lived in Detroit, but in the suburb of Livonia, in a neat brick house with a crab-apple tree in front of it. The tree had spreading branches that grew in luxuriant twists; in the spring it exploded with pink blossoms, and in the summer the lawn was covered with the flesh of its flowers. Megan and Susan ran through the yard with Kyle, the neighbor boy. Megan, seven, climbed the crab-apple tree, wrapping her legs around a branch and crowing for her mother to take a picture. Green, blue, purple. Red. It had not been a happy time for the family, and yet her memories of it were loaded with small pleasures. Dancing to the "Mexican Hat Dance" in the living room, the girls prancing around, and Mac swinging her in his arms, yelling, "A hundred pounds! A hundred pounds!" The willow trees on 8 Mile Road, the library with the model of Never Land, the papier-mâché volcano at the Mai Kai Theater, glowing with rich colors. Kyle and Megan putting on Gilbert and Sullivan's *Mikado* in a neighbor's garage with the little girls down the block—she had a picture of it in one of the photo albums: Kyle was very dashing in slippers and his mother's silk robe with black dragons on it. The little neighbor girls wore gowns with silk scarves tied around their waists. Megan, the director, wore a top hat and a mustache. Susan sat in the driveway with the other siblings and parents, her thin arms wrapped around her body, staring off into the sky.

At the end of the corridor was an escalator with people pouring onto it from all directions. Bea mounted it and stood still, while on her left people rushed facelessly past her. Going up, she felt as if she were falling, but falling where?

She had just come from a visit to Megan in upstate New York.

Megan was a forty-two-year-old lawyer married to a travel writer—no children yet, but Bea hadn't given up hope entirely. They had driven to Manhattan to see a play, the windows down and country music on the CD. She was at first disappointed to see that they were seated in the mezzanine, but it was all right—the actors' limbs were as subtly expressive as eyebrows or lips or the muscles of the neck. Afterward, they had dinner in a big open-faced restaurant on a cobbled street with tables spilling out, women sitting with their legs comfortably open under the tables, their bra straps showing a little and their chests shining slightly in the heat. There was a huge bar with the artful names of drinks written on a board above it, and a mirror behind it, and a great languidly stirring fan on the ceiling. Young men courted girls at the bar; a small girl with one knee on a tall stool leaned across the bar to order a round of drinks, and her silvery voice carried all the way to their table. They started with french fries served in a tin cone, with mayonnaise on the side. Bea wondered aloud what it would be like to have a glass of sherry, and Jonathan called the waiter, a grave-faced young man with an entire arm tattooed. "I like the casual air of this place," she'd said. "I like the rough napkins instead of linen."

"It's a nice place," said Megan. "Though I've been noticing there's an awful lot of really ugly people here right now."

"You think?" asked Jonathan. "You think it's changed over already?"

"Just look," said Megan. Her voice was strangely hot, the way it would get as a little girl when she was overtired and about to get hissy. "That guy is like an anteater in leisure wear. That girl, she can't wear that dress; look at her stomach."

"You sound like Tomasina and Livia," said Bea, "at Woolworth's and the Greyhound bus terminal. 'Look at her, look at her.' "

"What?" said Jonathan.

"Mom's talking about her sisters," said Megan. "They would go on purpose to places where ugly poor people would be and comment on them. We didn't come here to do that; it's not the same thing."

Not far off, thought Bea. Megan hated her aunt Livia, but here she was, saying, "Look at her." Except without Livia's lightness. It was dead serious to Megan. At some other point during dinner, she'd said to her daughter, "You've always been so beautiful," and Megan had said, "I certainly never thought that was your opinion."

"How could you say that?" said Bea. And Megan was silent. A woman at the table next to them turned to look at Megan, then at her. Was this woman ugly, badly dressed? Bea had no idea. The waiter came back and informed them that they were out of sherry.

She looked up and saw the woman with the little boy halfway up the escalator; the boy was gazing intently down into the corridor of light. He was six or seven years old, heavyset, with dark, glowing skin, possibly Hispanic or part black. His mouth was full and gentle, and his eyes were long-lashed and deep, with a complicated expression that was murky and fiery at the same time. The child disappeared with the movement of the escalator; a moment later, Bea stepped off the clanking stair, unknowingly buoyed by his bright face. She looked at her watch; she had a layover of an hour and a half before her flight to Chicago. In front of her was a snack shop, a bookstore, and a store that sold knickknacks, decorative scarves, hats, and perfume. Decorative scarves and hats, thought Bea. The most gallant members of the accessory family.

Inside, the shop gleamed with glass and halogen light and dozens of little bottles. Shallow cardboard boxes of scarves were displayed under a glass countertop with neat shelving; whimsical hats sat atop Styrofoam dummy heads. She tried on hats before a mirror in a plastic frame, and the finale from act 2 of *The Mikado* played in her head—she knew it from the recording Mac used to have, which had somehow disappeared after the funeral.

"That looks good," said the woman behind the counter.

"Thank you," said Bea, and good feeling rose through her. Characters were threatened with boiling in oil and beheading and forced marriage—and in between, the full cast was onstage, singing with urgent joy. "As I drew my snickersnee!" sang Livia. "My snickersnee!" Ten-year-old Beatrice pretended to cower on her knees before her sister's snickersnee. Pitty-Sing, the cat, tore through the room. Tomasina whooped and forgot about the play; their mother was coming up the walk, stripping off her clothes because it was hot and she was too imperious and impatient to wait till she got through the door. Her daughters ran to the window, bursting with admiration for the long, slender limbs that were as strong and beautiful as the flowering dogwood she walked past. Thirty years later, Megan, chin up and arms outstretched, presented the little neighbor girls, who were bowing and tittering in their gowns and silk scarves. And she was strong and beautiful, too.

"Here," said the saleswoman. "This scarf has a Brazilian flavor that really works with the hat." *Brazilian* was a ridiculous word for the scarf, but it *was* arresting, with bold wavy stripes of gold and brown, and the saleswoman's brown eyes were warm and golden when Bea met them with her "Thank you."

That weird snapshot of Susan—what had she been looking at anyway? You couldn't tell from the picture. Her big glasses had caught the glare of the sun, so that in the camera's eye she was intently blind; her small body, tensile and flexible as wire, expressed buzzing inner focus. She certainly didn't seem to be looking at the play.

"You're right," said Bea to the lady behind the counter; "this scarf does do something for this hat."

"On you it does." The woman's hair was an ostentatious bronze; her skin was damaged and overtanned. But her jewelry was tasteful and her makeup perfect.

An old-school sales type, thought Bea approvingly. You don't expect to find that at an airport. "I'll take them both," she said.

Pleased with her purchase, she continued down the corridor toward her gate, past more gleaming eateries and shops. Her thoughts now were suffused not by *The Mikado,* but by the look Susan had on her face when her sister presented that childish spectacle in the garage. It occurred to her that although Susan had become many things since then, that particular look of blindness and glaring sunlit vision still described her. She was a sort of therapist, and it was part of her therapy to read people's "auras," and, by moving her hands some inches above their bodies, to massage these auras. She read tarot cards, believed in past lives, and occasionally phrases like "astral plane" versus "physical plane" appeared in her conversation. It was nonsense, but harmless and—

Should she stop and get something to eat? Here were people at an Internet café, humped over keyboards and dishes of fried food, typing with one hand while they gobbled with the other, writing e-mails and surfing chat rooms while televisions blared from every corner. How interesting it was to be a person who, while considering eating at the airport Internet café, could remember riding a mule on a mud road to get the bus to school. You used to sit in the Greyhound terminal, waiting for the bus, and except for the roar and wheeze of the buses, it was quiet and you had to really look at the people across from you. You had to feel them, and if it was hot, you had to smell them. There might be children chasing each other up and down, or men playing chess on a cardboard table set up on the sidewalk outside, or a woman holding a beautiful baby. But there was nothing to make you think you were anyplace but the

Greyhound waiting room. Now people waiting to travel crouched over screens, hopping from one outrageous place to the next, and typing opinionated, angry messages—about the war in Iraq or a murder in Minneapolis or parents who were keeping their daughter alive even though she'd been in a coma for ten years—to strangers they would never see, let alone smell. Above their heads, actors silently sang and danced and fought; scenes of war and murder flashed like lightning, and heads of state moved their lips as chunks of words streamed over them. You could sit there on the physical plane, absently loading piles of fried food into your mouth while your mind disappeared through a rented computer screen and went somewhere positively astral.

No, Bea thought as she walked on. She just wanted to go to the gate. She wanted to think about riding to the school bus on her grandfather's mule, Maypo. That had happened the winter they had stayed at their grandparents' farm while their parents looked for a place to live in Chicago, and the farm was way off the main road, on a dirt path that had treacherous ice patches in the winter. Their grandfather put all three of them up on Maypo and led them down the path to where the school bus was. It was fun to sway on the hairy, humpy back, knowing that Maypo's feet were sure. Bea remembered the way the mule's heavy hooves would make blue cracks in the ice; she remembered boughs of pine brushing against her body, thick with snow that fell off in clumps as she passed.

Megan had no patience for Susan's past lives and tarot cards. She thought it was precious and self-indulgent, and Bea could see why. When Megan was fifteen and Susan thirteen, Aunt Flower, their stepgrandmother, who hated cats, told them that Granddaddy had killed Pitty-Sing's litter by putting them in a bag and swinging them against the side of the house. In fact, more than one litter had been killed, but none so brutally, nor so late in life, and Bea saw no reason for the children to hear about any of it. Susan was already crying when she came to Bea, with Megan trailing sulkily behind, upset about the kittens, too, but provoked by Susan's wild, high-pitched sobs.

"She said . . . she said that Pitty-Sing was crying," said Susan, weeping. "She said Pitty-Sing was crying, and grabbing his pant leg, begging him to stop."

"She told us as an example of a time she had sympathy for cats," explained Megan. "Even *she* was sad when Granddaddy told her about it. Because of Pitty-Sing grabbing the pant leg."

"That is cruel; it's wrong!" cried Susan. "Granddaddy is mean!"

"Honey." Bea put her arm around Susan's hot back. "It's not the same as it would be now. There was no birth control for cats back then, and you couldn't keep all the kittens. You had to kill them; otherwise, they'd starve."

"That's what I told her!" said Megan. "I think it's awful too, but—"

"But like that? Bashing them against the side of the house?" Susan pulled away from her mother and searched her face with wet, hysterical eyes. What was she looking for? "Something was wrong there. Something was wrong!" She turned away, her voice rising. "I hate Granddaddy, I hate him!"

"Oh shut *up!*" said Megan.

Bea stopped thinking for a moment and looked at the stream of faces pouring past her, young, old, middle-aged. Their expressions were tense and lax at the same time, and they moved mechanically, without awareness, focused only on getting somewhere else.

In fact, Susan had been right. Something was wrong. There were only three kittens in that litter and their mother had told

them they could each have one; she had already given each of them
a particular kitten. Then they came home from school and she told
them that Daddy had decided that having four cats was too much,
and that the kittens had been taken away. It was the same summer
she had come up the walk, smiling and triumphant as she stripped
off her clothes, the dogwood flowering as she came.

Here was her gate, A6. It seemed that she always departed from
gates that were low alphabetically and numerically—an example of
something to which Susan might attach mystical significance. She
sat down with a proprietary "Oof." Well, Susan had made her
beliefs work for her. She had made a life. She had a "partner," a
woman named Julie, who managed a bookstore. Susan had worked
on Bea's "aura" several times, and if the "therapy" didn't help, it
was still pleasant to have her daughter's hands working above her,
close enough to feel the heat of her palms, working to give her
mother healing and happiness. She took out her book-club novel—
something literary from another century, the name of which she
had a hard time remembering—and a newsmagazine. She looked
through her purse, found her glasses, looked up, and—there he
was again, the little dark-skinned boy she had seen earlier. He was
singing as he fooled around on some plastic chairs, hopping neatly
over each armrest, his face glowing with pleasure. Bea smiled to
see him.

She put her glasses on, remembering Susan at his age, when she
and Mac found her in their bedroom, leaping up and down on
their big bed as if it were a trampoline, ecstatically whipping her
hair about and crying, "Eeee! Eeee! Eeeeee!" Bea was about to
make her get down, but before she could, Mac kicked off his
shoes and climbed up onto the bed with his daughter. "Eeeee!" he
yelled, jumping once, landing on his rear, and bouncing from there.
Bea said, "Careful, Mac, careful!" but she was smiling. Dinner

was about ready to come out of the oven; she could still remember the meaty smell of it, and the big green leaves of the bush
outside pressing against the windowpane. "Daddy!" shouted Susan.
"Daddy!" His shirt had come out of his pants, and his face was pink
and joyous.

Nothing but contempt—

Bea put her book down and felt her face flush. It was Megan
who had contempt. Contempt for her father's sadness and his failure at medical school and his job at a pharmacy. Contempt for his
rage, especially for his rage; when he lost his temper and slapped
her, her blue eyes were hot with scorn. It wasn't that his violence
didn't hurt her—it did. His sarcasm and ignoring hurt her, too. But
in adolescence, scorn rose up from her hurt like something winged
and flaming. At fourteen, she lectured Bea on sexism as if her
mother were a perfect idiot. When Bea drove her to a sleepover, or
to buy new shoes, or any other time they were alone together,
Megan would say, "It's unfair. He acts like a big baby and then he
bosses you! You should stand up to him or leave!"

It was true that Bea in some small way had liked to hear her
daughter say these things. It *was* unfair, his constant complaining,
his throwing the fork across the dining table and expecting her just
to pick it up, get him a new one, and act as though nothing had
happened. Somebody littered the edge of the yard, and he yelled,
"I'll show you littering!" and then went out and dumped a bag
of potatoes in the neighbor's drive. When Bea came home from
the hospital with newborn Megan, she'd come early on Monday
evening instead of on Tuesday morning, because she'd been eager
and Tomasina had unexpectedly been there to give her a ride. They
had no phone at home, so she couldn't call ahead, and she thought
she might surprise him—but when she and her newborn child
arrived, young Daddy wasn't at home. He was out having drinks

and dinner with Jean, a woman he worked with. Bea had waited until after he was dead to tell it: how she was there all alone with her baby and how, when he finally got back after midnight and found her there, he *ran* into the laundry room, taking his shirt off as he went, stammering nonsense about wanting to help the lady they'd hired to do the laundry. The next day, Bea had looked in the hamper and seen it: his shirt covered with sticky lipstick kisses.

The air filled with floating announcements directing everyone every which way: *Flight 775—ready for boarding—Gate A4. Flight 83—Memphis—delayed until further notice. Cincinnati—flight—*

Her mother came up the walk, stripping down to her slip in the heat, flowering all around. She announced her adultery in public, in glorious secret. They didn't know until they found the love letters after she died. But looking back, it was there in her proud walk, for anyone who had eyes to see. Mac scuttled and hid, when he hadn't even succeeded at cheating!

"Jean was a smart cookie," said Bea, "and she never would've kissed him all over the shirt like that if she'd done anything untoward. I think she meant that as a message to me."

"*That's* what you think?" said Megan.

"Yes. I think he tried and she said no."

"And you're telling me you don't have contempt for him?"

"Stop it, you little idiot! You little—"

Aware that people were staring, the mother of the dark-skinned boy lowered her voice to a furious mutter as she dragged her child back to his seat by the crook of his elbow. Was she even his mother? She was pale, with thinning blond hair and a small mouth—on the other hand, her body was heavy like his, tall and voluptuous. Bea tried to catch the child's eye, but he was looking down, all the life gone out of his face.

"Honey," said Bea. "You don't understand. I felt sorry for him. It's different."

Megan stared, and her face grew remote.

Flight 775—final call. Bea picked up her book and remembered Prue Johannsen, the oldest member of the book club, who had twice, when she meant to say "the cemetery," said "the airport" instead. The memory gave Bea a sensation that she could not define. Prue was a beautiful ninety-year-old woman with bright eyes and a long, still-elegant neck, sloping and gentle as a giraffe's. She was a widow and she visited her husband's grave often. "I went to the airport this afternoon," she'd say. "I think I'll have them plant some purple flowers instead of the red."

What a strange world, thought Bea. A strange, sad, glowing world. In this world, she had married a boy who courted her with a vision of the two of them traveling together, in the jungle, in the desert, in the mountains of Tibet, bringing healing to the sick and learning from life. In this world, her boy husband became a man who got up in the morning and said, "I think I'll just kill myself," and who at night threw a fork across the dining room table. It was the same world, but now he was dead and yet she was not a widow. At night, her darkness came while she lay alone watching light and shadow on the wall: streetlamp, telephone wire, moths, bits of leafy branch; sometimes a pale rectangle of light suddenly opened its eye, revealing a ghost of movement inside it as someone in the apartment across the street used the toilet or the sink.

"I feel so old and so worthless." Beautiful Prue Johannsen had said that one night after a discussion about *Mrs. Dalloway.* Everyone said, "No!" But they all knew what she meant.

Bea got to her feet, full of sudden energy. "You can still do good," she'd said. "Prue, you can still—" She went to a nearby kiosk attended by a long-fingered East Indian bent like a pipe-cleaner man. She bought a bottle of water and a candy bar with caramel and nuts. Instead of going directly back to her seat, she walked around the gate area and approached the little dark boy and his blond mother. The mother looked up, not unpleasantly. Her eyes were deep, long-lashed, and fierce. Well, thought Bea. She is his mother after all.

"Excuse me," she said, smiling. "You look familiar to me. Did you ever live in this area?"

"No. But my sister does."

The little boy, still looking down, bumped his feet together and hummed.

"Hmmm—" Bea nervously half-laughed. "Do I look at all familiar to you?"

"I don't think so." The woman's eyes were civil, but her voice was vaguely tinged with common sarcasm.

Coarse, thought Bea, and unobservant. "Well, I guess when you've lived as long as I have, a lot of people look familiar to you."

"I know you," said the child, still looking down. "You were in the magic cave. Downstairs."

His mother looked irritated. "The *what?*"

"He means the walkway connecting the terminals," said Bea. "It *is* like a magic cave, the way they've done it up."   .

At this, the boy looked up; his gaze was alive and tactile, like a baby touching your face with its hands.

"What a beautiful little boy," said Bea. "And imaginative, too!"

"A beautiful little pain in the butt, you mean." But the mother's face was grudgingly pleased. Her name was Lee Anne; her son was Michael. They had been visiting her sister, who lived in a suburb called Canton, and were now waiting for their return flight to Memphis, which had been delayed. Bea and Lee Anne talked about

Canton and Livonia, where Bea's family lived; Bea described the crab-apple tree, with its hard dark fruit and soft pale flowers. While they talked, Michael walked around and around them, as if he was dying to run or dance. Could you eat the crab apples? he wanted to know. Could you throw them at people? Could you put them on the floor at night, so crooks would slip and break their butts?

"Michael, sit down," said Lee Anne.

He sat, and immediately began to rock and nod his head.

"Well," said Bea, "I—"

"You talk to yourself," said Michael, rocking. "In the magic tunnel, you talk to yourself."

"Don't be rude!" snapped Lee Anne. She whacked her son on the head with the flat of her hand. "And quit rocking like a retard."

"It's all right," said Bea. "I probably was."

"That doesn't matter; I still don't want him being rude." She stood, looming over Bea with an air of physical dominance that was startling before Bea realized it was habitual. "Listen, could you just watch him for a minute? I want to see if I can talk to these jackasses here." She gestured at the check-in counter, where a man and a woman in short-sleeved uniforms made automaton motions.

"Certainly," said Bea. Lee Anne held her eye for a second as if to make sure of her, then went on toward the check-in counter, her hips expressing a steady, rolling force.

"She's the one who said you talk to yourself," said Michael sullenly. He was still now, and very sober.

"It's okay, honey. I do talk to myself sometimes."

He raised his head and touched her again with his tactile gaze. Except this look did not have the feel of a baby's touch. It was warm and strong, curiously adult. "Who do you talk to?"

"Somebody who's gone. Somebody I used to love."

Used to. He turned away, but still she felt it coming from him, warmth as strong as the arm of a man laid across her shoulders. Feeling came up in her.

Attention: Those passengers waiting for flight 83 to Memphis—

"I talk to my father sometimes," he said. "Even though he's gone."

She started to ask where his father was and then stopped herself. Feeling came up.

—will be boarding in approximately five minutes.

"My father is fighting in Iraq," said Michael. He looked at her, but his eyes did not reach out to touch her. They looked like they had when he rode above her on the escalator—deep and fiery, but murky, too.

"You must be proud," she said.

"I am proud!" His eyes were bright, too bright. He was beginning to rock. "My father is our secret weapon! He's fighting on the shoulders of giant apes! He's throwing mountains and planets!"

Impulsively, Bea knelt and took the boy's shoulders to stop him from rocking. She looked into his too-bright eyes. "And he is proud of you," she said. "He knows he has a very good boy. He is very proud."

"Okay, Mikey, it's time to go." Lee Anne was back, and full of business. "We're outta here." She hoisted a backpack up on a chair and slipped one arm through a strap. She glanced at Bea. "Nice talking to you." She shouldered the pack with a graceful swooping squat, then picked up a bulging canvas bag.

"Yes, you, too. And best to your husband in Iraq."

Michael shot Bea a look. Lee Anne's face darkened unreadably. "He's been telling you stories," she said. "I don't have a husband. I don't have anybody in Iraq."

And they were gone. Bea saw Lee Anne slap her son on the head once more before they disappeared. Oh, don't, thought Bea. Please don't. But of course she would. The woman was alone and over-worked, had probably never married, probably hadn't wanted the child. At least I talked to him, thought Bea; I talked to him and he responded—he responded almost like an adult speaking a child's language.

And she got on the plane. The stewardess smiled at her, and she slowly made her way down the neutral space of the aisle. She found her seat, stowed her bag, then took out her book and opened it. Children had always responded to her. When Megan and Susan were little and they fought, she rarely had to punish them; she just talked to them in her love voice, and usually they would forget their fight and look at her, waiting to see what she would say next. She could say, "Let's go out into the yard and see what we can find. Maybe we'll see a field mouse or a four-leaf clover!" And quietly they would take her hands and go.

The stewardess came down the aisle, closing the overhead com-partments, making sure they were tucked into their seat belts. What luck: She had the whole row to herself.

Before they went to sleep, her children would talk to her about anything, artlessly opening their most private doors so that she could make sure all was in order there. When Megan wet the bed, she would go, half-asleep, to her parents' room, pull off her wet gown, and get between them in her mother's chemise, a little white sardine still fragrant with briny pee. Even at thirteen, Susan would run to her, crying, "Mama, Mama!" Once she sank down on the floor and butted Bea's stomach like she wanted to get back inside it.

The plane pushed back. Now no private door was open to her;

not even Megan's face was open to her. Susan hadn't come to her even when she was raped in the parking structure, hadn't even told her about it until ten years later, when she could say, clipped and insistent, that it wasn't "such a big deal."

The plane turned on the runway like a live thing slowly turning in heavy water. Sunlight glinted on its rattling, battered wing. Still, Megan had flown her out to visit, and taken her to a play. Susan and her girlfriend were coming for Easter. Both girls came to visit every Christmas, and had since they'd moved away from home. When she left Mac and was living from apartment to wretched apartment, the girls divided their Christmas time with scrupulous fairness. Megan spent two nights in Bea's apartment, while Susan spent two nights with Mac; then they switched. The two of them spent Christmas Eve with her, and Christmas Day with him, then the other way the next year.

But she knew they'd rather see her than Mac. Sometimes Susan even sneaked in extra time with her mother, pretending to Mac that she'd left on Tuesday, when she had really stayed through Wednesday with her mother. It was cruel, but so was Mac. When the girls stayed with him, he walked through the house, yelling about how terrible Bea was or declaring that he wanted to die, and that if it wasn't Christmas Eve, he'd kill himself that night. When he did calm down and talk to one of his daughters, it was about grocery-store prices or TV shows. "And I tell him over and over again that I don't watch TV!" said Susan, laughing. Susan laughed, but Megan got mad and fought with him. "Oh give it a break!" she yelled. "You've been talking about how you're going to kill yourself for the last ten years, and you know you aren't going to!" And then she told her mother and Susan about it.

"When I was there, I did a meditation with him," said Susan.

"With him?" asked Megan. "Or at him?"

"I told him I was going to pray," said Susan. "And we sat together in the dark."

They were in the living room, she said, at night with the shades open so they could see the heavy snowfall. Susan went into "a light trance." In this light trance, she "connected" with Mac as he lay on the couch, seemingly in a light trance of his own. She connected with his heart. In his heart she saw a small boy, maybe five or six years old, alone in a garden. The garden was pleasant, even beautiful, but it was surrounded by a dense thicket of thorns, so that the boy could not get out and no one else could get in.

"I asked him if he wanted to come out," said Susan. "And he just shook his head no. He was afraid. I told him I loved him and that other people out here love him, too. He looked like he was thinking about it. Then Dad got up and went to the bathroom."

Megan sniggered. The plane picked up speed. Bea thought, Mac was six when his parents died. But she didn't say it.

Stop it, you little idiot! You little—

That child, playing on the chairs, full of hope and life. Making up a hero father whom he could be proud of, longing for him, longing to be worthy of him. Didn't the mother see? *How dare you?* said Megan. *How dare you disrespect his service?*

The plane steadily rose, but she felt as if she were falling.

Mac died in his apartment, with the girls taking care of him, or trying to. She did not spend the night there; she did not sit at his side. But during the day, she went there to be with Megan and Susan. They had a hospice nurse who monitored him, washed him, and told them how much and how often to give him morphine. The nurse's name was Henry, and they all liked him—Susan said that Mac seemed to like him, too. When he was finished upstairs,

they made coffee for him, and he would sit in the living room, talking and looking at pictures of Mac when he was young. Megan
showed him the picture of Mac in his army uniform, just before he
shipped out. "He volunteered," she said. "Before he was even eighteen, he signed up."

"That's not true," said Bea. "He was eighteen. And he only
signed up because he knew he'd be drafted anyway."

Televisions came down from the ceiling in whirring rows.
White-faced, Megan left the room. Henry looked at Bea, looked
away. Colors flowed across the rows of dark screens, making hot
rectangles, oblongs, and swirls. In the kitchen, Megan faced her,
eyes glittering with tears of rage. "How dare you? How—" Bea said
no to a beverage but accepted the packet of peanuts. She looked
out the window, holding the nuts. The sky was bright, terribly
bright, but still she felt the darkness coming. *Do you remember the first
time, Beatrice? How you were scared and I held you? You were so beautiful and so
innocent. But you scared me a little, too, did you know that?* Mac had written
these things on brown grocery bags, cut to the size of notepaper to
recycle and to save money. He never sent them; she found them,
stacks of them, when she and the girls were going through his
things. *We could have that passion again, I know it. Remember, Beatrice, and
come back. Please, Beatrice, remember what we had.*

Faces bloomed on the overhead screens, clever, warm, and
ardent.

She did remember. She remembered that she had been frightened and that he had held her; that he had bruised her body with
the salty, spilling kisses of his sex, that each bruise bloomed
with pleasure, and that pleasure filled her with its hot dissolving
blossoms.

And still she couldn't cry. A stewardess came down the aisle, headphones draped gracefully over her arm. It had been two years and she had not cried for him once. The stewardess smiled and offered her draped arm. Bea shook her head and turned away, into the darkness. I am old and worthless, and I am going home to shadows on the wall. Susan— Megan— She raised her fists and weakly beat upon her forehead. Why are they so far away? Why don't they have children? Why does Megan stare at me so coldly when I tell her she is beautiful?

Shadows on the wall: streetlamp, telephone wire, moths, bits of leafy branch. A pale rectangle of light. When the darkness came, these things lost their earthly meaning and became bacteria swimming in a dish or cryptic signaling hands or nodding heads with mouths that ceaselessly opened and closed, while down in the corner, a little claw pitifully scratched and scratched. Loving, conceiving, giving birth; if human love failed, it was bacteria swimming in a dish, mysterious and unseeable to itself. From a distance, it was beautiful but also terrible, and it was hard to be alone with it night after night, without even an indifferent husband lying with his warm back to you.

Hard to bear, yes. But she could bear it. She had been a child herself, and so knew the cruelty of children. She knew the strength of giving, even if you did not get what you wanted back. She had thrown her body across a deep, narrow chasm; her daughters had walked to safety across her back. They had reached the other side, and she had stood again, safe and sound herself; all was as it should be. The darkness passed. She picked up her book. And he came to her: Michael, the little boy.

He came first as a thought, a memory of his face that interrupted her reading in the middle of the second page. He had so much in his eyes, and so few words to express it. How could his mother give him the words? Or the music or pictures? She thought of him. And then she felt him. She felt him in a way she would later find impossible to describe.

"He was looking for me," she would say to Susan some time after. "He needed me."

But it felt more specific than that. She felt what was in his eyes, hot and seedlike and ready to unfurl. Waiting for the right stimulus, like a plant would wait for the sun. Vulnerable but vast, too, like a child in her arms.

When she told Megan, Megan surprised her by saying she'd had experiences like that, too. "But you never know," she said, "if it's really the other person communicating with you, or if it's just your mind."

"No," said Bea. "It wasn't my mind. It was him. It felt just like him."

Love me. See me. Love me. He had no words, but what he said was unmistakable.

"What did you do?" asked Susan.

"I answered him," said Bea. "I tried, anyway. I tried so hard, I wore myself out."

I see you, she answered. You are a wonderful boy and you will grow into a wonderful man. I love you; I love to look at you. She put her arms around him, gently, not too tight. She held him and talked to him until finally, she felt him ebb away, as if he were going to sleep. She reclined her seat and closed her eyes. Just don't get lost in the thorn garden. We need you right here. Don't go behind the thorns. A tear rolled down her cheek, and she turned her head to hide it. We need you right here.

She waited a long time to tell Megan because she was afraid of being sneered at. She waited a long time to tell Susan because she was afraid Susan would talk about the astral plane. But she didn't.

She just said, "I've heard people who had abusive childhoods say they survived because they had a good experience with an adult outside the family. Even one, even if it was tiny."

Bea opened her eyes. Before her were clouds, vast and white, their soft clefts bruised with lilac and pale gray. She wiped her eyes with her little peanut napkin. She leaned back in her seat. *Good night, Mama.* Closing her eyes, she remembered the sudden warmth and heaviness as Megan sat on the edge of the guest bed in the dark. She remembered her singing "The Sun, Whose Rays Are All Ablaze" from *The Mikado,* her voice off-key but still piercing in the dark. She sang and then bent down, and her nightgown fell open slightly as she kissed her mother good night. Beatrice crumpled the peanut napkin with an unconscious hand as she began to dream a dream that began with that kiss.

The Arms and Legs of the Lake

Jim Smith was riding the train to Syracuse, New York, to see his foster mother for Mother's Day. He felt good and he did not feel good. Near Penn Station, he'd gone to a bar with a green shamrock on it for good luck. Inside, it was dark and smelled like beer and rotten meat in a freezer—nasty but also good because of the closed-door feeling; Jim liked the closed-door feeling. A big white bartender slapped the bar with a rag and talked to a blobby-looking white customer with a wide red mouth. A television showed girl after girl. When Jim said he'd just gotten back from Iraq, the bartender poured him a free whiskey. "For your service," he'd said.

Jim looked out the train window at the water going by and thought about his white foster father, the good one. "You never hurt a little animal," his good foster had said. "That is the lowest, most chicken thing anybody can do, to hurt a little animal who can't fight back. If you do that, if you hurt a little animal, no one will ever respect you or even like you." There had been green grass all around, and a big tree with a striped cat in it. Down the street, ducks had walked through the wet grass. He'd thrown some rocks at them, and his foster father had gotten mad.

"For your service," said the bartender, and poured him another one, dark and golden in its glass. Then he went down to the other end and talked to the blob with the red mouth, leaving Jim alone with the TV girls and their TV light flashing on the bar in staccato bursts. Sudden flashing on darkness; time to tune that out, thought Jim. Time to tune in to humanity. He looked at Red Mouth Blob.

"He's a gentle guy," said Blob. "Measured. Not the kind who flies off the handle. But when it comes down, he will get down. He will get down there and he will bump with you. He will bump with you, and if need be, he will bump *on* you." The bartender laughed and hit the bar with his rag.

Bump *on* you. Bumpety-bump. The truck bumped along the road. He was sitting next to Paulie, a young blondie from Minnesota who wasn't wearing his old Vietnam-style vest. Between low sand-colored buildings, white-hot sky swam in the sweat dripping from his eyelashes. There was the smell of garbage and shit. A river of sewage flowed in the street and kids were jumping around in it. A woman looked up at him from the street and he could feel the authority of her eyes as far down as he could feel, in an eyeless, faceless place inside him, where her look was the touch of an omnipotent hand. "Did you see that woman?" he said to Paulie. "She look like she should be wearing jewels and riding down the Tigris in a gold boat." "That one?" said Paulie. "*Her?* She's just hajji with pussy." And then the explosion threw them out of the truck. There was Paulie, sitting up, with blood geysering out his neck, until he fell over backward with no head on him. Then darkness came, pouring over everything.

The bartender hit the bar with his rag and came back down the bar to pour him another drink.

He looked around the car of the train. Right across from him there was a man with thin lips and white finicky hands drinking soda from a can. Just up front from that there was a thick-bodied woman, gray, like somebody drew her with a pencil, reading a book.

Behind him was blond hair and a feminine forehead with fine eyebrows and half ovals of eyeglass visible over the frayed seat. Beyond
that, more foreheads moved in postures of eating or typing or staring out the window. Out the window was the shining water, with
trees and mountains gently stirring in it. She had looked at them
and they had blown up. Where was she now?

"Excuse me." The man with thin lips was talking to him. "Excuse
me," he said again.

"Excuse me," said Bill Groffman. "You just got back from Iraq?"

"How did you know?" the guy replied.

"I got back myself six months ago. I saw your jacket and shoes."

"All right," said the guy, like to express excitement, but with his
voice flat and the punctuation wrong. He got up to shake Bill's
hand, then got confused and went for a high five that he messed up.
He was a little guy, tiny really, with the voice of a woman. Old,
maybe forty, and obviously a total fuckup—who could mess up a
high five?

"Where were you?" asked Bill.

"Baghdad," said the guy, blatting the word out this time. "Where
they pulled down Saddam Hussein. They pulled—"

"What'd you do there?"

"Supply. Stocking the shelves, doin' the orders, you know. Went
out on some convoys, be sure everything get where it supposed to
go. You there?"

"Name it—Ramadi, Fallujah, up to Baquba, Balad. Down to
Nasiriyah, Hillah. And Baghdad."

"They pulled down the statue . . . pulled it down. Everybody saw
it on TV. Tell me, brother, can you—what is this body of water out
the window here?"

"This is the Hudson River."

"It is? I thought it was the Great Lakes."

"No, my man. The Great Lakes is Michigan and Illinois. Unless you're in Canada."

"But see, I thought we *were* in Illinois." He weaved his head back and forth, back and forth. "But I was not good in geography. I was good in MATH." He blatted out the word *math* as if it were the same as *Baghdad.*

But he was not thinking about Baghdad now. He was tuned in to the blond forehead behind him, and it was tuned in to him; it was focused on Jim. He could feel it very clearly, though its focus was confused. He looked at its reflection in the window. The forehead was attached to a small pointy face with a tiny mouth and eyeglass eyes, a narrow chest with tits on it, and long hands that were turning a piece of paper like a page. She was looking down and turning the pages of something, but still, her blond forehead was coming at him. It did not have authority; it was looking to him for authority. It was harmless, vaguely interesting, nervous, and cute.

When Bill was gone, he realized that nobody at home would understand what was happening. He realized it, and he accepted it. You talk to a little boy in broken English and Arabic, make a joke about the chicken or the egg—you light up a car screaming through a checkpoint and blow out a little girl's brains. You saw it as a threat at the time—and maybe the next time it would be. People could understand this fact—but this was not a fact. What was it? The guy who put a gun in his mouth and shot himself in the portable shitter, buddies who lost hands and legs, little kids dancing around cars with rotting corpses inside, shouting, "Bush! God Is Great! Bush!"—anybody could understand these events as information. But these events were not information. What were they? He tried to think what they were and felt like a small thing with a big thing inside it, about to break the thing that held it. He looked out the window for relief. There was a marsh going by, with soft green plants growing out of black water, and a pink house showing between some trees. House stood for home, but home was no relief. Or not enough. When he came home, his wife told him that the dog he'd had since he was sixteen was missing. Jack had been missing for weeks and she hadn't told him. At least six times when they'd been on the phone and he'd asked, "How's Jack?" she'd said, "He's good."

"Hey," said the little guy. "You sure this a river?"

"Positive."

Positive. She said she didn't tell him about Jack because he had only a few weeks left and she wanted him to stay positive. Which was right. They both agreed it was important to stay positive. And so she'd said, "He's good," and she'd said it convincingly, naturally. He hadn't known she was such a good liar.

"The reason I'm asking is, it looks too big to be a river. A lake is always going to be bigger than a river. I remember that from school. The river leads to the lake; the river is the arms and legs of the lake. Only thing bigger than the lake is the ocean. Like it says in the Bible, you know what I'm saying?"

Bill didn't answer because the smell of shit and garbage was up in his nose. The feel of sand was on his skin, and he had to try not to scratch it, or rub it in public like this crazy ass would surely do. Funny: The crazy ass—he should have some idea of what it was like, even if he was just supply. But even if he did, Bill didn't want to discuss it with him. All the joy you felt to be going home; how once you got home you couldn't feel it anymore. Like his buddy whose forearm had been blown off, who still felt his missing arm twitch—except it was the reverse of that. The joy was there, almost like he could see it. But he couldn't feel it all the way. He could make love to his wife, but only if he turned her over. He could tell it bothered her, and he didn't know how to explain why it had to be that way. Even when they lay down to sleep, he could relax only if she turned with her back to him and stayed like that all night.

"But that don't look like the arm or the leg. That look like the lake. Know what I'm sayin'?"

Bill looked out the window and put on his headset. It was Ghostface Killah, and he turned up the volume—not to hear better, but to get his mind away from the smell and the feeling of sand.

Like it says in the Bible, you know what I'm sayin'? The white guy across the aisle laughed when he heard that, a thick, joyless chuckle. Puerile, thought Jennifer Marsh. Like a high school kid. Probably racist, too. Jennifer had marched against the war. She didn't know any soldiers; she had never talked to any. But she was moved to hear this guy, just back from war, talking so poetically about rivers and lakes. I should reach out to him, she thought. I should show support. I'll get up and go to the snack car for potato chips, and on the way back, I'll catch his eye.

The idea stirred Jennifer, and made her a little afraid. Afraid that he would look at her, a middle-aged white woman, and instantly feel her to be weak, artificially delicate, a liar. But I'm not weak, thought Jennifer. I've fought to get where I am. I haven't lied much. Her gaze touched the narrow oval shape of the soldier's close-cropped head, noticing the quick, reactive way it turned from aisle to window and back. Sensitive, thought Jennifer; delicate, and naturally so. She felt moved again; when the soldier had stood to shake hands with the guy across the aisle, his body had been slim and wiry under the ill-fitting clothes. He looked strong, but his strength was wiry and tensile—the strength of a fragile person made to be strong by circumstance. His voice was strange, and he blurted out certain words with the harshness of a sensitive person trying to survive the abrading force of the world.

See me comin' (blaow!) start runnin' and (blaow! blaow!) . . . Phantom limb, phantom joy. Music from the past came up behind Ghost's words; longing, hopeful music. *Many guys have come to you* . . . His son, Scott, had been three when he left; now he was nearly five, healthy, good-looking, smart, everything you would want. He looked up at his father as if he were somebody on TV, a hero, who could make everything right. Which would've been great if it were true. . . . *With a line that wasn't true* . . ."Are you going to find Jack tonight, Daddy?" asked Scott. "Can we go out and find him tonight?" . . . *And you passed them by* . . .

"The lake is bigger—but wait. You talkin' 'bout the ocean?"

Jennifer's indignation grew. The soldier's fellow across the aisle was deliberately ignoring him and so, stoically adjusting to being ignored, he was talking to himself, mimicking the voice of a child talking to an adult, then the adult talking back. "The ocean is bigger than the lake," said the adult. "The ocean is bigger than *anything.*"

———

He hadn't meant to look for Jack; the dog was getting old, and if he hadn't come back after two weeks, he must be dead or somewhere far away. But Wanda had done the right thing and put up xeroxed flyers all over their town, plus a town over in every direction. He saw Jack's big bony-headed face every time he went to the post office or the grocery store, to the gas station, pharmacy, smoke shop, office supply, department store, you name it. Even driving along back roads where people went for walks, he glimpsed Jack's torn, flapping face stapled to trees and telephone poles. Even though the pictures showed Jack as a mature dog, he kept seeing him the way he was when he got him for Christmas nine years before: a tiny little terrier, all snout and paws and will to chew shit up. He greeted Bill every day when he came home from school; he slept on his bed every night. When Scott was born, he slept in front of the crib, guarding it.

Jennifer tried to imagine what this man's life was like, what had led him to where he was now. Gray, grim pictures came half-formed to her mind: a little boy growing up in a concrete housing project with a blind face of malicious brick; the boy looking out the window, up at the night sky, kneeling before the television, mesmerized by visions of heroism, goodness, and triumph. The boy grown older, sitting in a metal chair in a shadowless room of pitiless light, waiting to sign something, talk to somebody, to become someone of value.

The first time he went out to find Jack, he let Scott go with him. But Scott didn't know how to be quiet, or listen to orders; he would suddenly yell something or dart off, and once Bill got so mad that he thought he'd knock the kid's head off. So he started going out alone—late, after Scott and Wanda were in bed. They lived on a road with only a few houses on it across from a stubbly field and a broken, deserted farm. There was no crime and everybody acted like there could never be any. But just to be sure, he took the Beretta Wanda had bought for protection. At first, he carried it in his pocket with the safety on. Then he carried it in his hand.

Jennifer grieved; she thought, I can't help. I can't understand. But I can show support. This man has been damaged by the war, but still he is profound. He will not scorn my support because I'm white. As if he had heard, the soldier turned around in his seat and smiled. Jennifer was startled by his face—hairy, with bleary eyes, his mouth sly and cynical with pain.

"My name's Jim," the soldier said. "Glad to meet you."

Jennifer shook his proffered hand.

"Where you headed today?" he asked.

"Syracuse. For work."

"Yeah?" He smiled. His smile was complicated—light on top, oily and dark below. "What kind of work?"

"I'm giving a talk at a journalism school—I edit a women's magazine."

"Yeah? An editor?"

His smile was mocking after all, but it was the sad mocking men do when the woman has something and they don't. There was no real force behind it.

"I heard you talk about being in Iraq," she said.

"Yeah, uh-huh." He nodded emphatically, then looked out the window as if distracted.

"What was it like?"

He looked out the window, paused, and began to recite: "They smile and they say you okay / Then they turn around and they bite / With the arrow that fly in the day / And the knife in the neck at night."

"Did you make that up? Just now?"

"Yes, I did." He smiled again, still mocking, but now complicitous, too.

"That's good. It's better than a lot of what I read."

Did you make that up? Just now? Stupid, stupid woman, stupider than the drunk nigger she was talking to. Carter Brown, the conductor, came down the aisle, wishing he had a stick to knock off some heads with, not that they were worth knocking off really. That kind of white woman—would she never cease to exist? You could predict it: Put her in a car full of people, including black people who were sober and sane, hell, black people with Ph.D.'s, and she would glue herself, big-eyed and serious, to the one pitiful fool in the bunch. He reached the squawk box and snatched up the mouthpiece.

"To whoever's been smoking in the lavatory, this message is for you," he said into it. "If you continue to smoke in the lavatory, we will, believe me, find out who you are, and when we do, we will put you off the train. We will put you off, where you will stand on the platform and smoke until the next train comes sometime tomorrow. Have a nice day." .

Not that the sane and sober would talk to her, it being obvious what she was—another white jackass looking for the truth in other people's misery. He went back down the aisle, hoping against hope that she would be the smoker and that he would get to put her off the train.

"Did you talk to the Iraqis?" she asked.

"Sure. I talked to them. I talked mostly to kids. I'd tell 'em to get educated, become a teacher. Or a lawyer."

"You speak their language?"

"No, no, I don't. But I still could talk to 'em. They could understand."

"What were they like?"

"They were like people anywhere. Some of them good, some not."

"Did any of them seem angry?"

"Angry?" His eyes changed on that word, but she wasn't sure how.

"Angry at us. For tearing up the country and killing them."

She thinks she's the moral one, and she talks this way to a soldier back from hell?

Mr. Perkins, sitting behind, could hear the conversation, and it filled him with anger. Yes, the man was obviously not playing with a full deck. No, the war had not been conducted wisely, and, no, there were no WMD. But anyone, *anyone* who knew what war was should be respected by those who didn't. Perkins knew. It was long ago, but still he knew: The faces of the dead were before him. They were far away, but he had known them. He had put his hands on their corpses, taken their personal effects: Schmidt, Heinrich,

PFC, 354th Fortress Artillery . . . *Zivilberuf: Oberlehrer.* He remembered that one because of those papers he'd kept. God knows where they were now, probably in a shoe box in the basement, mixed up with letters, random photos of forgotten people, bills and tax statements that never got thrown out. *Schmidt, Heinrich.* His first up-close kill. He'd thought the guy looked like a schoolteacher, and, by Christ, he had been. That's why he'd kept the papers—for luck.

Yes, he knew, and obviously this black man knew—and how could she know, this "editor" with her dainty, reedy voice? More anger came up in him, making him want to get up and chastise this fool woman for all to hear. But he was heavy with age and its complexity, and anyway, he knew she just didn't know better. As an educated professional, she ought to know better, but obviously she didn't. She talked and talked, just like his daughter used to do about Vietnam, when she was a seventeen-year-old *child.*

"Angry?" said the soldier. "No. Not like you."

She said, "What do you mean? I'm not angry."

The soldier wagged his finger slowly, as if admonishing a child. "The thing you need to know is, those people know war. They know war for a long time. So not angry, no. Not like you think about angry."

"But they didn't—"

The finger wagged again. "Correct. They don't want this war. But they know. . . . See. They make a life. The shepherd drives his animals with the convoy. The woman carries water while they shoot. Yes, some, they hate—that's the knife in the neck. But some smile. Some send down their good food. Some appreciate the work we do with the kids, the schools. . . ."

———

He could walk for hours, every now and then calling the dog and stopping to listen. He walked across the field and into the woods and finally into the deserted farm. When he walked, he didn't think of Iraq always. He thought of Jack when he was a pup, of wrestling with him, of giving him baths, of biking with the dog running alongside, long, glistening tongue hanging out. He thought of how patient Jack was when Scott was a baby, how he would let the child pull on his ears and grab his loose skin with tiny baby fists.

But the feeling of Iraq was always underneath, dark and liquid, and pressing up against the skin of every other thing, sometimes bursting through: a woman's screaming mouth so wide, it blotted her face; great piles of sheep heads, skinned, boiled, covered in flies; the Humvee so thick with flies, they got in your mouth; somebody he couldn't remember eating a piece of cake with fresh offal on his boot; his own booted foot poking out the doorless Humvee and traveling over endless gray ground. In the shadows of the field and the woods and the deserted farm, these things took up as much space as his wife and his child, the memories of his dog. Sometimes they took up more space. When that happened, he took the safety off the gun.

Like, an angry, cripple, man, don't push me! Ghost's voice and the old music ran parallel but never touched, even though Ghost tried to blend his voice with the old words. Sad to put them together, but somehow it made sense. Bill took off his headset and turned back toward the guy across from him, feeling bad for ignoring him. But he was busy talking to the older blonde behind him. And she seemed very interested to hear him.

———

"And the time I went out on the convoy? See, they got respect, at least those I rode with. 'Cause they didn't fire on people unless they know for a fact they shot at us. Not everybody over there was like that. Some of 'em ride along shooting out the window like at the buffalo."

"But how could you tell who was shooting?" asked Jennifer. "I hear you can't tell."

"We could observe. We could observe from a distance for however long it took, five, sometimes maybe even ten minutes. If it was a child, or somebody like that, we would hold fire. If it was an enemy . . ."

If it was an enemy, thought Bill Groffman, he would be splattered into pieces by ten people firing at once. If it was an enemy, he would be dropped with a single shot. If it was an enemy, she would be cut in half, her face gazing at the sky in shock, her arms spread in amazement as to where her legs might've gone. If it was an enemy, his or her body would be run over by trucks until they were dried skin with dried guts squashed out, scummed-over eyes staring up at the convoy driving by. *Oooh, that's gotta hurt!*

"Still," said Jennifer. "I don't see how they could not be mad about us being there."

Oooh, that's gotta hurt! Six months ago, he would not have been able to hold back. He would've gotten into it with this woman, shut her up, scared the shit out of her. The war was stupid, okay. It was probably for oil. But it was also something else. Something you could not say easily with words. There was enemy shooting at you and then there was the thing you could say with words. There was dead squashed enemy and there was the thing you could say with words. There was joking at squashed bodies and nothing else to be said.

"Here," said Jim. "Let me ask you something now."

"Okay," said Jennifer.

"Do you ever feel guilty?"

"What?"

"Do. You. Ever. Feel. Guilty." He smiled.

"Doesn't everybody?"

"I didn't ask about everybody. I asked 'bout you."

"Sometimes," she said. "Sometimes I feel guilty."

"Good. Because guilt is not a bad thing. Guilt can instruct you; you can learn from guilt. Know what I mean?"

"I think so." She felt something, but she didn't know if it was manipulated or real.

He smiled. "So here's what I want to say. Guilt, you can live with. But you can't live with regret. Can't learn from it, can't live with it. So don't ever feel regret."

The thing was, Perkins could not really understand this man, either. He didn't know if it was because he had forgotten, or because war was different now, or because the man was black, or because . . . well, the man was not right, that was obvious. But you

heard things about a lot of them that didn't seem right. You supported them, absolutely; you wanted to be proud; what happened
after Vietnam should never be allowed to happen again—but then
you read someplace that they didn't care about killing civilians,
that it was like video games to them. Stuff about raping young girls,
killing their families, doing sex-type things with prisoners, taking
pictures of it—and then you'd read somebody sneering that "the
Greatest Generation" couldn't even fire their guns, while these
new guys, they *liked* to kill.

"Now I have another question. Is that okay?"

"Yeah."

"When you look out that window, what do you see?"

Jennifer looked and thought; even though he was crazy, she
wanted to give a good answer. "Trees," she said. "Sky. Water. Plants,
earth."

He smiled. "All of that *is* there. I see it, too. But that is not all
I see."

"What do you see?"

In his head, Bill saw a horror movie. It was one he'd seen a long
time ago. It was some kind of fight between good—or maybe it was
just normalcy—and evil. Evil had gotten the upper hand, and good
was going to lose. "We can't stop them now!" cried the scientist.
But then by mistake the evil people woke up something deeper
than evil. They woke things underground called *Mogred* or some
shit, things who knew only destruction and didn't care who was
destroyed; they made the earth come open and humanoid mon-

sters without faces came out the crack. They weren't on anybody's side, but because evil had annoyed them by waking them up, they attacked evil.

Jim saw trees and shining water. He saw lake water, river water, sewage water. He saw the eyes of God in the water, and they were shining with love. In the eyes of God, even the sewage water in the street was shining. In the eyes of God, a woman came out on the street, moving very quick. She pulled up her robe and walked into the shining sewage and pulled a child out by the hand. She led the child and looked at Jim, and the mouth of God roared.

Outside the train window, the mouth of God was silent. It was silent and it was chewing—it was always chewing. That was okay; it needed to eat to keep the body going. And the eyes of God were always shining with love. And the nose of God—that was something you grabbed at on your way to the chewing mouth. Like those people in the old television movie climbing on the giant presidents.

The war was like the crack in the ground that let the Mogred out. The crack in the ground had nothing to do with arguments about smart or stupid, right or wrong. The crack in the ground was even sort of funny, like in the movie with shitty special effects, the monsters pouring out the hole like a football team.

Who told anybody they couldn't shoot their weapons? That's what Perkins wondered. If the American army couldn't shoot, who killed all those Germans and Japanese? True: Straight off the ramp, chest-deep in the ocean, fighting its sucking wet muscle toward the shore with machine-gun fire hammering down around you and shells slamming your eardrums, pushing on floating corpses as you got close—you couldn't see what to shoot at then. They hadn't been chasing a ragged Third World army with inferior weapons and they hadn't been wearing body armor. They came out of the ocean into roaring death, men exploding like bloody meat, and all of it sucked into the past before memory could grab on to it or the nerves had time to react. At least that must be why he could not recall most of it as anything but a blur.

The war was a crack in the ground, and the Iraqis were the Mogred, pouring out. Then somehow he and his buddies had become Mogred. Then it was nothing but Mogred all around, clawing and killing. Bill glanced at the guy sitting across from him; that was no Mogred. No way.

"I can't tell you what I see," said Jim. "And what I see you will never see. Because I have been touched by God." There was a wheel of colors spinning in his mind, gunfire and music playing. A little ragged boy ran down the street, a colored pinwheel in his hand. A ragged little boy tried to crawl away, and was stopped by a bullet. Laughter came out an open window. "You never hurt a little animal," his foster father said.

Unseeing and unhearing, she stared impassively in his face. "By Jesus, you mean?"

He felt himself smile. "Not by Jesus, no. Lots of people have been touched by Jesus. But I have been touched by God."

Unfeeling spread through her face like ice, stilling the warmth and movement of her skin. With unfeeling came her authority. "How'd you get to skip Jesus?" she asked.

"If I told you that, we would have to be talking all day and all night. And then you'd be like me." He smiled. Ugliness bled through his smile, the weak, heartbreaking ugliness of the mentally ill. Dear God, could they really have sent this man into combat?

When his daughter was a little girl, sometimes she would ask him to tell her a war story, her eyes soft and shining with trust, wanting to hear about men killing one another. But he never told her about killing. He told her about the time he was standing guard one night, when he thought he heard an enemy crawling through the brush to throw a grenade; just before he squeezed the trigger, a puppy came wiggling into the foxhole with him. He told her about the time in Italy, when he and his buddies saw a tiny woman carry-ing a great jug of water on her head, and he'd said, "Hell, I'm going to help that woman!" He'd stopped her and taken the jug off her head and almost collapsed, it was so heavy; his buddies had fallen about laughing. . . .

"Were you in the National Guard?" she asked. "Were you a reservist?"

"Naw," he said. "I was active duty."

"Well," she said. "I really appreciate talking to you. But I have to get back to my work now."

"All right." He extended his hand across the seat.

"And thank you for your service," she said. "Even if I don't agree with the cause."

This pitiful SOB had been in *Iraq*? That was one fucked-up piece of information, but it made all the sense in the world, thought Carter Brown as he took the ticket stub down off the overhead. They deliberately went out and got the dumbest, most desperate people for this war—them and kids like his nephew Isaiah who *were* in the National Guard so they could go to school. Isaiah, who got A report cards all through community college and who would be in a four-year school now if he wasn't busy being shot at. He tapped the spooky-looking white guy on the shoulder maybe a little too hard to let him know his stop was coming up and—hell, everybody on this train was nuts—the man just about jumped out of his seat.

Perkins was relieved to hear her finally become respectful. Even if the guy was half-wrapped. At least liberals had changed since Vietnam. Everyone had changed. His daughter, who used to fight him so hard about Vietnam, supported this war less equivocally than he did. She told him about attending a dinner for a returning soldier who, when he got up to speak, said, "I'm not a hero. I'm a killer. But you need killers like me so that you can go on having all the nice things you have." Some of the people at the dinner had been disturbed, but not her. She'd thought it was great. She'd thought it was better than platitudes or ideals; she'd thought it was real.

He looked at his watch. When they got to the station, he'd go to the bathroom for another smoke.

———

One night when there was a full moon, out in the field across from
the house where his wife and child slept, he remembered his first
night in Iraq. He remembered how good he'd felt to be there.
There had been a full moon then, too, and its light had made a
luminous path on the desert, like something you could walk out of
the world on. He remembered thinking, We are going to do something great here. We are going to turn these people's lives around.

"Your stop, comin' up."

Now there was the man across the aisle, talking to himself and
nodding. Now there he was in the dark field, holding a loaded gun
pointed at nothing. There were all the people criticizing him for
not getting a job, for being cold to his wife, for yelling at his son,
for spending so much time looking for a dead dog. He put away his
iPod, shouldered his pack. They didn't get it, and he didn't blame
them. But alone in the field or in the woods, looking for his dog,
was when he could feel what had happened in Iraq and stand it.

The train was pulling into the station; people were getting up with
their things; conductors were getting ready to work the doors. The
silent soldier stood up with his pack and briefly clasped hands with
the crazy soldier. Perkins fingered his packet of cigarettes.

He had been a returning hero; then people forgot the war had
ever happened. Then war was evil and people who fought it were
stupid grunts who went crazy when they came back. Then people
suddenly went, "Hey, the Greatest Generation!" Then just as suddenly, they were the assholes who couldn't even shoot their weapons. No, not even assholes, just nice boys who didn't know what
was real. These guys now—some people said they were killers,

some said heroes, and some said both. What would they be in fifty years?

When people got off the train, Jim got up and wandered away, and for a moment Jennifer thought he'd gotten off. But then she saw him wandering toward the back of the car, apparently talking to himself as well as to other people as he went. She tried to pay attention to the short essay she had been working on before her conversation with him. It was by a novelist who was in love with a vegetarian and who had gone to great lengths to pretend that he was even more "vegan" than she was in order to impress her. It was light and funny, and she felt too bitter now to appreciate those things.

Coming out of the bathroom, Perkins noticed the couple, the woman first. She was black, and normally he didn't like black, but she was beautiful and something else besides. Her soft eyes and full presence evoked sex and tenderness equally, and he could not help but hold her casual gaze. Or he would have, if she hadn't been sitting next to a giant of a man with quick, instinctive eyes.

Old white fool look away quick—good. Shouldn't have looked at all, and wouldn't if they were anyplace else. Chris put one hand on Lalia's arm and worked the game on his laptop with the other. He wasn't mad; old man couldn't help but look. Lalia was all beauty beside him, shining and real in a world of polluted pale shit. He killed the dude crawling at him in the street, then got the one coming out the window. He moved down her arm and put his hand over hers; her fingers responded as if linked to him. His feelings grew huge. Dudes came rushing at him in the hallway; he capped 'em. He was looking forward to tonight, to the hotel room he'd reserved, the one that was supposed to have a mirror over the bed and a little balcony where they'd drink champagne with strawberries in chocolate. He killed dudes coming out the door; he entered the secret chamber. He wanted it to be something they would always remember. He wanted it to be the way it had been the first time with her.

It was humiliating to be old, to shrink before the glowering eyes of a stronger man. But just mildly. He understood the young gorilla— you'd have to protect that woman. He thought of Dody, when she was young, how it was to go out with her; he'd always had to be looking out for trouble, for some idiot wanting to start something. You always had to watch for that if you were with a good-looking female, and it could become automatic. Sometimes it had made him scared and sometimes angry, and the heat of his anger had gotten mixed up with the heat in her eyes, the curves of her small body, the heat she gave off without knowing it. That was all gone now, almost. They still kissed, but not with their tongues, just on the lips. Still, he remembered. . . .

It took a long time to get with her, years, but when it finally happened, it was like the song his aunt used to listen to when she sat by the window, her glass of Bacardi and juice tilted and the sunlight coming in, her knees opening her skirt—the song that made him run and hide in the closet the first time he heard it, because it was too much of something, something with no words, but somehow living in the singer's voice and words, high-voiced sweet-strong words that made him remember his mama, even though everybody said he was too young to remember. *If I ever saw a girl / That I needed in this world / You are the one for me* . . . The words were like the poems on cheap cards, like the poems nerds wrote to get *A*'s in class—but the way this singer said them, they were deep and powerful, and they said things no words could say, things his mama said with her hand, touching his face at night, or his aunt, just brushing against him with her hip. . . . A trapdoor opened; the secret chamber was flooded with dudes wearing masks.

Oh, my little love, yeah . . . He had her every way, with no holding back, with his shirt over the light to make it soft. She was a quiet lover, but the warm odor that came off her skin was like a moan you could smell, and though she moved like every other woman, she said things with her moves that no other woman said. When they finished, she turned around and pushed the hair off her dazed eyes, and—*oh, my little love*—took his face in her hands. Nobody ever touched his face, and the move surprised him so that he almost slapped her away. Then he put his hands over hers and let her hold his face.

He remembered that when the war ended, the Italians invited the victorious Americans to come see a local company put on an opera. They went for something to see, but it was mostly boring, too hot, everybody smelling bad up in the little balcony, the orchestra looking half-asleep, flies swarming—but then there was this one woman singing. He made his buddies quit horsing around, and they did; they turned away from their jokes and listened to the small figure on the stage below, a dream of love given form by her voice and pouring from her to fill the room. When he and his friend Bill Steed went backstage to meet her, it turned out she was older than they'd thought, and not pretty, with makeup covering a faded black eye. But he still remembered her voice.

In the essay Jennifer was editing, the writer claimed that sometimes whom you pretend to be is who you really are. He said that sometimes faking was the realest thing you could do.

"Bitch! What you think you doin', bitch!"

Her heart jumped; she looked up, to see a huge black man looming over somebody in the seat behind him, yelling curses—oh no, it was him. He was yelling at Jim. A woman stood and grabbed the huge man's shoulder, saying, "Nuh, nuh, nuh," a beseeching half word, over and over. She meant no, don't, but the big man grabbed Jim, lifted him up, and shook him like a doll. The woman shrank back, but she said it more sharply, "Nuh, nuh!" Ignoring her, the man stormed down the aisle to where Jennifer sat, holding Jim up off the ground as if he were nothing. Jim was talking to the man, but words were nothing now. She felt the whole train, alert with fear but distant, some not even looking. She stood up. The man threw Jim, threw his whole body down the aisle of the train. She tried to speak. Jim leapt off the floor with animal speed and put his arms up as if to fight. She could not speak. Next to her, an old man stood. "Ima kill you!" shouted the big man, but he didn't. He just looked at the old man and said, "He touch my wife's breast! I look over and see his hand right on it!" Then he looked at her. He looked as if he'd waked suddenly from a dream and was surprised to see her there.

"It's all right," said the old man mildly. "You stopped him."

"It's not all right," said the young man, but quietly. "Nothin' all right." He turned and walked the other way. "You ruinin' my vacation," he said as he went. "Pervert!" He didn't look at his wife on his way out of the car.

The old man sat down. Jennifer looked at Jim. He was pacing back and forth in the aisle, talking to himself, his face a fierce inward blank.

There's no God, no face, you weak, lying—*you lying sack of shit!* There is just the woman and the roaring and the world and the pit. Jim fell into the pit, and as he fell, all the people in it screamed things at him. Teachers, foster parents, social workers, kids, parents, all the people he'd ever known standing on ledges in gray crowds, screaming at him as he fell past. He landed hard enough to break his bones. He was under an overpass, standing with his backpack and crying while his father drove away, with his mother yelling in the front seat and his sister crying in the back, looking out with her hands on the window. Paulie sat next to him with no head and blood pouring up. His uncle said, No, I cannot take those children. Paulie fell backward and blood ran from him. Dancing children lay in pieces; guns shot. The woman and the child ran, fell, ran, far away. His foster mother opened the door and let in the warm light of the living room; the bed creaked as she sat and sang to him. The trees shivered; the giant fist slammed the ground; they shivered. The long grass rippled in the machine-gun fire. The pit opened, but Jim stayed on the shivering ground. He did not fall again. His sister came to him and held him in her arms. *La la la la la la la la la means / I love you.* He closed his eyes and let his sister take him safely into darkness. She could do that because she was already dead. He didn't know it then. But she was.

The door between cars exploded open and they came rolling down the aisle, two conductors and a human bomb, the bomb saying, "And we on our honeymoon! In Niagara Falls! The only reason we even took the train is she's afraid to fly—and this happens?"

"I know just the one you mean." The black conductor sighed. "I know just the one."

"And she's pregnant!"

"Don't worry, we'll get him off," said the white conductor. "We'll have the cops come get him. He won't bother you no more."

Carter had no pleasure in putting the man off the train. He could barely look at his sad, weak-smiling face. He even felt sorry for the blond woman sitting there with her dry, pale eyes way back in her head, looking like she'd been slapped. He got the clanking door open, kicked down the metal steps, handed down the man's bag, and thought, Cheney should have to fight this war. Bush should have to fight it, Saddam Hussein and Osama bin Laden should fight it. They should be stripped naked on their hands and knees, placed within striking distance of one another, each with one foot chained to the floor. Then give them knives and let them go at it. Stick their damn flags up their asses so they can wave 'em while they fight. "Utica," he yelled, "this stop, Utica."

He didn't seem to mind being put off the train; he was even pretty cheerful about it. Jennifer looked out the window to see what happened to him once he got off, and saw him talking to two policemen who stood with folded arms, nodding politely at whatever it was he was saying. She heard the big guy up ahead of her, still going over it. "I heard him talking to you," he said to someone. "What was he saying?"

"Crazy stuff," replied a woman. "I was real quiet, hoping he'd go away, but he just kept on talking."

"Why did he *do* that?" asked the big man. "I don't usually do nobody like that, but he—"

"No, you were right," said the woman. "If you hadn't done something, the next person he grabbed might've been a little girl!"

"Yeah!" The big man's voice sounded relieved. Then he spoke to his wife, loudly enough for Jennifer to hear him several seats away. "Why didn't you *say* anything?" he asked.

Because he like my brother. I could feel it when he touch me. My brother grab a teacher's butt in the sixth grade; he do it for attention, it's not even about the butt. I can't talk about it here, Chris, with all these people listening; I can feel them, and this is too *private*. But my brother coulda turned out like this man here. Kids beat on him when he was like six, he had to be in the hospital, and for a long time after, he talked in this whisper voice that you can hardly hear, like he's talking to himself and to the world in general, talking like a radio with the dial just flipping around, giving out stories that don't make sense, but all about kicking and punching and killing people. He gets older and anything anybody says to him, he's like, "Ima punch him! An then do a double backflip and kick him in the nuts! An then in the butt! An then—" It so annoying, and he still doing it when he gets older, only then he talks 'bout how somebody does this or that, he's gonna pull out a gun and shoot him. He talks like he a killah but he a *baby,* and everybody knows it. My brother now, he works as a security guard in a art museum, where he sits all day and reads his books and plays his games. But he coulda got hurt real bad—and looked at one way, he talk so stupid, he almost deserves it. But look the other way, Chris. You do that, you see he lives in Imagination, not the world; shit don't mean for him what it do for us. You see that and you wanna protect him even if he is a damn fool, and also I don't want you into any trouble over me; our baby is in me, and it is *our day*. I love you; that's why I don't say nothin, Chris—

She put her hand on his arm and felt him withdraw from her without moving. Her heart sank. She looked out the window; they were moving past people's yards. Two white kids, just babies, were standing in wet yards with their mouths open, looking at the train, one with his fat little legs bare, only wearing shoes and a hoodie. Her heart hurt. Please come back, she said with her hand. I love you. Don't let this take away our beautiful night.

Disgraceful all around, thought Perkins. That they would treat a vet like that, that a vet would act like that. He looked out the window at small homes set in overgrown backyards: broken pieces of machinery sitting in patches of weeds, a swing set, a tied-up dog barking at the train, barbed wire snarled around chain link. A long time ago, he would've gone home and told his wife about the guy being put off the train; they would've talked about it. Now he probably wouldn't even mention it to her. They used to talk about everything. Now silence and routine were where he felt her most. He looked out on marshy land, all rumpled mud and pools of brown water with long grasses and rushes standing up. His reflection in the glass floated over it, a silent, impassive face with heavy jowls and a thin, downward mouth. And there, with his face, also floated the face of Heinrich Schmidt, PFC.

He didn't touch that lady's breast; he touched her shoulder. Maybe the train rocked or something, made his hand move down, but he was just trying to talk to her. The conductor knew that—he told him so—but they'd had to take him off the train anyway. It wasn't good, but it wasn't that bad. The police said there would be another train, sometime. But there was no lake to look at here. Where you sat down here, there were just train tracks and an old train that didn't work anymore. He would sit for a while and look at them and then he would call his foster mother. He would tell her there'd been a problem he'd had to solve, a fight to be broken up, and he couldn't get back on the train. His foster mother had strong hands; she could break up fights, using the belt when she had to. She served food; she rubbed oil into his skin; she washed his back with a warm cloth. She led a horse out of the stable, not her horse, the horse of some women down the road, the one that sometimes his sister, Cora, would ride. She was so scared to get up on it at first, but then she sat on it with her hands up in the air, not even holding on, and they took her picture.

They said Cora died of kidney failure and something that began with a *p*. They had the letter when he got back to the base. He read the letter and then he sat still a long time. Before he left for Iraq, she'd had her toes cut off, and she said she was going to get better. When she took him to the airport, she walked with a fancy cane that had some kind of silver bird head on it. He couldn't picture her dead. He could picture Paulie, but not Cora. When he came home, he still thought he might see her at the airport, standing there looking at him like he an idiot, but still there, with her new cane. He thought he might see her up in Syracuse, riding her horse. Even though he knew he wouldn't. He thought he might see her on her horse.

Riding her horse across a meadow with flowers in it, riding in a race and winning a prize, everybody cheering, not believing she'd really won, cheering. Then they'd have a barbecue like they used to have, when the second foster father was there, basting the meat with sauce and Jim helping out. The cats walking around, music turned up loud so they could hear it out the window, his foster singing him a dirty song to the tune of "Turkey in the Straw." It was mostly a funny song, so it wasn't dirty, and his foster always told him not to hurt anything, so it wasn't bad. Or his other foster father did—he wasn't sure. He'd tell his foster about lying on the ground and feeling it shiver in terror, watching the grass and the trees shiver. He might tell him about seeing a little boy trying to crawl away and getting shot. Because his foster father had known Jesus. But he did not know the face of God.

Or did he? Softly, Jim sang, *Way down South where the trains run fast / A baboon stuck his finger up a monkey's ass. / The baboon said, Well fuck my soul / Get your fucking finger out of my asshole.* A family came down the stairs, little girls running ahead of their mother. They wouldn't think his sister would win the prize, but she would; she would race on her horse ahead of everybody, her family cheering for her. Not just her foster family, but her real family, Jim's real family. Like the Iraqis had cheered when they first came into the town. Before they had shot.

Description

Joseph and his friend Kevin were driving to New Paltz for a hike. Kevin was driving with one hand, elbow out; Joseph had his whole arm out, hand on roof. They had finished their M.F.A.'s in creative writing weeks earlier and they felt great. Kevin had just published an essay in a big-deal magazine that paid. Joseph's mother had been really sick, but now she was getting well. It was a bright spring day; the car windows were down and the breeze smelled good. They were drinking sodas from cans and arguing about literary junk.

"It's like what John Ruskin wrote about architecture," Kevin was saying, "a style that allows for flaws may not be the most beautiful, but it's the most engaging because it reveals a human handprint."

"I hate that," said Joseph, "the whole 'human' thing. It's a euphemism for mediocre, and anyway, it's meaningless. Only humans build buildings; only humans write books. Those things are human by definition."

"You're mimicking Braver," said Kevin; he meant Professor Janice Braver.

"How? Janice never said that; *I* said it," said Joseph.

"She said it. Maybe in private conversation with me, but she said it."

"Since when were you having private conversations with her?

You didn't like her. Anyway, horrible things are human—rape and murder are human."

"Don't change the subject," said Kevin. He took a sharp, slow curve that made the car feel unwieldy and boatlike. "To say art is human doesn't mean it's morally good; it means it engages you. It's not static, with everything in place; it's everything, including flaws and clumsiness."

" 'It's everything,' " mimicked Joseph. "That's vague and grandiose."

"Bellow and Roth write about everything."

"That's not why they're great. They're great because—"

Kevin swerved into the park so sharply that the soda popped out of Joseph's can and splashed his face. Joseph yelped "Shit!" then wiped his chin with his shirt and said, "I *said* they're great because—"

But Kevin was already out of the car and rummaging in the back for water and lotion. Joseph got out, saying, "Bellow and Roth are great because—" Two girls in shorts and hiking boots came walking down the trail, cool and laughing, as if they'd just come out of a movie theater. "They're great because they're deep," said Joseph, looking at the smaller of the girls.

Kevin straightened and the girls both turned to look at him; even at a distance, Joseph could see them spark up. Kevin was tall and athletic; he had broad shoulders and a wide mouth. Aware of them but not looking at them, he flexed his chest as he shouldered a light pack. "They write about particular things deeply," said Joseph, and threw soda in Kevin's face. Kevin shook the bright drops off him and swiped at Joseph; Joseph swiped back. The taller girl looked back and smiled. Smiling, Kevin lunged forward, throwing air punches; Joseph danced back, feinting. The girls got in their car, talking to each other.

The boys quit playing. They rinsed away the sticky soda with bottled water and rubbed on bug lotion; Kevin put his foot up on the hood of the car to better rub his long half-naked leg. The girls pulled out of the lot, one of them smiling from the window as they went. Kevin put his leg down and gazed after them. Now he looks, thought Joseph. A family pulled up in an SUV, radio blaring, two little boys in the back, one of them twirling something bright and multicolored.

They started up the trail.

Kevin and Joseph had grown up in Westchester. They became friends in junior high because both were bookish boys obsessed by horror comics in which bad things happen to girls until the hero comes. Then Kevin grew nearly two feet and began to play basketball; in high school, he made the team. Smiling girls crowded around the new hero, while Joseph looked on with dangling hands.

Then Kevin's family moved to Manhattan. The boys drifted apart, but not right away; the move happened just weeks after Joseph's parents divorced, and it was somehow because of this that Joseph doggedly visited Kevin in Manhattan whenever he could. He liked being in a home with two parents. Kevin's mom, Sheila, was not pretty, but her eyes were warm, and her soft, pouchy cheeks were somehow warm, too. Sometimes they wrestled in front of her, and once they pretended to have a real fight: Joseph put pieces of white candy in his mouth, and when Kevin socked him, he roared and spat the candy out like teeth. Sheila pretended to be horrified, then burst out laughing. Afterward, they took the subway to Chinatown, where they went to a cheap place and ate an enormous meal, trying everything on the menu, until they couldn't eat any more. A waiter with tattooed hands sold them illegal beers and then they walked all the way back to the West Side.

On the mountain, Joseph still remembered walking in China-town, the neon signs speaking bright-colored Chinese on each side of them, the dead fish and vegetables heaped in alleys and spilling out onto the pavement. As high school went on, they saw each other less often. After graduating, they so lost touch that neither realized they'd gotten into the same writing program until they both showed up at the orientation party. Even in the same pro-gram, until today, they had not spent much time together, at least not alone. Still, Joseph looked at Kevin's back and remembered the wrestling, the laughter, the tattooed hands, the beers—

"So who do you think will be the next to publish something big?" asked Kevin, he having been the first.

"Adam," said Joseph. "His thesis was so strong, and he's a hard charger."

"Nah," said Kevin. "I mean he's good, but he has a long way to go. I think it'll be Tom." He paused, lunging slightly as the path steepened. "Or Marisa. I think it could easily be Marisa, with those last stories of hers."

Marisa: the name was still a small, smartly struck bell. Joseph had been with her for three weeks and then she'd dumped him. He didn't think her recent work was that good, but he was afraid of what it would sound like if he said so. Instead, he said, "What about Andy? He's gotten good."

"Are you kidding?" said Kevin. "He's weak. And he got weaker listening to Braver."

Joseph sighed. "I don't think you understood what she was say-ing some of the time."

"*I* didn't understand what *she* was saying? About how important it is to describe how characters *look*?"

How to tell Kevin that sometimes he was so busy being smart, he couldn't understand anything? Once in class, Janice said to him, "If you closed your mouth and opened your mind, you might actually learn something." Kevin replied, "Maybe I would, if there was anything to learn here." The room was quiet. Janice's face stiffened, then relaxed. "Wow," she said. "You're a real pisser, aren't you?" People laughed. Kevin flushed. Joseph suppressed a smile.

"Why do you even care?" he said. "The semester's over."

"I care about writing whether the semester's over or not." Kevin's voice was mild, but feeling came off his slightly hunched back. "And what's important in writing is what's happening between the characters, what they are *doing*, not what they look like or what *things* look like."

How Marisa looked: narrow-framed and supple, giving the appearance of coiled quickness, like a pretty weasel; small lips, short unpolished nails, blue eyes, poised, expectant posture. On the street one night, a homeless guy sitting on the sidewalk had yelled as they passed. "Hey chickie! Little chicklet! Come sit on me; you'd fit me like a glove!" She'd said, "He sounds so wistful," her voice hitting *wistful* as if it were two words, one pitched high, the other low.

He wondered what kind of girl would preen at sexual praise from a homeless guy—but it was true: Marisa *was* supple and functional as a glove. There was no waste, nothing excessive in her words or movements, not even during sex. When she broke up with him and he tried to make her change her mind, she said, "Don't make me feel sorry for you." And that was that.

Then he had to sit through a three-hour class with her every week. It was Janice's class. Two days after the breakup, they read a story by Chekhov in which a cruel woman scalds a girl's baby to death. Janice read aloud the part where the girl is returning home from the hospital on foot, at night, in the woods. She wanted them to notice the "soft and open quality" of the description, of the darkness and its sounds—animals, insects, the voices of men. Joseph sat across from Marisa, immersed in darkness. He was astonished that such pain could have been roused by this small alert girl who would not meet his eyes. He told himself it would pass, that he only had to ride it out. "Yours is not the worst of sorrows." An old man in the story said that to the young girl who had lost her child; he said it to comfort her.

Janice asked them whether they could imagine such a scene written now. The suffering girl walking in the live darkness, the vast world of creatures all around. The girl and her suffering a small thing in this mysterious, still-soft, and beautiful world. Through this description of physical life, said Janice, mystery was bigger than human feeling, and yet physical life bore up human feeling as with a compassionate hand.

Joseph slowed his pace and looked at physical life: bushes, mountains, stones. The warm sun dappling the path, a tiny red rag someone had tied to the branch of a small tree. Grasses. Bugs. He could not connect any of it with Janice's talk about mystery or compassion. But at the time, her words had moved him. He had looked at Marisa and had known with certainty that his was not the worst of sorrows.

Two weeks later, his mother had called and said she had cancer.

"Am I walking too fast for you?" Kevin was turned around, walking backward.

"I'm just not in a hurry," said Joseph, picking up his pace.

Kevin slowed to wait for him; the path was now wide enough for them to walk abreast.

"I'm thinking about what I'm going to do," said Joseph, "like for a job."

"Yeah," said Kevin, "I know. I am, too. People think it's going to be easy for me because of the essay. But I doubt it."

Easier for you than for some, thought Joseph. He looked up at the tree line on a ridge above them, at the branches moving gently against the sky.

"What is it?" asked Kevin.

"When my mom was sick, I would sometimes come out of the apartment at night and watch the trees move against the sky. It made me feel better. I don't know why."

"I understand that," said Kevin. And his back gave off a different kind of feeling.

Joseph's mother and father had been divorced for eight years. His younger brother, Caleb, was in Ohio studying theater. His mother lived alone in Westchester, where she ran an upscale women's clothing store that made money. She did not have a lover, but she had a lot of friends. She told her friends about the tumor in her breast before she told anyone in her family. When she told him, she'd known for nearly a week.

"Why?" he asked, astonished. "Why did you wait?"

"I was afraid you might cry," she said. "I didn't want to make my sons cry."

God, how ridiculous was that? Ridiculous and theatrical. He hadn't cried since he was about ten. He felt guilt for being annoyed with her, then sick-making pity.

She said that the prognosis was good, that they were doing the mastectomy just to be sure. She was going to have a reconstruction done at the same time; they would use tissue from her stomach. "I hope you don't think that's grotesque," she said. "But fifty is the new forty, and forty-three is too young to be disfigured like that." She laughed. He said he would come to be with her. She said he didn't have to do that, that she didn't want him to miss school.

"Don't be silly!" he snapped. "I'm going to come."

"I think of Max when I hear certain songs on the radio," said Kevin. "Songs I know he really likes."

Kevin's brother, Max, was a marine; he'd been in Iraq almost a year. "How's he doing?" asked Joseph.

"Okay, I guess." Kevin paused. "I'm not sure. He calls. But I'm not sure he tells us what's really going on."

When Joseph called his brother to talk about their mom, Caleb said, "This could not have come at a worse time. I guess stuff like this always does."

"Are you coming to New York?" asked Joseph.

"No," said Caleb. "She said she didn't want me to."

"She says that, but she doesn't mean it; it's obvious."

"Joseph, I can't. I'm playing Ricky Roma in *Glengarry Glen Ross*. I'm rehearsing nonstop. She's going to be all right; she said the doctor said that. It's awful, but breast cancer is so common now, it's practically normal for a woman her age."

He had to call his father several times before he got him on his cell. He was driving in his car, going somewhere with his wife, who was almost twenty years younger than Joseph's mother. When Joseph told him, he was quiet for a long moment. Then he said, "Well, I never would've wished that on her. She was so vain about her body, it's going to be bad for her." Joseph rolled his eyes, but it was true: His mother *was* vain. She had reason to be. Just five years ago, his friends had said, "Dude, your mom is hot," and they were only half-joking.

"Call me anytime," said his father. "I don't want you to be alone through it."

"Can you call Caleb?" asked Joseph. "Can you tell him to come? Mom told him it was okay if he didn't, but I know she wants him to. And if something happens to her, he's going to feel horrible."

His father sighed. "I know how you feel, Joe. But I don't think you can tell someone to do something like that."

"You ought to be able to," said Joseph. "If you're his father." And he hung up.

The path narrowed, but they continued to walk abreast, so close that their shoulders rubbed together. "Ruskin's ideas are pretty ironic," said Joseph, "considering the way he treated his wife."

"What do you mean?"

"He refused to have sex with his wife. After courting her for years, starting when she was something like twelve. He'd written these passionate love letters to her when she was a child. Then she got old enough to marry and—forget it. Wouldn't touch her. It went on for years. Finally, when she was nearly thirty, she said, Enough. It was the most notorious divorce trial of the time."

He went to see his mother a day before the operation. She met him at the train station, smiling and waving. She was wearing tight pants and a down jacket, like a woman in her twenties might wear. They went to the store to shop for "nice ham and tomatoes"; she wanted to make sandwiches the way she'd made them on some occasion that he could not remember. She loaded the cart with ice cream, imported cookies, sardines, artichoke hearts, paper towels, and cleansers. She got upset because the fancy-ham counter was closed, then angry because there weren't any good tomatoes. Angrily, she chose processed slices of ham and hard, pale tomatoes. "I'm so sorry," she said. "I should've come earlier, and now it's too late. Our night is ruined."

"Really, it's not."

On the way home, they rented a comedy about a dysfunctional family and watched it while eating the sandwiches from plates on their laps. Then he put things in the dishwasher while she talked to Caleb on the upstairs phone. When he turned off the water, he could still hear her voice through the ceiling. He went into the living room and finished up the rest of the artichoke hearts.

The path opened onto a small meadow of pale grasses with a single tree standing in its middle. It was a large tree, with branches stretched in all directions; roughly half the branches were alive, with flourishing leaves and rich-colored bark, but the other half looked dead—blackened, dry, naked of bark or leaves.

"Want to hear how he explained himself?" asked Joseph. "Ruskin, that is."

"Sure."

"He said, 'It was not made to excite desire.' Meaning his wife's pussy. Or maybe her breasts. Or maybe just her body, period."

———

She was in surgery for fourteen hours. She came home with plastic tubing attached to the wounds in her stomach and chest, tubes that functioned as drains, collecting the pus in detachable plastic bulbs. He could see the tubes under her clothes; he was aware that she took the bulbs off, emptied them of pus, put them back on. While he was with her, he was not squeamish about the tubes and bulbs— if she'd asked, he would have detached, emptied, and replaced the bulbs himself. He didn't mind the new breast made out of stomach either. He scarcely thought of it, and when he did, he was glad it was there, if it made his mom feel better. He couldn't help feeling superior to Caleb, who obviously squirmed even to hear about it on the phone.

" 'It was not made to excite desire,' " repeated Kevin.

"I guess it was a little too human," said Joseph.

"A little too old, it sounds like."

"It amounts to the same thing," said Joseph. "Anyway, public opinion was overwhelmingly on her side. She won the case and married Ruskin's protégé, Millais. They had eight kids."

"Something poignant about the whole situation," said Kevin. "For both of them."

In Westchester, it was okay. But the first night he got back to Albany, he had a nightmare in which his mother's breast was a piece of gnawed cake. He woke from the dream feeling depressed. He didn't think his mother was going to die. But it was weird to think that men in surgical scrubs had labored to take some of her stomach off and put it where her breast had been, to think of her sleeping with plastic drains sewn into her soft, gowned body, of the bulbs pressing against her when she turned. In the past, they would've just cut the breast off and left it that way. Deeper in the past, she just would've died.

⋅

He ran his hand across the rough foliage growing beside them; it stirred in his wake.

"How would you describe this?" he asked.

"Why would you describe it?" replied Kevin.

"Feelings," said Joseph. A dragonfly lighted on a wildflower and made it bob. "It would bring feelings into the story." The dragon rose off the bobbing flower and lilted in the air.

"Feelings come from people," said Kevin. "Not bushes. Bushes don't have feelings."

"I know bushes don't have feelings." He wasn't actually sure that they didn't, but he wasn't going to say that to Kevin. "It's the character who sees the bushes and has feelings about them."

"Sure, that's fine," said Kevin. "But think of Don Watson. His stories are filled with emotion, but it comes from what the people in the story are doing, an engagement with the human world. They come from the work he does with Israeli and Palestinian writers who deal with the psychotic shit that's going on there. Not from bushes."

Emotion was coming off Kevin again; Joseph wondered why. Probably there was no why. It was just Kevin's nature to always be stirred and needing something to butt up against. It was obnoxious, but even so, he respected the feeling coming off his friend, wanted to stand with it. That was his nature.

Abruptly, the path steepened. They both fell silent and began to hike in earnest.

———

When he returned to the university, he decided to write a story about a young man whose mother had cancer. The young man would be some kind of business executive, maybe in advertising, or an architect just starting out. He would not have time to go home and care for his mother, and his do-gooder brother would be giving him grief about it. Over the course of the story, his deeper feelings would be uncovered.

He went to Janice's office to discuss his story idea. He told her that his mother had cancer; he told her about his father and his brother and the way his mother had been about the ham. She listened and her face grew soft, much softer than it was in class. Her receptive silence felt to him like touch.

But when he told her that he wanted to write about his experience for his next workshop story, she spoke adamantly. "Don't do that, Joseph," she said. "It's such a vulnerable time. More than you know. I'm sure no one would be deliberately cruel about your story. But it's too raw now for public discussion." Again, he felt touched by her eyes, even the signs of age around them, the soft sagging of the lids.

"I don't think I can write about anything else," he said.

"It's fine to write it," she said. "But don't turn it in to the workshop. Please. Turn it in to me and we can discuss it privately. Workshop something old, just to keep up appearances."

And so he workshopped something he didn't care about and took the real story to Janice in various pieces and drafts.

They had been hiking for nearly an hour when the path forked; they argued about which way to take. Finally, they decided that both ways would come to the same end and they split up. Joseph intuitively chose the smaller trail, which quickly proved steep and jumbled with loose rock.

———

In the story, it was revealed that the architect who was just starting out was not merely indifferent to his mother. He was angry at her. He did not even fully believe that she had cancer. She had a history of acting out and hypochondria and had ruined his tenth birthday party by saying she couldn't breathe, insisting that their father break up the party so that he could take her to the hospital. He was also angry at his brother, who was still living at home and didn't have to make any sacrifices to look after her, angry at the way this brother had bought into her self-mythologizing—the myth of the beautiful woman who could've been an actress if she hadn't been stunted by early marriage and children.

The trail became increasingly chaotic. There were flat sunbaked outcrops with cool, wet fissures full of mashed pine needles. Bushes, mosses, and little trees grew out of the fissures, pushing their way out of huge rocks. Smaller, broken chunks of rock wobbled under his feet, forcing him to slow his pace; some were dry, some slippery with mud.

In real life, there were two positive lymph nodes in his mother's body, and she needed chemo. In the story, she needed chemo, too. In real life, she lost her hair; in the story, she lost her hair, too. In the story, she screamed and cried about losing her hair. In real life, she made jokes and shopped for wigs with her friends. In the story, the architect finally came home, and was forced to confront his angry brother. In real life, Caleb came home and delighted their mother by acting out scenes from *Glengarry Glen Ross.* In the story, the dutiful son was the favorite. In real life, it was Caleb.

He came suddenly close to a coiled snake and, stepping away from it too fast, stumbled and fell, banging his knees and hands. Too quickly, he clawed for purchase and cut his palm on a rock. The snake slithered away. He cursed as he stood.

In the story, the brothers got drunk and had a fistfight on the lawn. In real life, they did the dishes together. In the story, the architect makes the do-good brother realize he's giving himself away to win his mother's love. The do-gooder makes the architect realize he's riding free while his brother does the work of keeping the family together. In real life, no one realized anything.

"It's very good," said Janice. "Though I'm not sure the mother's feelings would be so clear-cut."

Sweating and irritated, he emerged from the path. Here was a clearing, an overlook. There was no way to go farther up, though there was another way down. He sat on a rock and breathed deeply. Either he had reached the top ahead of Kevin or he was lost. Either way was okay. From somewhere came rustling, the sound of rubbing cloth and parting limbs; Kevin had come. "You beat me," he said.

"For once," replied Joseph.

Kevin smiled and sat beside the rock, dropping his pack beside him. Joseph passed the water; Kevin drank. They sat a long time silently, looking at the grass, the trees, the sky. A bird, black in the distance, flew gracefully from one point to the next, dipping almost out of sight before rising again. Kevin leaned back on his elbows, legs stretched out before him. Joseph felt warmth for his friend; he felt good that they had finally reconnected.

"So, do you think you'll stay in touch with Janice?" Kevin tilted his head slightly up and back, glimpsing at Joseph with a sliver of eye.

"I don't know, maybe a little. It wasn't a social relationship; she was my professor."

"Students keep in touch with teachers."

"Are you going to keep in touch with anyone?"

"Yeah, Don and I will definitely be in touch. I want to follow his work in the Middle East, maybe go over there with them."

"Wow," said Joseph, "that would be incredible." He thought of Kevin's mother, one son already in Iraq. The *Odyssey* rushed to the front of his thoughts; he remembered how, when a soldier had been killed, the narrative had stopped to say who his mother was and what kind of blanket she had wrapped him in when he was a baby.

"I have to tell you something," said Kevin. "I feel like I have to tell you."

"What?"

"I slept with Janice."

"*What?*"

"I fucked Braver."

"You're lying."

"Why would I lie?"

"But you didn't like her. She didn't like you."

"She liked me."

"When did this supposedly happen?"

"The weekend before the graduation ceremony."

That weekend: Joseph had been at that party, too. Everyone was at that party, all the grad students and most of the faculty. Everyone was drunk. Late at night, he had been surprised to see Janice and Kevin talking in a corner: Kevin was leaning close to Janice and she was looking up at him with a strange naked expression on her face. He had not paid further attention because he was trying to get a girl to give him her number.

"But you said you didn't like her." Joseph stood up. "You made a whole huge point of not liking her."

Kevin stayed sitting on the ground. "I didn't like her as a teacher. I liked her as a woman."

"She's *married*. She's old enough to be your mom."

"No, she's not. She's forty-eight."

Kevin stood up. "Why should I care about that? It was good, for one night. We both understood it was for one night."

"I don't want to hear details."

"Who said anything about details?"

Kevin turned away abruptly. He walked to the edge of the over-look and bent to pick up a rock. Joseph wanted to kick him. Kevin threw the rock over the edge, hard, like a little boy with something to prove. Joseph wanted to kick him in the ass. Kevin turned around; his face was startled and soft. The kicking urge went away. Kevin spoke mildly. "Do you want to go back down your way?" he asked.

"No," said Joseph. "It's all slippery rock."

But Kevin's way was slippery, too; almost immediately, Joseph stumbled and fell against him. Kevin staggered and nearly went down; anger flashed in his eyes.

Joseph said, "Why didn't you tell about Janice until now?"

"She made me promise not to."

"But you're telling it now."

"The semester's over. You just said you're not really going to stay in touch with her. It doesn't seem like it matters now."

Joseph tried to concentrate on his footsteps. Instead, he thought of Janice naked, in sexual positions. He had never thought of her that way before.

"So, how was it?" he asked.

Kevin didn't answer. His broad back expressed an upright reticence that was somehow dirtier than dirtiness.

"Did she like it?"

"It seemed like she did." He paused and then added, as if he couldn't help it, "Even though she cried."

Semicrouched, Joseph stopped. "Why? Why did she cry?"

Kevin turned and slipped a little. "I thought you didn't want to hear details."

"I don't."

"What's wrong?" asked Kevin. "Did you like her or something?"

"Not like that," said Joseph.

"Then what . . ."

"It isn't anything, I just . . ." He thought of Janice with her legs spread. He did not see her face or her upper body, only her spread lower half. "I just want you to go on down," he said quietly. "I'll come in a bit."

"Okay."

The sky had changed. The clearing was now covered with soft shadows broken by slow-moving light. Joseph sat on the stone and put his head in his hands. His thoughts of Janice faded. He thought of Marisa, how she had asked not to feel sorry for him, when it was clear she didn't. He thought of holding her from behind, her breasts in his hands. He dropped his hands and leaned forward with his elbows on his knees. In truth, no one knew if his mother was well, or if she still had cancer. They could not find cancer now, but one day she might go to the doctor to check and cancer would be there again. She would have to check and check always.

He stood up, looking into the valley. Giant broken rocks fell motionless down the incline, harsh gray stippled with black moss, shadow deeply pitting the spaces between the raw chunks. Broken trees stumbled down the slope, half-living, half-dead. At the bottom, only the living parts were visible, converged in the crease of the valley like virile hair at the fork of the body.

He pictured Caleb acting for his mother in the living room, making her laugh. It wasn't what Caleb said that made her laugh; it was something in his voice that, without his trying, touched her somewhere that Joseph couldn't reach.

He looked up at a flat field of clouds hanging low in the sky, rippled with soft gray; above them, bright light massed together as if trying to give itself a shape, like a sound trying to form a word. Above this light rose pale sky that deepened and turned blue as it rose higher into cloudlessness. He thought, Kevin would always win. That's just how it was. Radiance shone, receded, and shone again.

Don't Cry

_____

Our first day in Addis Ababa, we woke up to wedding music playing outside the hotel. We had traveled for twenty hours and we
were deeply asleep. The music entered my sleep in the form of
moving lights, like fireflies or animate laughter, in a pattern, but a
loose and playful one. I was dreaming that I was with Thomas. In
the dream, he was very young, and we were chasing a light that had
come free of the others, running down a winding path with darkness all around.

When I woke, at first I did not know where I was. The music
seemed more real than the dingy room; its sound saturated me
with happiness and pain. Then I saw Katya and remembered
where we were and why. She was already up and standing at the
window, lifting a shade to peer out—the sun made a warm place
on her skin and I felt affection for her known form in this unknown place. She turned and said, "Janice, there's weddings going
on outside—_plural!_"

We went outside. All around our hotel were gardens, and in the
gardens were crowds of people dressed in the bright colors of
undiluted joy. Brides and grooms were wearing white satin, and the
streets were lined with white limousines decked with flowers, and
together with so much color, the white also seemed colorful. Little
girls in red-and-white crinoline ran past, followed by a laughing

woman. Everyone was laughing or smiling, and because I could not tell where the music came from, I had the sensation that it was coming directly from these smiling, laughing people. Katya turned to me and said, "Are we in heaven?"

I replied, "I don't know," and for a second I meant it.

My husband, Thomas, had died six months before the trip to Addis Ababa. The music that woke me that first day touched my grief even before I knew it was wedding music. Even in my sleep, I could hear love in it; even in my sleep, I could hear loss. I stepped out of the hotel in a state of grief, but when I saw the brides and grooms in their happiness, wonder spread slowly through my grief. It was like seeing my past and a future that was no longer mine but that I was part of anyway.

In the dirty hotel restaurant, we had dry bricklike croissants and lots of good fruit—papaya, mangoes, bananas, oranges, and pineapple. The coffee was burnt, so we decided to go to the espresso place we'd been told was just a few blocks away. We never found the place, although we walked a long time. At first, we walked on a crowded street made of pavement, with department stores, an Internet café, and a grocery with a big Magic Marker drawing (green and red) of fruit and vegetables in the window. Starving dogs wandered freely. The pavement abruptly fell off and gave way to rocks. We saw another wedding party, in a Mercedes decked with rich-colored flowers, moving through a herd of donkeys, the herders lagging behind, talking on their cells. Beggars swarmed around us, shouting and showing us their deformed limbs, their blind eyes. We forgot our espresso. The rocky street gave way to dirt with pools of muddy water. Houses, patched together with tin, plastic, canvas, and wood, bulged out, sagged in, lurched and leaned this way, then that. Beggars swarmed us, chanting. Wedding guests in gold pants and silky shirts pushed their broken car through slowly parting pedestrians. A little boy marched along blowing a horn; he was followed by a smaller boy, who was shouting and rhythmically shaking a clutch of bells on a strap. The smell of fresh shit rose up suddenly and mixed with the odors of sweat and cooked meat. An old woman seated in the roots of a giant tree sold bundled sticks and dresses mounted on smiling white mannequins. Trees made soft, blunt, deep green shapes with their boughs. Katya turned to me, her face dazed. "We'd better go back," she said. "We're getting lost."

Katya was in Ethiopia to adopt a baby; I was there to help her. Katya had asked me to go with her because I am one of her oldest friends, going back to our waitressing days in Manhattan. She is a narrow little woman with a broad, bossy air: ugly-beautiful, full lower lip a bit too pendulous, hips and breasts small but highly charged, black hair big, curly, and shining with secreted oil. The restaurant we'd worked in was run by Mafia thugs, and they would sometimes come in before the shift to do coke with us. The head thug really liked Katya; he would confide in her and ask her advice and she would console him and boss him around.

In those days, I was putting myself through a writing program; she was having experiences. I got married and turned into an English professor who publishes stories in quarterly magazines. She started various businesses, which she either failed at or got bored with and sold. She had family money to begin with, and in spite of the failures along the way, she has actually amassed some money of her own. She now runs a boutique in D.C., which is where she lives. She has made some Ethiopian friends, one of whom, a woman named Meselu, runs a "big woman's" store across the street from Katya's business.

Katya had been thinking of adoption for some time; she didn't want to go through an agency in America because it pissed her off that while agencies gave the birth mother full disclosure regarding the adoptive parent, there was no reciprocity. She didn't want to go through a foreign agency because most of them required a two-year wait, and she felt that, at forty-nine, she was already too old. She had learned through someone on the Internet—a woman in California who'd already adopted an Ethiopian child—that independent adoptions there were relatively easy. It helped, of course, that Meselu could hook her up with people in Addis Ababa, including a driver named Yonas, who specialized in clients there to adopt.

When Katya asked me if I would go to Africa with her, I said yes, because Thomas had died four months earlier and I had still not gone back to teaching. In the emptiness of my life, it didn't seem to matter what I did; between doing nothing and doing something, it seemed better to do something. Thomas and I had never had children, and, maybe without thinking about it, I wanted to help my friend give a child safe passage. Katya had never been lucky with men and I knew she had always envied my marriage; perhaps I was hoping to balance my loss with something good for her. In any case, before I left I took Thomas's wedding ring from the altar I had made in our bedroom, took my own ring from my finger, and put them both on a gold chain around my neck.

When Yonas came to pick us up at the hotel, he told us that every Saturday at this time of year, people in Addis Ababa come out to get married, and that our hotel was an especially popular spot because of the gardens. Yonas was a young man with a beautiful face and a profound feeling of age about him. When we told him how heavenly the weddings had seemed to us, he gravely bobbed his head and made the quick, sharp inhalation that we were beginning to understand meant yes. He held the door of his rattling Soviet car for us and said something I couldn't understand. We got in, sank into the broken, reeking cushions, down almost to the floor.

We couldn't go to the orphanage on a Saturday, so Yonas took us up into the mountains, a trip I remember in the way I remember my dream that morning. I remember getting out of the car to stand at the top of a steep street, with big broken stones on each side of us, and looking down at a jumble of shanties and tiny houses careering up and down a hill. Farther out of the city, we saw houses made of mud and gray thatch that appeared soft as hair from a distance; there was one house surrounded by a beautiful fence made of light, slender branches of all shapes and sizes linked in a winding, nearly musical pattern, varied by the curves of certain branches that suddenly and softly digressed before returning to the music of the pattern. Big flowers grew through the branches in random places, spilling their pink petals. There was a woman in the yard with a bright red scarf on her head. The sky was full of soft, swollen clouds.

That night, we had dinner with Meselu's relatives. We were taken to the house by Meselu's uncle, who spoke a little English; we brought huge bundles of clothes, batteries, and toiletries that Meselu had sent. The house was behind a high stone wall with an archway bowered by thick-growing plants.

The head of the family was a matriarch named Zeyneb, who served us a spread with dozens of little meat dishes—goat and lamb in a variety of sauces with a grain called teff. Zeyneb sat at the head of the table in a crimson dress and passed the dishes in a formal manner. Most of her family was there—one of her two daughters, three of her four sons, and six grandchildren. The uncle translated as well as his skill would allow. We couldn't understand a lot of it; we heard something about the election and the government. Zeyneb said something about adoption and things being different than they had been. The grandchildren talked loudly and happily among themselves, listening sideways to the translations of our speech. Zeyneb asked how many children I had. When I said none, one of the little girls looked at me piercingly.

That night, we went to bed early—we had to. The power was out and it got too dark to read by 8:30. We lay in the dark and talked for a long time. We talked about the jumbled streets, Zeyneb, the mountains, and the fence—which, we agreed, would cost thousands of dollars in the States. It was almost cold, and so we slept with the windows shut; the muffled street sound had a lulling effect. Katya said she was too excited to sleep, but she drifted off quickly; it was I who stirred all night, unable to sleep or to stay fully awake. The wedding music from the morning crowded my mind, the bright colors and smiles, the running girls, the laughing woman. Cars mingled with donkeys; a little boy blew a horn. Beggars came bursting out of the wedding crowd, shouting. One of them was a boy I had seen that morning, and tried not to notice, a boy with a gouged-out eye socket. We emptied our purses—I gave the gouged boy handfuls of coins—but it was not enough.

I touched the wedding rings around my neck; Thomas appeared to me and sat on the bed. I stretched out my hand to him; the street crowd vanished. I remembered Thomas inside me. Once I'd said, "I want you inside me all the time," and he'd replied, "I will be." Children peered around a dark corner—first they were

Zeyneb's grandchildren; then they were unborn children waiting for Thomas and me to conceive them. Among them was the boy with the gouged eye, not begging, but waiting to be born. "I want you now," I whispered. Thomas replied, "I am here," but faintly. Chanting sounded. It was haunting, stern, implacable as a machine made of powerful feelings cut away from their source. Rules, I thought. Punishment: it's coming. Chanting filled the suffocating room. "Shut up!" I hissed. "Just shut the fuck up!"

Katya stirred and murmured, "What?"

"This noise, what is it?"

"Zeyneb said it's from the churches. Go back to sleep; it's going to go on all day."

That morning, Yonas drove us to the first orphanage on our list. It was Catholic. It was a compound made of cement, with a tin door, heavily patched with roofing tile, that, had it been open, would've been big enough to drive a car through. A girl pocked with open sores and dressed in filthy rags was huddled near it, a baby in her arms. I thought she would beg from us, but she didn't have the strength; she didn't have the strength to swat the flies from her. We tried to give her money—I bent down and put it in her face—but she didn't even look at it. She just looked at the door. We tried the door and found it locked. Katya knocked. No one came. I looked at the girl's baby; its eyelids were encrusted with parasites and swarmed by flies. Katya knocked again, louder and longer. Street traffic went back and forth. Again, I tried to give the girl money. She stared at the door as if I weren't there. I tried to look into the baby's eyes, but its little face was numb with suffering; it didn't see me, either. Katya knocked again. We waited. I imagined children peering from behind the door. Still no one came. Finally, Katya turned away, her face very pale.

When we got back into the car, we asked Yonas if there was something we could do for the girl with the baby.

He shook his head. "I don't think we can help her. Probably she's dying—she knows she's dying and she wants her baby to be taken into the orphanage when she does."

His tone was gentle and matter-of-fact, and there was no response to make to it.

At the next orphanage, we knocked and the door was opened. We were escorted through a barren courtyard—we heard children singing but didn't see them—and into a large office with a cement floor. A young child dressed in shabby Western clothes passed by the open door, craning her head to look at us as she did. We waited a half hour before a young woman came to tell us that the head of the orphanage was not available. We asked when she might be available and the young woman shook her head no. Katya asked if we might meet some of the children anyway; again the young woman shook her head. "They are busy," she said.

No one of authority was available at the next orphanage, or the next one, or the next after that; all the children were busy. When we got back into the car, Katya said to Yonas, "Get us out of here. Please. Take us someplace out of the city. Someplace where we can breathe."

We drove down a street of tin shanties and stalls hung with bananas and talismans that appeared to be made of hair; a dim electrical buzzing began in my ears. *"He can't breathe."* Elena, Thomas's daughter, had said this just before he died. His breath had become faster and shallower. He was still alive, but decompo-sition had begun—I was so used to it that it didn't even seem hor-

rible to me. I was so used to it that, even then, when I touched him,
I could feel him. His warmth, his personality, everything I had
thought of as his physical energy—I still felt it when I put my
hands on him; it was moving in him still. Though maybe moving
out of him instead of through him.

We passed a street that looked like a dark pit letting loose its
buildings and people; smiling and talking, they came out of the pit.
There was garbage strewn all around. A woman in a huge hat
crouched in it, selling what looked like prepared food. I thought of
Thomas's old aunt Lucinda in her big hat, picking through somebody's garage sale. Lucinda had raised Thomas, because when he
was seven, his mother had gotten on a bus one day and never come
back. Lucinda was the only one of his family to really accept me,
and she was half-senile. When Thomas showed her a picture of me
days previous to her meeting me, she thought it was a picture of his
mom. "Where'd you get this?" she asked.

The car thumped as the concrete ended and the rockiness
began. When Thomas and I met, Elena was already a young
woman; I'd see her and her brother, Frank, on holidays, and it was
mostly polite. But when Thomas got sick, she rented an apartment
to be near us. She was there for her father, but her feeling for me
had changed then, too; I could tell it by the way her hip would
touch against me when she kissed me good night.

The car thumped again as the rocks gave way to dirt. But Frank,
the son—at the beginning he flirted with me, and by the end he
was screaming at me about money. Especially he screamed about
my having redone the bathroom with a luxury marble shower
while his dad was sick—but that damn shower was one of the
last things that Thomas had been coherent about. *He'd* wanted it,
not me.

The buzz in my ear grew louder. "Look!" cried Katya. We were passing monster anthills, three feet tall, shaped like weird pricks with live streams of ant semen pouring out. The buzzing sound subsided, as if my ear had suddenly realized it was just the sound of my own body and I did not have to pay attention to it after all. Suddenly, there was a smiling lion carved on a stony hill, climbing a three-stepped stair, at the top of which a carved Coca-Cola bottle announced a refreshment stand. We parked and Yonas hired two teenagers to take us up into the mountains for three U.S. dollars.

We walked for about two hours. The landscape was more densely beautiful, wilder and less populated than the place we'd gone the day of our arrival. The sky was a soft rolling gray, deep and full of round shapes amid stretches of radiant blankness. Beneath us was a valley in which grew dark clumps of bushes and trees, pale grasses, and deep patches of turned earth. We passed farmers plowing the earth with wooden plows drawn by oxen, turning up earth and chunks of stone so crystalline, they gave light back to the sun. I wished that Thomas were there to see it.

And then he was there, in the sky; I felt him there. I was flooded with memories of our first meeting: I was twenty-four and he was fifty-two. People say that young women are attracted to older men because of social power. But my response was like strong weather—not chosen, not social. I was a graduate student and he was a visiting writer, and a party was held for him in the house of some faculty eminence. It was dull, and I went out into the yard to play with somebody's dog, a chocolate-spotted terrier with a chewed-up ball that I threw until it landed in a pond with a skin of chartreuse scum . The dog and I were looking through the weeds at the water's edge when the guest of honor appeared with a drink in his hand. "Did you lose something?" he asked. He wore an elegant suit and expensive shoes. He was ripe, confident, bursting with sex. "The dog's ball," I said. "It went in the water, I think." And, still holding the drink, he walked into the water in his suit and his expensive shoes and got it for me.

I shifted my eyes. White seeped through the soft gray of the sky; the earth hummed through the waving hairs of its pale grasses, its bright leaves, the pores of its dark flesh. My body remembered the flesh of my husband's arms, the warm intelligence of his chest, his willful, goatish belly. As my memory embraced him, his body changed: I felt his muscles grow soft, his will diffuse and fade, his chest become sad hairy boobs.

One of the boys turned to us and said something. I dried my eyes. Yonas said, "Okay, we're here."

He had brought us to a church built into the earth. The church was in a ravine; looking at it was like looking down into a ruined palace without a roof, a system of courtyards, chambers, and antechambers that, instead of being built into the air, had been carved into the earth. There were footholds going toward it that had probably once been steps, but they were eroded and over-grown now. Still, we made our way down slowly, crouching and clutching at bushes and vines that felt alive enough to close over our heads and swallow us, not like an animal, but an element. We reached the bottom and looked up at the lip of the gully and the sky, and it looked to me like something temporal and far away from this place that had the power to swallow us and not give us back.

Inside, the church seemed to have originally been carved so that it would appear nearly natural, an expression of the earth's mind. In its decay it was covered with lichen, deep-colored moss, and small trees; it smelled like rock and hummus. There were remnants of stone arches in the roof, thickly overgrown with clinging vines.

Niches were carved into the walls, and in the niches were stone figures with the faces worn away. There were stone benches, too, like
pews. Farther inside, there was another short descent into a grotto,
a chapel with a stream of water running through it like a vein of
shining blood. The steps descending into the chapel were intact
and so the descent was not that difficult. We reached the bottom
and stood there, wordlessly absorbing a feeling of power opposite
to the sky, embodied by earth but bigger than earth. Again came
the fear of being swallowed, but also a desire to be swallowed, as if
by a seducing lover. I clasped my hands and bent my head as if to
pray. Instead of prayer, a memory came to me, half-blotted in darkness; a memory of my cheek on the floor, my spread knees on the
floor, eyes closed, naked.

I loosed my hands and looked up. The darkened memory
passed, or became a memory of something else, someone else—
someone I had not thought of for years, someone I had not really
thought of at all. She was Thomas's first wife, the mother of Frank
and Elena; he had left her to be with me. I never met her, but I saw
her once, when Thomas and I were walking down the street in
Manhattan. He'd taken my arm abruptly and muttered her name
under his breath. I looked and saw a small middle-aged woman in
glasses looking fixedly ahead as she passed. I had turned away,
embarrassed. But now I saw her vividly. I saw her and felt her loneliness. On the street, she had looked about fifty—the same age I
am now.

The power was on that night, and we were more comfortable. Still,
I couldn't sleep for a long time. Again, Thomas came to sit on my
bed. But this time his presence did not comfort me. I thought of
the girl outside the orphanage, dying publicly while my friend and

I stood over her, knocking on the door. Katya might go back to America with a healthy baby. I would go back home and lecture writing students on the importance of specificity, and the role of description. "I want you to describe it in the way only you could see it," I would say, "you *specifically.*" In the dark, I hit myself with my fist—how stupid I had been. Did it matter who this girl was specifically, even to her? Her baby was sick and she was dying. Nothing more specific than that mattered, and life had made that plain to her. It was I who had been fooled.

For two days, wherever we went, no one was available to speak with us. Finally, we went back to the first place we had tried. This time, the dying girl was not there—though I thought I could make out a shadow, perhaps an indentation or soft mark where she had lain. We were about to turn and go, when the door was opened.

The head nun was a tall, erect woman with a still, cold face and fiery eyes—but the fire seemed to come from far away, far down in the hole of herself. We sat with her in her office and she told us the story of another woman who had come to do an independent adoption; the story took almost an hour to tell, and in the end, the woman had left Addis Ababa to look elsewhere. As an afterthought, the nun added that, at present, she had no babies.

"But what about the girl who was outside the door a few days ago?" asked Katya. "She was obviously very sick and she had a beautiful baby and I was wondering if you took that baby in?"

The head nun said that if the girl was sick, she was probably with her family now. And then she made it clear we were to leave.

Some version of this episode was repeated for several days at several different orphanages. Sometimes we were not allowed in at all. Sometimes we were allowed in but not allowed to see anyone

in charge. Finally, Katya went to the ministry that oversees adoptions to meet with the man that everyone referred to as "the head";
we never discovered his actual title. He suggested that we go to an
orphanage on the outskirts of town, but when we got there, we
were told that they had no babies available, either. Just as the
supervisor, or whatever she was, told us this, a baby began crying in
the next room.

Katya stood up, one hand on her hip, the other pointed toward
the sound. "And what," she demanded, "is *that?*"

"Obviously, that is a baby," said the woman stiffly. "But as this
baby has AIDS, he is not up for adoption in America."

Katya sat back down; she put her head in her hands. "I'm sorry,"
she said. "I don't mean to be rude."

The supervisor sighed and leaned back in her chair. She looked
out the window for a long moment. When she looked back, she
said, "I should not tell you this, but I am going to tell you. The
head of Social Services explicitly told us that you were coming.
And he explicitly told us that we were not to do any independent
adoptions. That's it. No independent adoptions."

Katya jumped up. "But he told us to come here!"

"If he has changed his mind," said the woman, "then he needs to
put it in writing. You need to get a letter from him stating that he
gives permission. And I doubt that he will give it to you."

The next day, Katya was sick with diarrhea and couldn't eat anything but clear tea and a banana. Still, we went to see the head of
Social Services. Katya went in to meet him in his office; I stayed in
the car with Yonas. He talked to me about the election; he said the
government had lied about the results in order to hold on to power
and that people were going to fight about it. I asked him how he

had learned to speak English so well. He said that he had studied it
at the university and that driving had given him the chance to prac-
tice. He had studied for only a year, even though he loved it; his
brother and sister had children and he needed to help make money
for them, so they could get the best education possible. He also
volunteered for an organization specifically for the education of
girls. "Like that girl we saw outside the orphanage," he said.

When he asked about my family, I told him about Thomas: that
he wrote books about Spanish literature, that he had been an ama-
teur bullfighter when he was young. I described for him a film clip
of Thomas leaning into a bull, his brow pressed against the brow
of the animal, as if both to conquer it and passionately kiss it. It
wasn't as daring as it looked; the animal was about to die. In fact,
the next moment, Thomas stepped away from it, and the animal
fell and died.

Katya came out and said, "What a prick!" She got in the car and
slammed the door. "Sorry for my language, Yonas. The agencies
must've gotten to him; that's the only explanation. He said I don't
need a letter, so why should he write me a letter. I said, 'How am I
going to get a child?' He said, 'That's your concern, not mine.' "

Yonas drove us back to the hotel. "I just don't know what to do,"
said Katya. "We can't stay here forever. I don't know what to
do. God I feel sick." She took out her cell phone and began rifling
through her purse.

"Who are you calling?" I asked.

"A guy named Kebede. Meselu gave me his number. He's a sort
of liaison between the hospital and orphanages in Arba Minch. I
didn't want to call, because he's in a whole other city. But I don't
know what else to try."

Yonas muttered unhappily; we were suddenly floating in a flood
of people and donkeys. Katya got Kebede on the phone. Music

came from somewhere, lots of instruments blended energetically. I smiled; I remembered the first time Thomas and I had had great sex. Right after, he'd put on an old pop song and danced in his underwear. He danced comically but also intently. The song went: "I've got a hard-ass pair of shoulders / I've got a love you can't imagine." Katya frowned, covering her other ear. "Really?" she said. "You know the head of Social Services?" Suddenly, her voice was round and shining. A boy shot past us on his bike, no-handed, beating time to the music with plastic bottles. Thomas danced; the car bucked forward; we rolled past a graveyard of white tombs and faceless angels standing guard over the dead. Katya hung up the phone. "He has a child," she said. *A love you can't imagine.* "A boy. Almost two. His mother dropped him off at the local hospital and hasn't been back for six months. The hospital just gave the child to Kebede and he's at Kebede's house, he hasn't gone into the orphanage yet. The rules don't apply to him. Kebede says to call back tomorrow." She looked like she'd been struck by lightning.

Two days later we were on a plane to Arba Minch. The weather was turbulent and the small jet bucked like an open boat on choppy water. Katya clutched her armrests and for the dozenth time went over the details of her conversation with Kebede. She had been too sick to her stomach to eat for several days, and her thinness made the taut, tense nature of her will more visible.

The plane banged around; a woman gasped so loudly it was nearly a scream. I stood slightly and looked at the cockpit; it was open and I could see the pilots. They were leaning back in their seats, laughing and talking as if they were sharing a very good joke.

I said, "The pilots look drunk."

"Oh, sit down," said Katya.

I sat down and looked out the window; the wing was vibrating ferociously. I began to sweat.

"I loved Thomas," I said. "I loved him right up until the end."

"I know," said Katya. "I know you did."

The plane dropped suddenly, then steadied, then rose above the clouds. The sun hit the wing with piercing brilliance.

"I loved him," I said.

"Yes," said Katya.

"But I was unfaithful."

Katya turned to face me, her fear interrupted by her surprise.

"It was only once. One person, once. A student. Not even technically a student—he had just graduated." I spoke rapidly, almost pattering. The plane jerked quickly to the side, then righted itself.

"How did it happen?"

"He was someone I really disliked—rude in class, so arrogant that it made him stupid. It was clear that he disliked me, too. I was glad to be getting rid of him. Then we saw each other at the graduation party and he came over to talk to me. I was surprised at first. Then I realized after about two minutes that it wasn't exactly dislike he felt for me. And I didn't dislike him, either. And Thomas wouldn't be surprised if I came home late."

"Was Thomas sick by then?"

It was a blow, but I could not be angry at her for striking it. "Yes," I said, "but I didn't know it yet. He had become very bad-tempered and strange—he was always starting fights and yelling at me—cursing at me, which he'd never done before. I was really mad at him. That partly explains why I did it, but not fully. I can't explain it fully. I wanted sex and I wanted it to hurt. Not physically but . . ."

"I know," said Katya. She said it quickly, as though to stop me from saying any more. "That was there, in the situation."

I looked out the window. Below us was a forest of textured green, a still mass of depth and roughness, of mesmerizing sameness. I looked at it and my thoughts dissolved like foam on an ocean. Again came the image of my face and spread knees on the floor. Unthinking darkness rose inside me, darkness and numbness. The plane steadied.

"I didn't know that he was sick," I said. "But I could tell that something was changing, that he was leaving me. The parts of Thomas that I knew as Thomas were leaving."

Katya put her hand on my arm and stroked it. Beneath us the forest fell away. We flew over bare ocher earth. I sat on the bed next to Thomas and tried to coax a spoon of soup into his mouth. He would not take it. I closed my eyes. On one side of me was the dark image of my grief. On the other side was bright sky, a rattling plastic window, and the torn edge of my seat cushion. How strange the contrast. How strange that I wished I could return to that moment of sitting on the bed, trying to get Thomas to take a spoon of soup.

We began our descent. I turned away from the window and saw Katya sitting very erect and tense; I was struck by the intensity of her thinness and paleness, the swollen darkness under her eyes. Her face said, Don't desert me. Link with me. Link your will with mine. With a mental side step, I did. The plane hit the ground with an exuberant thud; a woman burst into laughter.

Kebede was waiting for us in an old pickup truck. He was a small fine-boned man with a high-bridged nose, unsmiling, his eyes quick and clear. He asked whether we wanted to see the baby now, or go to the hotel first. Katya said, "The baby, please."

———

I had wanted Kevin to hurt me. I also feared it terribly. We went to a hotel. I was so afraid, I couldn't walk without trembling. If he had not taken my hand at the threshold of our rented room, I might have stopped and walked away—but he did take my hand. I looked at him and saw that his eyes were wide and determined, which made me understand that he was actually uncertain and possibly a little afraid himself. I put my arm around him and leaned my head against his shoulder. We went into the room.

As we neared the town, the vegetation became more lush. We glimpsed a great blue body of water between the trees and rich greenery. We turned down a street of stone houses mostly hidden behind walls and gates; we saw courtyards through the gates; we saw somebody's garage painted with flamboyant brown spots, like the hide of a cow.

Kebede's house was small but elegantly constructed of big smooth stones, contrasted by a door made of rough wooden planks. His young daughter greeted us and led us into a long, narrow, vaguely furnished room. A woman in a vermilion dress emerged from a side room with a crying baby in her arms. "This is Sofia, my wife," said Kebede. Smiling, Sofia handed the baby to Katya. The baby stopped crying. Cradling him, Katya looked at us, grinning as if she had given birth.

The baby was beautiful, fragile and small for his age, with a severe mouth, a high forehead, almond-shaped eyes, and slightly pointed ears that made his gaze seem radically attuned. When you held him, you felt the pure unprotected tenderness of an infant, but in those eyes there also was something uncanny and strong, nascent and vibrating with the desire to take form. He had come to the hospital half-starved from pneumonia and parasites, and although he was now healthy, he was still undernourished and weak. I thought, It matters who this child is, specifically. Sofia made us all a pasta dish with spicy onion puree, so spicy that I could barely eat it, so spicy that Katya didn't dare eat it. I wouldn't have expected even a robust baby to eat something so strong, but this baby ate it. He ate and conveyed with each bite, I intend to thrive. "Son," said Katya. "Sonny. I'm going to name him Sonny."

When we were done eating, we took Sonny back to the hotel. Sofia and her other daughter, an eleven-year-old in braids, whose name was Mekdes, went with us. Mekdes was amazed at the hotel's plumbing; she kept turning the water on and off. Katya was itching to buy baby food and clothes—what Sonny had on was filthy—and so Sofia made Mekdes calm down and instructed her to watch the baby while we went shopping.

"Can she do that?" asked Katya. "At her age?"

"Of course she can," said Sofia. "She's cared for children younger than this one."

The clothing store was a dark little hole stuffed with boxes of ridiculously ugly baby clothes from Eastern Europe; Katya loaded her arms with them. Sofia's phone rang and she turned her back to us to answer it. A small girl capered as she walked in behind her mother; the mother frowned, planted herself in front of a box, and started digging. Still capering, the child made a beautiful gesture with her head, nuzzling the air the way a kitten might rub against its mother. Smiling, Katya held up an orange corduroy jumper with a lavender collar. Sofia turned to us. "Stop," she said. "You have to stop. This is my husband. The mother just came back to the hospital. She is very angry. She wants her baby back."

Kebede drove us to the hospital. Sofia held Sonny; Katya didn't want to. She had pulled into herself and become very contained. Kebede told us that the hospital staff was very upset with the mother for showing up after leaving the child for so long.

"Why?" said Katya tonelessly. "It's her right."

"She's a day laborer," said Kebede. "She lives outdoors; she lives from hand to mouth. The hospital staff say she's retarded. The baby will die with her."

There was a crowd of hospital staff gathered in front of the hospital, and they came forward to meet us when we got out of the car. They were all talking loudly, but my eyes went to the only silent one among them: a small beaten-looking woman with long dirty hair and flat breasts hanging way down her body. She was dressed in filthy ragged clothes and the earrings had been torn from her ears. Her eyes were small and hot and I could not read their expression; it came from too far back in her head. I looked at her and thought, This woman is not retarded. Her eyes went past me and fell on Katya; her deep expression came forward slightly. Katya steadily returned the look; I could not read her expression, either. Sofia went forward and put the baby in his mother's arms. Everyone fell silent. The mother glanced at Sofia, went toward Katya, and tried to hand the baby to her. Everybody burst out talking. Katya automatically reached for the baby, but before she could take him, Kebede stepped in and took him. The baby screamed and reached for his mother. Looking meaningfully at the mother, Kebede gave the sobbing baby to a female hospital staffer. The staffer handed the child back to his mother. The mother took the child, walked around the staffer, and tried to approach Katya again. Everybody was yelling then. Kebede moved in front of the mother, blocking her. The baby screamed. Katya hung her head and turned back to the car, both hands pressed against her chest.

It was over in less than five minutes. After the mother walked away with the baby, Sofia went to the car to comfort Katya. I was too stunned by the scene to leave it that quickly. Kebede stood for a while talking with the hospital people, but I could not understand what they were saying.

When we got back to the hotel, Katya lay down in bed. It was getting dark, but I did not turn on the lights. The room was stifling, but I made no move to open the windows. Katya spoke with her back to me.

"This was a mistake," she said. "An arrogant mistake. People told me that, and they were right. I have been lazy and selfish all my life and I think I can just come and buy a kid after living in a world that stole the ground out from under their parents and their grandparents and sucked the blood out of them and—"

I said, "Don't start with that. You aren't buying a kid; you're not giving anyone money. Even as a metaphor, it doesn't work; Ethiopia never sold slaves."

"Don't give me that shit. This isn't an English class. You know there's truth in what I say. And anyway, I am sick of everything always being wrong. With every relationship I've ever had, there's been some reason it can't work. Even with sex half the time, there's something in the way; somebody is scared or married, or you touched him the wrong way, or he said the wrong thing and it's gone. Or it's there for six weeks and then it's gone. And now this. Maybe I deserve it."

"Katya," I said. "That mother wants you to have her baby. I saw it. You saw it. Wait and see what happens."

She turned to face me. Her lips and eyelids were swollen pitifully. Unable to breathe, I got up to open the windows and saw there were no screens. The air was thick with mosquitoes; it was

malaria season and we had not brought any antimalarial drugs with
us. I closed the window. Katya reminded me that she had packed a
mosquito net, but when she got up to help me with it, we discovered that there was no way to put it up over the bed.

We lay in the darkness and heat and talked about the baby and
the mother and how the mother had looked when she had seen
Katya; we tried to understand what her expression had meant.
Soon it was too hot to talk, too hot to think. The few mosquitoes
that had gotten in when I opened the window bit us, and we
itched. We sweated so, we soaked our sheets. Again and again, we
got up for water. Then we got up to piss and it came out scalding.
The dark and heat became a private maze we wandered, in and out
of a delirium that passed as sleep. Far away, I stood in front of
a classroom, talking about a girl carrying her dead baby through a
dark forest. There were a dozen students in that class, but Kevin
was the only one whose face I saw before me. He had been right to
despise me—I who had no child lecturing on this experience, like I
knew. *Yours is not the worst of sorrows.*

But it was. I had wanted him to hurt me and he had. Or at least
I thought he had. In fact, the real shock and pain came later, along
with something worse: Weeks after I went into the hotel room,
Thomas was diagnosed with Alzheimer's. Now he was hurt and I
had done it to him. Or at least it felt as if I had.

I touched the rings on the chain around my neck; I felt Thomas
there, and his presence was not reproachful. But it was painful anyway. It was painful to know that even if my mind saw him, he wasn't
there, that my mind was at odds with reality, and that my mind
could do nothing to change reality. I could see him. He wasn't
there. The emptiness between the two states was pitiless.

Katya stirred and talked in her sleep. I felt protective tenderness, a feeling that could not fill the emptiness, but softened it. I thought of the little girl I had seen in the store, the touching movement she had made with her head, and a single word came to me: *faith.* This is not a word I use often or hear used often except lightly, ignorantly or manipulatively. But there it was, standing singly in my head. This word has meaning, I thought. Whatever it has faithlessly been made to mean, it has actual meaning. But it was very little to hold on to: the image of a graceful girl in a dirty store in a hungering, wounded country—so small, so light, so surrounded by darkness.

In the morning, I opened the windows a crack. We showered; the fixtures in the shower were heavy brass, the tiles were thick with mold, and the loofah in the soapless soap dish was worn and moldy, too. Wordless, we went down to the dining room for breakfast. I ate fruit and a little plastic container of vanilla pudding; Katya had coffee and a piece of bread. There were some Italians talking about the election a few tables over; we heard them say something about getting out of the country. Then they glanced at us and fell silent. I thought, The world is tipping over, like a table, and everything on it is falling off. It doesn't matter if it's round; it's tipping and we're falling. We took our coffee and went outside on the terrace. The air was warm, thriving and dense with the smell of earth and minerals. We sat quietly for a bit. A car drove by, blaring pop music. Two boys walked by, driving two skinny cows, lustily slapping their bony haunches with whiplike branches.

Katya said, "Being here is like being in biblical times and modern times at the same time. Like all times are happening at once, and people are just walking back and forth between them."

Not walking, I thought, falling.

I said, "Did I ever tell you that Thomas was the first man I came with?"

"No," said Katya. "I didn't know that."

"It's true. Not immediately, but yeah. First time for me."

"The first time I came—I mean with a person, not myself—it was with a stranger," said Katya.

"A total stranger?"

"Almost—I'd known him a day and a half. It was when I was sixteen. He was, like, twenty-five. He was probably more skilled than I was used to, or maybe he wasn't. I've no idea why it happened. We were doing it and—this huge feeling came and grabbed me up. Like a wave picked me up and put me on top of a building, and before I had a chance to look and see where I was, it took me back down. He was looking at me and smiling, because I'm sure my face was saying, What did you just *do*? And then the next day, he was gone. If that had happened with somebody I loved, I would've thought I came because I was in love. Sex would've been all about love in my mind. But as it was, it was impossible to make that mistake. I fell in love after that, and I came with people I loved. But I didn't think I was coming because of love."

"It wasn't always about love with Thomas," I said.

She started to respond, but her cell phone rang in her lap. Irritated, she picked it up. She listened; her attention went taut like a bow. She dropped the phone and shouted, "The mother brought the baby back!" and she grabbed the phone up again. It was Kebede. The mother had slept outside the hospital all night with the baby. She wanted to put him up for adoption, and she wanted Katya to have him.

It took a few days for the mother to do the paperwork, but we got Sonny right away. We went back to the store of ugly clothes and bought a little suitcaseful. We bathed Sonny and dressed him. But he would not stop screaming. It seemed to Katya that the baby screamed most when she tried to hold him. Sofia came to help us. She brought more of the spicy pasta dish that Sonny had devoured on the day we had met him, but the baby refused it with a frown that was deep and imperial. He refused to eat at all. "Maybe he wants to go back to his mother," Katya said. "Do you think that's what he's saying?" "Nonsense," said Sofia. "Don't even think it. They were sleeping outside during malaria season. Do you know what that means? The baby is already weak; if he stayed with that woman, he would die."

"And besides, he's bossy like you," I said. "Did you see the frown on him?"

And so we came before the judge. We took Sonny back to Addis Ababa. He screamed the whole flight. But Katya was unfazed; the strength of her doubt was now transformed and feeding her determination. We had fully entered our endeavor, and now, exhausted but almost mechanically activated, we were carried forward on a current of will that we had initiated, but which had become a force of its own.

We met Yonas at the airport and he took us to a bed-and-breakfast exclusively for people who were in Addis to adopt. The place was a compound with barbed wire and shards of glass atop its high walls. The massive gate was opened by a wizened man with clawlike hands and eyes like clouded marbles, a single twist of opaque expression coloring their center. The house was a weird combination of sparse and luxurious; it resembled a brick two-story you might find in Queens, but the oversized door was polished mahogany and, inside, the floors were made of large marble tiles. The owners were a haughty upper-class Ethiopian woman and a neurasthenic Italian man who had written several unpublished children's books; his mother, an opinionated lady with a pug dog, was also there, visiting from Rome.

Because Sonny tended to get carsick, I stayed at the B and B with him while Yonas drove Katya around the city to get letters proving who she was and who Sonny was, translations of these letters into English and/or Amharic, a birth certificate, a passport, and a visa for Sonny. Katya mounted a daily assault on the Head, from whom she needed to get a letter of approval for an orphanage to sponsor the adoption. Each of these tasks was, of course, impossible. When I tell the story to people, I make it sound as if Katya flowed through the city, coursing around the obstacles in her path with the smooth determination of water. But she was not water and she came home bruised and furious from bumping her head against every damn thing. She paced around, telling great tales of wild, shape-shifting bureaucracy, of crawling through its narrow mazes, up endless stairs and down fun-house chutes, confronting at every turn hydras made of obdurate, obfuscating, lecturing, lying, malicious, misshapen Ethiopian heads, plus some idiotic American heads thrown in. The Head was a pig and a bitch, and sometimes, so was I. When Katya came home tired out, still too sick to have an appetite, I would be desperate to leave the compound for something to eat, and she would not want to go. We quarreled about it until we were exhausted, breaking to feed, change, or walk the child, who, when he didn't sleep through it, watched the drama with interest. Then Katya would get up the next day and leave the house to do it all again.

My time alone was a different sort of maze: dreamlike and lullingly dull, the surreal darkness of grief blended with the bright reality of caring for a frail child. Sonny was not only frail; he was underdeveloped from his early life of illness and malnourishment. We had not seen the extent to which this was true, possibly because his spirit had stood out to us with such force. But our first day at the B and B we saw him with another child close in age, and, in comparison, his movements were weak, uncoordinated, somehow partial. He couldn't walk more than a few steps and his gaze was intense but not quite focused, as if he was suffering from a mild psychic fever. He didn't walk well, and at first he didn't want to walk at all. He just wanted to be carried around the house, out into the yard and back, again and again.

The first day, I carried him until I couldn't take any more; then I lay on the floor and rolled back and forth with him as he clung to me weakly, but with a hint of triumph in his raised head. I rocked him and crooned to him and dreamed of Thomas: of rocking him and crooning, of being rocked by him. Of straddling my husband and kissing him, bending to touch my breasts against him; of straddling him and struggling to reposition him on the bed, Thomas cursing me with strange half words because he could no longer position himself.

Sonny put his hand on my face and it came away wet. I kissed his tiny palm and held it. Thomas had lost motor control and could only get into bed by taking a sitting position over it and then letting himself flop backward. I had to let him do it that way—it was important for him to do what he could. But I had to reposition him, because if I left him as he fell, he woke in pain. It made Thomas furious to be straddled and positioned, and it hurt me to feel that. Yet I treasured it; I treasured his anger as a vestige of his pride, treasured that it could still make *me* angry, make me feel once more like a normal wife with a strong husband to quarrel with. I gave Sonny my finger; he squeezed it and I rolled into a seated position, cradling him.

I wondered if the baby wanted so much to be carried because his mother, a day laborer, had carried him strapped to her body. Or if it was something even more basic—that he was like a plant and I a random patch of earth from which he wanted to draw all the nurture he could get lest he be uprooted again. I looked into his eyes and remembered Thomas's eyes: restless, strangely shapeless. At the end, he still had the childish pleasure of sweet tastes, of touching the soft fur of Zuni, the cat; to see that pleasure was a kind of sadness I had never felt before. Sonny fluttered his lids, then half-opened them—checking one more time—then slept, his dear soft fist against my chest.

Friends ask me when I suspected that something was wrong with Thomas. I don't know how to answer; I think I knew before I knew. There were indications, most of them disguised as age and its eccentricity. But at least once the disease paraded itself garishly before me, and I didn't see it because I couldn't categorize it. Four years before he was diagnosed, we went to Spain for three weeks. We got back home in the evening, left our bags in the front hall, and went to bed. The next morning, I found him sitting in the kitchen, visibly afraid. He had no memory of our trip, yet he realized when he saw our bags in the hall that we had been somewhere. I made breakfast; I described for him everything we had done on the trip. He said he remembered, and I made myself forget it. Because nothing quite like that happened again, I could.

After a few days, Sonny began to eat in earnest—mashed bananas, cereal, formula, pasta, all of it. He built pyramids of empty film containers and prescription bottles and then knocked them down. He unscrewed and screwed the top on the milk bottle over and over. He discovered he wanted to walk and then—as if a bomb had gone off in his brain—he discovered that he might walk up and down the stairs. I passed through a sad and enchanted mirror: I walked Sonny like I had walked Thomas, his hands in mine, giving him a footstep pattern to follow, holding his eyes with encouragement. Everything depended on the slow movements of his blunt feet, of their exact position, trusting it, finding it again.

Everything depended on it: I pulled my husband out of bed to a standing position and led him backward, holding hands. I smiled at him and he smiled back at me. I got him on the john, waited for him to finish, and wiped him. I bathed him in the marble shower, which was so big, it made the whole room a shower where we could be naked together. We sat on the fancy marble floor and played, passing the hose back and forth, spraying, laughing. . . . And Sonny, with his little forehead blazing, several times nearly falling, climbed the stairs, leaning heavily into my hands. His hands radiated into my hands, imparting his being and sampling mine. "Look," I said aloud. Look, my husband, my father, my lover, my child: Look at this little boy and bless him.

When Katya came home, she would jealously take the baby from me—of course jealously. Every day, she walked in and saw me having intimacy she couldn't have because she was out doing the shit. What she didn't see: It didn't matter. Sonny knew that Katya was his mother and that I was his nurse; the uncanny gleam we had seen the first day had found mental form quickly. But still Katya grabbed him jealously and fed him and talked angrily about the Head while I ate dried fruit and nuts. I half-listened. I looked at the spoon going in and out of the baby's mouth. I thought, If I am the nurse and Katya is the mother, who or what is the birth mother

to him? Is she the earth of Sonny, the sky? The unseeable place
the child walks when he sleeps? When I asked Thomas what he
remembered about the birth mother who had abandoned him,
he just said he liked her. He said he liked to picture her getting on
the bus with a battered suitcase, in a long coat and flat shoes, her
large eyes bold and intense, her hair like a movie star's. She was an
adventurer, he thought, and he didn't blame her for leaving.

On our seventh day in Addis, Katya succeeded; she came back with
a letter from the Head and another letter from an orphanage (run
by a friend of the Head) that said they would sponsor the adoption. Out of fighting mode, she was dazed and unsure of how this
had happened. "We were going at it as usual," she said. "I told him I
would be back in his office every day until I got permission, and he
said, 'Fine.' And then a stomach cramp doubled me over; my head
went between my legs, my teeth were gritted, and my intestines
made this indescribable sound—I thought I was going to have
diarrhea right there. The only reason I didn't leave was that I was
worried about what might happen if I got up suddenly. He didn't
say anything. He just looked at me—almost like he felt sorry for
me! Then he got a piece of paper and wrote the letter and pushed it
across the desk."

That night, we finally went out for dinner. We wore the dresses
we had brought to celebrate in; Sonny wore his orange jumper. I
chose an Italian restaurant we'd walked past several times, because
the people in it always looked lively. But it wasn't lively this time.
On the way there, the streets were nearly empty, and the few people who were out seemed angry and tense. We were the only
people in the restaurant. Katya didn't feel well enough to eat more
than a few bites of pasta and she was too tired to talk much.

The next day, Katya and Sonny went to the American embassy in the morning and returned early in the afternoon. Sonny was tired and cranky, so Katya wanted to rest before going to the travel agency to arrange our flight out the next day. They napped together while I went to the laundry room and washed our clothes. While I was in the dining area, waiting for the clothes to come out of the washer, I met our host's Italian mom. She was feeding her pug dog sliced fruit from a dish in her lap. I told her we were about to leave; she said it was a shame that we hadn't gotten to Lalibela. "I hope you can get out," she said. "You choose a terrible time to come. You didn't know about the election?" I pointed out that she was here. She shrugged and meticulously peeled the skin off a fig. "I grew up here," she said. "I know the place. You don't."

I woke Katya and we tried to call Yonas. We couldn't reach him. This was unusual. We waited an hour and tried again; nothing. We waited another hour. We heard the huge gate open; people came in, talking loudly. Someone ran up the stairs, past our door. Katya and I stared at each other. Sonny stirred. It wasn't right then that we heard gunfire, but maybe ten minutes later. It wasn't close by. But close enough to hear. Not steadily, but off and on, during the afternoon and into the night.

Much closer than the gunshots was the machine of my body, buzzing inside me. It came from inside me and also enclosed me like the darkness and the warmth of the night. It said, It doesn't matter if you die here. It might be better if you die here. But Katya and Sonny have to get home. It won't be better if they die.

The next day, Yonas came in his uncle's car instead of his taxi. We saw him pull into the driveway, and we ran out to meet him. From the car, he held up a hand to indicate he was talking on the phone. We stopped; he had never signaled for us to wait before, and this signal scared me more than anything so far. But he didn't keep us waiting long. He put the phone down and got out to tell us: There had been a demonstration about the election. Twenty-five people had been killed. The city was under martial law. He could not take us anywhere. He would be in touch. He had to get home as quickly as he could.

We played with Sonny all day, both of us, going up and down the stairs, knocking the film containers all over the stairs, then picking them up again. When we heard shots, we looked up and then went back to what we were doing. The buzzing said, Your parents are dead; your husband is dead. You should be dead. But Katya and Sonny don't deserve to die.

In the early evening, Katya said, "We have to get something to eat. We haven't eaten for almost twelve hours."

"We can't go out," I said. "It isn't safe."

"Sonny is out of food. He hasn't eaten for eight hours."

"Katya, nothing is open; you heard Yonas."

"The fruit stand will be open. There's no way they'll close. They're just down the street."

"We're hearing guns."

"The shots aren't close. I have to go out. If you won't go, I'll go alone."

We took Sonny; I carried him because Katya was too weak. Outside on the street, people and animals were walking around like normal. Who were these people? I felt half-scared of them, half-linked with them, and didn't know which feeling was most real. I reached inside my shirt and held the rings for a moment in my cupped hand. Thomas's face, flat and beautifully misshapen, rippled in me like a reflection in water. There was a boy at my side, trying to push a cow out of the way. Thomas's face stretched unrecognizably on the moving water. The boy came suddenly around the cow and tore my chain off my neck. I screamed; the boy flashed down the street. I was after him. My legs are long and I almost had him, but I couldn't grab him because Sonny was screaming, forgotten, in my arms. I darted back to Katya, who was standing motionless, and thrust Sonny at her. The boy was a quick pixilation of limbs, disappearing. Katya shouted, "Janice!" and I ran. The boy was bright movement that I chased like an animal with a single instinct. I turned a corner, stumbled into a pothole full of warm brown water, and nearly fell. I staggered and bent to catch myself with my hands. I looked up; he was gone. I whipped my head around, looking, my instinct trying to leap in every direction—but it had nothing to leap at. I panted raggedly, sweat running in my eyes, my instinct exiting through my eyes as I stared around, wild. Women holding children stared back at me. Faces peered from the broken hole of a window. Skeleton dogs, fierce and cringing, watched with starving eyes. My instinct felt them all as it felt itself: quick force in slow mammal bodies; soft brain in hard bone; a machine of thoughts; a machine of sex. The dark radiance of emotions; the personality; eyes, nose, mouth. *You, specifically.* A little boy with a large round head pointed at me and said words I couldn't understand. My instinct broke; everything that had been joined was now in pieces again. I put my face in my hands and cried like an animal.

I came out of the alley to find my way back to Katya. I tried to stop making noise. I couldn't. I felt people following me. I understood. The current had reversed. As I had chased the boy, they would follow me. They would kill me. I heard myself sobbing. Thomas was dead. I had let him die. They would kill me. It was right.

"Miss? Miss?" A small voice was at my side, gently tugging me without touching me. "Miss? What's wrong, miss?"

I looked at the voice. There were two young girls, maybe thir-

teen years old, tagging at my side. They were dressed in school uniforms. Their faces were soft but intensely focused. I wiped my
face; I glanced behind me. There *was* a small crowd following me,
made up mostly of teenage girls and a few boys with curious faces.
I turned to face them. "My husband died," I said. "He died and
somebody stole our wedding rings. Now I don't have anything."
Tears ran down my face—human tears now. "I have to find my
friend and her baby. Thank you."

The girls nodded gravely. I continued to walk. One girl followed
me. "It will be all right," she said. "God will help you."

I said, "Thank you, honey." Machine-gun fire sounded in the
distance. The girl dropped away.

"Janice!" It was Katya, rounding a corner, Sonny in her arms.
She said, "What happened? Why did you do that?"

"I was robbed. That boy took my wedding rings. I couldn't catch
him."

"Then we need to call the police."

If she hadn't been holding Sonny, I would've slapped her. "Do
you know how stupid you sound?" I said. "Call the police?"

"Janice—"

"Look around you!" I was trembling, still dripping tears with no
force. "They're in the middle of a war and you think the police are
going to come because of my rings?"

"Janice—"

"Shut up!"

I turned to get away, to go back to the B and B. In my head was
Thomas well and virile, Thomas sick, our house with its marble
shower, its riches of detail, its condiments and candies, paintings
and knickknacks, baskets on the wall, baskets from all over the
world, from places we had traveled together, shelves of books, the
books he had written, the languages he had spoken, his children,

my students— *Now I don't have anything.* But once I'd had everything;
I had betrayed everything so I could fuck somebody I didn't love.

"Stop." Someone touched my arm from behind; I turned. A very
small old man stood before me.

"What?" I asked, or thought.

"Stop," he said. "Don't cry. Please. It's okay." He said "Please,"
but his eyes had an expression of command. I lifted my hand to
wipe my eyes. He reached out and took it. He held it palm up; he
put my rings in my hand and closed my fingers over them. "Okay?"
he said.

"But how—"

He shook his head and said, "Just don't cry. Okay?"

I stopped crying. He turned to go.

"Wait," I said. "There was a chain, too?"

He turned his head and looked hard at me.

"The rings were on a chain. Do you know about that?"

He shook his head and walked away.

Years later, I told this story at a party at the university. I told it to
a woman who had traveled extensively in Africa. She was a big
woman, very grand, with a high chest and a chunky necklace made
of precious stones. When I told her how I had lost my rings and
how the old man had given them back, she made a face. She said,
"Really, you make too big a fuss of yourself. You should not go to
Africa and then make such a fuss." I answered her vaguely. I let
myself be chastised. Because in that room, she was right. In that
room, I was a privileged and foolish woman running around bawl-
ing about rings while a whole city fell apart and people were killed.

But I didn't meet the old man in that room. I met him in a place
of biblical times and modern times, where people walked back

and forth between times, all times. In this place, I walked back and forth between the time of the living and the time of the dead. In the middle of my walking, war broke out, and the path between the living and the dead opened up and everything dear to me fell down the crack. I fell, too, and I might've fallen forever—but the old man came and said, "Stop." And I stopped.

That same night at the university, another person asked, "Did you thank him?" And I was amazed to realize I didn't know. Probably I did not. How could I? Thanking him would have been like thanking an angel.

I sit in my darkened house sometimes, holding a glass of wine, and I thank him.

The next day, we rode through the streets, crouched on the floor of a car Yonas had borrowed from his uncle. We rode to the American embassy, sharing the car with five Ethiopians, women and girls whom Yonas was taking "to safety." He didn't dare drive his cab lest taxi drivers striking on behalf of the protestors turn it over and burn it. But there were no taxis in the street, no cars, no people. There were huge high trucks full of soldiers in camouflage with automatic weapons. Still, the Ethiopian women sat on the seat and we crouched on the floor, hiding the whiteness that declared us paying customers. One of the women, a girl really, held Sonny against her breast. A military truck passed close by, bristling with guns. The girl holding our baby looked at me with wide, frightened eyes. Katya pressed her forehead to the sweat-drenched seat and stretched her hand up to clasp Sonny's foot as though it were a hand.

Outside, the embassy was surrounded by guards with machine guns; inside, it was jammed with frightened people and officials behind windows. We took a number and waited. Waiting next to us was an American doctor who had been on emergency-room duty when gunshot victims began to come in. He was calm, over-calm, but he smelled like fear, and when he got up to one of the windows, he began talking loud and fast, telling someone, really everyone, that there had been many killings, many more than the reported twenty-five. The whole room smelled of fear. Something was missing from Sonny's file, and Katya was shouting at someone, her jaw moving like cheap animation on her stark chalk white face, her body giving off a smell that was nearly savage, the smell of something ready to attack. She turned to me suddenly and I flinched. "I've got to go," she said. "I'll be back." She was already dialing Yonas on her cell.

I went to take Sonny from her, but the child refused; he hadn't let me hold him since I'd handed him off and run down the middle of the street and come back howling in pain. So I held his hand and walked out to the hall with him. Thomas walked out of the sun-shadowy water, stepping on his elegant pants, damp and sagging, and his shoes squishy wet, smiling as he handed me the dog's chewed-up ball, the dog, standing on its hind legs, dancing. With an ecstatic face, Sonny took the steps two at a time. Thomas's mother smiled and boarded the bus, the sun shining on her beauti-ful hair. Sonny looked up at me, gurgling with pleasure, forehead shining with effort. I stroked his hair. I thought of his mother's beaten face, her torn ears, her breasts hanging down. The child grabbed my hem with his tiny fist. Katya came back beaming, papers in her hand, her sweat rank and innocent.

That night, I dreamed Katya and I were in a small dark house of mud and thatch. Thomas was there, too, asleep on a dirty mat, and so was Sonny's mother, who was terribly sick. Katya kept trying to nurse the mother, to suckle her at her breast, but the woman couldn't hold her head up, and I kept wanting to say, Stop. It's ridiculous. *She's* the mother. But I was distracted by Thomas's mother in the next room, laughing as she played with Sonny; I was distracted, too, by gunfire, which came closer and closer. . . .

I woke in the dark with my heart pounding; I reached for my wedding rings on the table beside me.

"Katya," I whispered, only half-expecting her to be awake, too.

She replied unintelligibly.

"When Sonny gets older, and he asks you about his mother, what are you going to tell him?"

She didn't answer. Shortly, she began to snore.

But the next day, when we were at the airport, she answered. She said, "If he asks, I'll tell him that his mother was a great woman. That she was a fighter, and because she had to fight so hard, she gave me her most precious child to keep him safe. Something like that. Here." Without thinking, she handed me the baby, and bent to pick up her bag. I stiffened, expecting Sonny to protest. But he didn't; he reached for me. For the first time since I'd run down the street, Sonny let me hold him. I thrive, his body said to mine, I will thrive. I put my hand on the back of his head and held it to my shoulder, my cheek against his hair. It was time to go.

ACKNOWLEDGMENTS

I would like to thank and acknowledge Pamela Laws, Tom Bissell, Maria Pallotta, Debra Losada, Beatrice Von Rezzori and Santa Maddalena, the MacDowell Colony, Jin Auh, Deborah Garrison, Deborah Treisman, Roger Hodge, Michael Ray, Eric Gottesman, Peter Trachtenberg, and especially my mother, Dorothy Jane Gaitskill. I am particularly grateful to Nuruddin Farah for his permission to use an excerpt from his novel *Secrets* in "The Agonized Face."

A NOTE ABOUT THE AUTHOR

Mary Gaitskill is most recently the author of *Veronica,* nominated for the National Book Award, and *Because They Wanted To,* which was nominated for a PEN/Faulkner Award in 1998.

A NOTE ON THE TYPE

The text of this book was set in Requiem, a typeface designed by Jonathan Hoefler (born 1970). It was derived from Ludovico Vicentino degli Arrighi's 1523 writing manual, *Il Modo di Temperare le Penne.*

Composed by Creative Graphics,
Allentown, Pennsylvania

Printed and bound by R. R. Donnelley Harrisonburg North,
Harrisonburg, Virginia

Designed by M. Kristen Bearse